COUP

The guard quit ogling the gorgeous woman before him, cleared his throat, and glanced at the ceiling of the wooden guardhouse trying to collect his thoughts. "How'd you get into the grounds, anyway?" he asked.

"Like this," she said. She reached into her purse. He found himself gazing at the muzzle of an automatic.

He clutched at the emergency alarm.

The silenced pistol coughed twice as he reached for the button.

The first slug caught the guard in the throat, causing him to jerk his hand back. The second bullet left a quarter-inch gaping third eye.

Andrea listened.

Silence—except the humming of insects and the sounds of light traffic and music drifting from the city.

She removed her tiny CB radio and thumbed its switch.

"One, go!" she whispered into it.

Hobbs received the message. He signaled the men. They charged the Presidential Palace.

Night STALKERS

DUNCAN LONG

Harper Paperbacks

Harper & Row, Publishers, New York
Grand Rapids, Philadelphia, St. Louis, San Francisco
London, Singapore, Sydney, Tokyo, Toronto

This is a work of fiction. The characters, incidents, and dialogues are products of the author's imagination and are not to be construed as real. Any resemblance to actual events or persons, living or dead, is entirely coincidental.

Harper Paperbacks   a division of Harper & Row, Publishers, Inc.
10 East 53rd Street, New York, N.Y. 10022

Cover art by Edwin Herder

First printing: July, 1990

Printed in the United States of America

HARPER PAPERBACKS and colophon are trademarks of Harper & Row, Publishers, Inc.

10 9 8 7 6 5 4 3 2 1

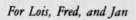
For Lois, Fred, and Jan

ACKNOWLEDGMENTS

I must extend my gratitude to those who helped me locate the technical odds and ends of information along with the various manuals, magazines, and reference books needed to obtain information about the aircraft covered in this story. Among these kind folks are James R. Bowman of United Technologies/Sikorsky Aircraft; Major Donald Riffey (US Army, Retired); SPC Russell Kirby, US Army; Sgt. 1st Class Charlie Drake; and the fine librarians at the Wamego Public Library who went above and beyond the call of duty to obtain some rather obscure manuals for my perusal.

Many thanks must go to Ethan Ellenberg and my wife, Maggie, who developed some excellent plot devices and helped me get various types of "plotting bugs," typos, and other gremlins exorcised from my manuscript. Thanks should also go to Ed Breslin and Jessica Kovar who, as they say, made this book possible. It's doubtful that this book would ever have seen the light of day if it hadn't been for these people.

Finally, a thank-you must go to my in-house assistants, Kristen and Nicholas.

CHAPTER

1

The Caribbean sunset was purple as the evening smoldered to an end. A cricket chirped and then quieted at the rustle of the combat boots passing stealthily through the lush foliage. The armed men took their positions on the steep hill overlooking the Presidential Palace.

The humid air carried the fragrance of tropical flowers mixed with cloves, cinnamon, and moist vegetation. In the distance above the palm- and brush-covered hill, the island's volcanic mountain towered. Shadows darkened the verdant forest on the peak.

With the retreat of the sunlight, the nocturnal creatures crept from their sanctuaries. A bat flitted above a mercenary. Like the other mercenaries, he wore black nylon web gear. Scuffed pouches mounted to harness and belt contained heavy magazines of ammunition and grenades. The object of the mercenaries' attention was a decrepit colonial manor that the natives of the Republic of Palm Island generously called their "Presidential Palace."

Earlier that day, the gang had promenaded

1

through the port of entry to the Republic of Palm Island. They had carried their weapons in bags and suitcases, unquestioned and uninspected by the customs agent who had received a bribe greater than he'd ever earn in a whole lifetime on Palm Island. They had assembled their weapons in a large house rented a month earlier by their leader. By nightfall, they were divided into three bands. They proceeded to their three separate objectives in rented vans and cars.

A fourth group of five men was held in reserve, remaining in the rented house, listening to their CB. Should any of their comrades run into problems, it was their job to reinforce them.

And now the first group of ten mercenaries waited on the hilltop, sweating in the summer night. Most simply waited, shooing insects as the sky grew darker and stars twinkled. One fingered a crucifix chained to his neck. Hobbs held a walkie-talkie.

Hobbs was in charge of those on the hill. He checked his luminous watch for the hundredth time and then switched on his hand-held CB. He waited nervously.

Minutes passed.

The radio crackled. "Roll call," a husky female voice commanded.

"Number One," Hobbs said. "We're in place." He looked at the diminutive CB a second, then added, "It's clear." He licked his lips and listened. His scarred, pocked face resembled the moon. His black hair was filthy. Tufts of greasy locks engulfed his ears and stuck from his stocking cap. He hunched his slightly overweight frame and shifted the FN FAL that was cradled in his meaty arms.

The radio hissed like a snake and then spoke, "Two is home free."

"Three's clear," a third voice announced.

"All right," the female voice said with an eruption of static. "In three minutes." Static.

Hobbs switched off his CB and shoved it into an empty pocket in the black combat vest he wore. "Three minutes," he warned the line of gruff men who fingered their rifles, anticipating bloodshed.

Hobbs extracted a scratched pair of Bushnell binoculars from the case that hung from his neck. He brought the instrument up, adjusted the focus, and carefully scrutinized the brightly lit entry of the palace through a break in the foliage.

He gazed down the long walkway leading to the mansion. Floodlights buried in the earth lit the pathway. A woman with long, shapely legs strolled up the cracked sidewalk. Through the safety of the optics, Hobbs lustfully explored her snug dress. The man felt the tautness at the base of his stomach, the same feeling he had whenever he saw her.

Oblivious to the gunmen uphill from her, Andrea Todd studied her fingernail polish as she walked. She wore a frilly white blouse cut dangerously low to reveal the tantalizing hint of pendulous breasts barely hidden beneath its fabric. A delicate white skirt complemented the blouse. She had long, platinum hair and crisp features. Petite and graceful, she was aloof, cool, and self-possessed. With a hypnotic sway of hips and thighs,

she slinked to the guardhouse that stood beside the
entryway of the Presidential Palace. She paused
next to it.

A fat police private was nestled in the little
wooden shelter. Sweat glistened on his ebony skin
and stained his white uniform. He jumped to his
feet when he heard Andrea's footsteps. He tried
to conceal the girlie magazine he'd been reading
by rolling it into a baton. He stared at the woman,
swallowed, and stood as straight as his pudgy body
allowed. For a moment he toyed with the idea of
buzzing the alarm. No one should be on the presidential grounds after dark. But she looked harm-
less. And so beautiful.

"Uh . . . How can I help you?" the private
asked, trying vainly to hide his magazine behind his
back. "There are no more tours until tomorrow,"
he added, hoping he'd guessed her reason for the
long trek from the city to the palace.

"I'm lost," she replied. "Could you tell me
how to get to the Coopersville Hotel from here?"
Her eyes met his without blinking.

"Uh . . . Well, let's see . . ." He quit ogling
the goddess before him, cleared his throat, and
glanced at the ceiling of the wooden guardhouse
as he tried to collect his thoughts. "How'd you get
into the grounds, anyway?" he asked, looking back
at her.

"Like this," she said. She reached into her
purse and he found himself gazing at the muzzle
of an automatic.

He clutched at the emergency alarm connected to the police station in town.

The silenced pistol coughed twice as he reached for the button.

The first slug caught the guard in the throat, causing him to jerk his hand back. The second bullet left a quarter-inch gaping third eye that merely hinted at the pulped damage to his brain. The wound wept blood as the guard toppled into the wooden chair at the rear of the tiny guardhouse. He sat slack-mouthed, his facial muscles frozen in surprise.

"What's goin' on here?" a sleepy voice asked. Another guard stumbled up the walk, unsnapping his holster as he came.

Andrea swung around and jerked the trigger twice. The old man tumbled to the pavement with a groan. He extracted his revolver from its holster. The third projectile entered his eye and he slumped flat on his face.

Andrea listened.

Silence—except the humming of insects and the sounds of light traffic and music drifting from the city.

She carefully removed a loaded magazine of .22 Shorts from her purse. The woman exchanged the loaded magazine for the nearly empty one in her Beretta Minx, then hid the pistol in her purse. She removed her tiny CB radio and thumbed its switch.

"One, go!" she whispered into it.

Hobbs received the message. He signaled the men. They broke into a trot down the hill. Boots padded in the loam and clothing rustled as they passed through the brush and thick grass.

They charged the palace, ignoring the two bodies lying at its front. The men raced up the chipped marble stairs and through the heavy wooden front doors that Andrea held ajar for them.

They found themselves in a cavernous room. It was empty. Each man inspected it for a moment, standing with weapons ready.

The floor was checkered with large black-and-white tiles that were in need of cleaning and waxing. The empty couches and chairs lining the wide hallway were upholstered in cracking red leather. The potted palms along the far wall had nearly outgrown their tarnished brass bowls. A rusty elevator stood in the corner.

"OK. Go," Andrea Todd ordered.

As they had practiced, the ten men split into three small squads. Three raced up the curving stairs to the balcony, then on to the presidential family's quarters. Two mercenaries checked the kitchen. Hobbs and the remaining four crossed the large hallway and bulldozed through the double doors leading to the servants' quarters.

Moments before, Babblo Forest had stepped outdoors for a quick smoke before going to bed. Now the fifteen-year-old cowered behind a banyan tree, wondering what was happening.

CHAPTER

2

The pilot and copilot of the MH-60K Special Operation Aircraft sat tensely in the helicopter's cockpit. The CRT—cathode ray tube—screens and instruments glowing in the cabin tinged the two men an eerie green. The pilot, Captain Jefferson Davis "Oz" Carson, strained to keep on course; the wind buffeted the men and stirred the pitching sea below them. The lighting in the black mantle of clouds to the south hinted at the second ominous gale storming toward them.

Behind the pilot, in the crew compartment, the warrant officer and crew chief tried to spot the airman they were searching for. The lost airman had been in the water a full day—heavy seas and a storm had prevented him from being found. Adding to his problems, his radio beeper, which should have enabled rescue planes to home in on him, was working only intermittently. Time was running out. It was doubtful the airman could survive the night in the cold water. Either he was found during the first few hours after nightfall, or he would die.

At the rear of the compartment, five SF troops

sat forlornly, blind in the darkness that was as black as their rubber scuba suits. They huddled on the folding seats in silence, thinking their secret thoughts. The overbearing noise of the MH-60K SOA's twin engines was broken only by the splatter of rain on the shell of the cabin.

The four Night Stalkers crewmen wore olive-green Nomax suits. Their heads were encased in olive-green helmets, emblazoned with the logos of each man's "handle." Their faces were visored by night-vision goggles that enabled them to see distinctly in the dim moonlight that filtered through the thick clouds overhead.

Oz studied the rolling waves on the ocean's surface. The wind had picked up and the waves were coming dangerously close to the chopper. It was time to put more distance between the MH-60K and the churning ocean. "Hang on," the pilot warned his crew and the SF lieutenant, who wore an intercom headset.

The pilot waited a moment for the lieutenant to relay the message to his men. Then he pulled on the collective pitch lever in his left hand. The MH-60K responded smoothly and climbed higher. His swift maneuver put a sickening feeling at the pit of his stomach. A brief shower of rain splattered from nowhere and then vanished, leaving the Plexiglas windscreen coated with beads that twinkled from the CRTs in the cockpit. Oz switched on the windshield wipers as the wind shook the aircraft.

"Still haven't detected his emergency signals," said Oz's copilot, Lt. Chad Norton. Known as

"Death Song" to his friends, Norton analyzed the instrument display as if he were part of the circuits beneath its panel. Under his NVG—night-vision goggles—his exposed dark face and sharp features reflected his American Indian ancestry.

Oz kicked his left rudder pedal and nudged the control column to the left. The MH-60K angled a bit to counteract the buffeting wind that strained to shove them off course. The pilot glanced at the CRT once more to check their heading and then scrutinized the quaking sea outside. His NVG showed the swirling water in varying shades of green and white.

Somewhere there's a man dying, struggling for breath in the cold water, Oz thought. He tensed the stiff muscles in his long legs and wished he could reach the itch at the back of his head. All that showed of his face beneath his NVG was a muscled jaw, narrow lips, and a hawkish nose that had been broken more than once. His moody blue eyes and cropped blond hair were hidden.

Tired of the silence, Oz spoke with a drawl that betrayed his southern Virginian heritage. "You guys see anything?" Oz wondered what had motivated him to ask such a ridiculous question. Exhaustion, he decided.

"Still nothing," Lt. Harvey Litwin's voice crackled on the intercom. He rode on the other side of the partition behind Oz on the right of the crew compartment. Known as O.T., short for "Old-Timer," he was the oldest man on the MH-60K. He glanced back at the five members of the SF team. Their heads flopped in unison as the wind lashed the chopper. The one at the end is definitely getting airsick, O.T. told himself. He returned to his vigil at the gunner's port window.

"Nothing," SP4 Mike Luger concurred over the intercom. Luger had the body of a jogger with muscles so tight they almost twanged. He was the youngest man aboard—and looked even younger than his twenty years.

"There's the beacon again," Death Song interrupted, a hint of excitement in his low voice. "His emergency beeper's back. If it'd just stay on long enough for us to home in."

"What's the heading?" Oz asked.

"It's behind us."

"Behind us?" Oz slowly brought the control column to its center position. The chopper slowed and then hovered, shuddering in the wind like a giant black dragonfly. The rolling waves kicked foam at the aircraft. The pilot booted his right rudder pedal, leaning slightly in his chair as he swung the MH-60K to face the west. He watched his vertical situation display, or VSD, until he had the helicopter properly aligned and waited for the new heading from his copilot.

"Just a sec, I'll have it," Death Song said. He tapped a button to the side of his VSD and punched two buttons on his keyboard. After consulting the HSD, or horizontal situation display, he hit more keys on the chopper's computer console. The computer plotted the course between the MH-60K and the downed flyer.

"There," Death Song said finally.

Oz studied the glowing HSD in front of him.

"How'd he get behind us? In this cold water, his signature on the FLIR ought to stick out like a nudist at a revival meeting."

"We missed him because we never flew over him. He isn't *directly* to our rear. He's to one side of the path we took."

"But how could the SGPS be that far off?" Oz asked. Their satellite global positioning system received updates by locking onto two Air Force navigation satellites. "Our course heading should have been accurate to within several feet."

"Our SGPS isn't off. The problem is he's drifting. The wind and waves. We went over where he was when his beeper was on."

"Not where he was when we passed him," Oz finished. "But he couldn't drift that far."

"He didn't. But we'll need to be almost on top of him to see him with the height of these waves . . . Hang on . . . His signal broke up again."

Oz swore under his breath.

"Blackbird, can you read us? Over," the radio crackled in Oz's headset.

The pilot engaged the triggerlike radio switch on the control column.

"Roger. This is Blackbird, over."

"The weather sat shows a heavy rainstorm entering your area. Come on home."

"Negative, Control. We're about to zero in on Baby Bird."

"The weather's . . ." The transmission was lost in the crackling of lightning that intruded into the radio band.

"Say again," Oz said over the radio.

"The weather's deteriorating. You can't stay out."

"How much time?"

"Probably not more than five minutes. Ten at the most. You'll not be doing us a favor if we have to hunt ten instead of one tomorrow."

"I copy. We'll not fool around longer than we have to. We've got a fix, but this guy's radio beeper isn't cooperating. Over."

"It must be weak. We're not picking up anything in here."

"We're going to make one more pass."

"Good luck. Remember the clock's running. Over."

"Will do. Over and out."

Oz clicked the radio off and spoke through the intercom, "OK, where is that guy?"

"There's no way of telling exactly," Death Song said. "But we've traveled twenty-four klicks since the previous beacon reading. He's within that range."

Oz eased the control column forward and the MH-60K accelerated, pushing him back into his bucket seat. They hurtled above the water. "Too bad there isn't a second chopper out here. We could have vectored our two readings and pinpointed him." He checked the course on the HSD and then spoke, "Keep your eyes peeled, guys. This is our last pass before we head for base. Got to find him this flyby."

"We can still triangulate if he comes back on," Death Song said.

"Hmmm. Jump to one side of our path?"

"Right. Take a second reading and compare it to the first. It wouldn't be too precise, but it'd get us into the neighborhood."

"That'd work. *If* he comes on line."

"Speak of the devil," Death Star said.

"Hang on," Oz warned the crew. He stomped on the right pedal and cramped the control column to the right. The MH-60K lurched to the right, a gust of wind speeding it on its gut-wrenching way.

"That's far enough," Death Song said seconds later. "Come to a stop for a minute."

Oz pulled on the control column so the MH-60K hovered, vacillating in the gale of spray coming up from the dark ocean. The brine ebbed, then mounted upward and snatched at them. The wind slapped at the side of the helicopter.

"Lost it!" Death Song said. "No wait. There it is. Weak . . ." The copilot tapped the buttons alongside his VSD and again poked a button on the HSD. His fingers stabbed at several keys on the chopper's computer console and it plotted a second course between the MH-60K and the downed airman. "He's dropped off again. But I've got a fix. There. Where the two headings intersect."

Oz studied his HSD, then swung the helicopter to the new heading and locked onto the glowing path on display. "OK, everyone. We're going to be over him in a minute. Keep sharp."

As Oz watched the waves, he felt as if his helicopter hung immobile while the sea raced below him. He glanced at the HSD. Almost there. He tugged on the control column to decelerate.

"OK," he alerted the crew. "He should be right around here. Lieutenant, your guys ready?"

The SF leader's voice crackled on the intercom, "We're ready and waiting. I'll make the descent myself. I shouldn't need anyone else unless we run into trouble."

Oz studied the forward-looking infrared or FLIR. There! The pilot's body bobbed into view on the screen, a white blob in the cool green of the ocean. Twenty-four hours before, he'd woken up in a warm Pawtucken bed for a routine training mission; now he was lucky to be alive.

"There he is," Oz said, pulling on the control column bringing the MH-60K to a near stop. He fought a gust of wind to bring the chopper about, placing the flyer under the SH-60B-style rescue hoist mounted over the right crew compartment door.

"I see him, too!" O.T. yelled, staring out his port. O.T. staggered in the wind-shaken helicopter, making his way back to the passenger compartment. The warrant officer checked to be sure the SF troops were secure and then slid open the side door. Chilly rain splattered into the compartment and soaked O.T.'s Nomax suit.

"Get your goggles off," Oz ordered his crew. "I'm switching on the landing light." He turned off his NVG and then let them hang on the rubber cord draped behind his helmet. His head was pulled back by the counterweight at the back of his helmet. Except for his scopes and instrument panel, everything was suddenly black. He flipped the light switch and stared through the lower windscreen on the MH-60K's chin.

The pitching salt water below the hovering aircraft was bathed in a bright cone of light. The cold airman waved weakly as he bobbed up and down. The wash from the chopper made rippling rings radiating around him and splattered him with ocean spray.

"Lieutenant, we'll have to lower you on the hoist," Oz said. "The wind's too strong for us to descend to your twenty-foot drop height."

"OK," the SF lieutenant said over the intercom. He removed his intercom headset, inhibiting easy conversation with the crew. He got his harness arranged for the descent.

O.T. switched on the dim cabin light in the crew compartment. The lieutenant left his scuba tank under the bench where he'd been sitting. The wind rattled the MH-60K as the lieutenant grabbed a handhold. He staggered to the winch.

O.T. hooked the end of the winch to the soldier's STABO, or stabilized tactical airborne body operations, harness. "The lieutenant's secured," O.T. said.

"Has he got a spare STABO for the airman?" Oz asked.

"He's got the extra harness."

"You run the hoist, O.T. I can't see much with the rain splattering my windscreen."

"Will do." The warrant officer turned to the SF lieutenant. "Ready?" he yelled at the lieutenant.

The soldier lowered his goggles over his face and flashed a thumbs-up signal.

"Forward two meters," O.T. told Oz on the intercom. "Good. Right there. Hold her as steady as you can."

O.T. stood at the backup hoist controls in the crew compartment and slowly lowered the rubber-clad soldier on the end of the steel cable. As the diver neared the heaving surface of the inky water, he swung pendulumlike into the cone of light beneath the chopper. He skimmed the surface with a finned foot, then splashed in next to the flyer. A wave crashed over both men.

"He's in the water," O.T. told Oz.

It was essential that the MH-60K remained as motionless as possible. It's not going to be easy to keep us steady, Oz told himself. The wind rocked the chopper and—when the pilot compensated—abated unexpectedly, forcing Oz to sling the column over briskly to keep from plowing to the side.

Below, the SF trooper thrashed toward the airman. The two men struggled to encircle the downed pilot with the harness.

"I'm freezing," the pilot yelled, squinting in the bright light. The spray stung his eyes.

The lieutenant said nothing. He tugged at the harness he'd mounted on the airman to be sure it was secure, then kicked away and gave the ready-for-pickup signal by holding his right hand in the air, palm forward.

"Bingo," O.T. said. "He's hooked."

"OK," Oz said. "Bring 'em up." The pilot tensed his hand on the collective pitch lever. He'd need to counteract the sudden weight the helicopter would acquire when the men left the buoyancy of the ocean.

O.T. clicked on the hoist. The steel cable wound and the airman started to rise with the lieutenant cradled below him. O.T. felt a sense of déjà vu watching the two men rise. Years before, a newby in Vietnam, he'd rescued a pilot from the ocean. Only then the sea was calm. And things weren't as dangerous as they often were in his work as a Night Stalker.

In a few seconds, they were alongside. O.T. grabbed the steel cable and hauled them to the edge of the deck so they sat in the doorway.

"They're up," O.T. said. A gust of rain rapped across the warrant officer's helmet as he leaned over the soaked flyer. "Come on over here," he yelled, half carrying the young pilot away from the cable. O.T. felt the airman shiver. The warrant officer guided the rubber-legged pilot away from the open door toward Luger's station.

Luger took the airman and maneuvered him across the rocking cabin. The flyer settled into the chair that had been folded down for him from the wall. Luger draped a plastic emergency blanket around his shoulders.

After the SF lieutenant had slipped into his spot on the bench, O.T. slammed the door home and latched it. "All aboard and stowed away."

"Good job, O.T."

"Beers are on me at Jake's," the warrant officer offered.

To the puzzlement of the SF troops, a loud groan came from the other three members of the crew. The Night Stalker crew knew about the raunchy country-western music O.T. liked. He was always trying to lure them into some dive to hear a band no one else could stand to listen to. But they'd be there to celebrate a successful mission, once they returned.

"Let's switch back to NVGs," Oz said, a tired smile on his face. He clicked the landing light off. He raised his night-vision goggles and ascended to a safer altitude. Lightning flashing at their backs warned of the approaching storm.

The helicopter surged to its top speed and hurtled through the wet night. One thing about this job, the pilot mused to himself, it doesn't get boring.

C H A P T E R

![3]

At the same time Andrea Todd's first group had stormed the Presidential Palace, her two other bands of mercenaries had started their synchronized missions.

Andrea's second group consisted of two men.

Bruce Wetzel and "Smiley" Douglas left when the other teams did. As they neared their assigned objective, Wetzel slowed the rented Chevy.

"That it?" Smiley asked.

Wetzel eyed the cinder-block building alongside the road, nestled in a grove of rubber trees. On its side—in crude, faded letters—a sign proclaimed "Voice of the Island." The building was located on the mountain overlooking the capital city of Coopersville. The meager antenna stretching above the cement structure comprised the country's one and only radio station.

"Yeah," Wetzel growled. "There's the satellite dish next to it." The dish relayed all the off-island calls to and from a communications satellite high in space. A small building containing the automated equipment connecting the phone calls for the tiny city sat next to it. The dish antenna had been sited next to the radio station because the generator inside the station was more reliable than Coopersville's ancient power plant. Currently, the city's lights were working. They twinkled and reflected over the bay far below.

Satisfied that they'd found the station, Wetzel pulled the car over and parked it in front of the building. The car's tires crunched in the loose paving of gravel and sea shells.

Wetzel twisted the car key and the motor sputtered to a stop. Behind the steering wheel of the dented blue Chevy, he slouched with the demeanor of a bear. The big-boned mercenary wore a short-sleeved black T-shirt with a soiled collar. His animal eyes glowed in the dim light and his untrimmed beard rose almost to his eyes and fell to his prominent Adam's apple. Unconsciously, he pawed the .45 automatic and wirecutters lying on the seat beside him.

"Isn't it about time?" Smiley fretted.

"Quit whining," Wetzel snarled. "Or I'll wring your neck."

Smiley was quiet. He knew Wetzel didn't make idle threats. But Andrea would skin them alive if they missed their alert. He wondered how he'd had the misfortune of being saddled with Wetzel.

After letting Smiley fidget a few more minutes, Wetzel yanked the antenna from his radio, stuck it out the open window, and clicked the receiver on.

"Andrea's always punctual," Smiley warned.

"All right! We've got a few minutes. You just watch to be sure some fool islander doesn't stop to poke his nose into our business."

Shortly, the CB crackled. "Roll call," Andrea's husky voice commanded.

Hobbs's voice crackled on the radio, "Number One. We're in place. It's clear."

Wetzel pushed his radio's call button. He grunted, "Two is home free." He switched the radio off.

"Aren't you going to wait?" Smiley asked. "To see if there're other instructions?"

"We know our orders without waiting to hear more." He threw the radio onto the torn seat between them and jerked his car door open. Wetzel grumbled under his breath at the car's cramped size. He awkwardly unwound himself from the interior of the vehicle. He rose, the .45 in his hand. He turned slowly in a circle, studying his surroundings through squinting eyes. "No one snooping about," Wetzel declared.

"What about the joker in the building?"

There were lights on in the radio station. The local disc jockey, "Mambo Jumbo," was working as the DJ, manager, and engineer. He kept the station on the air eight hours every day except Monday.

"Don't worry about the disc jockey," Wetzel said. "He can't see us through those glass block windows. Get the wire cutters and take out the station and dish." The big man shoved his pistol into his belt and tugged at his T-shirt to conceal the weapon.

Wetzel stood lookout while Smiley sneaked toward the side of the radio building. In a few minutes, the mercenary had cut off both the transmitter and the satellite dish. Smiley had isolated the island nation from the outside world.

The two mercenaries stood in the darkness as the tiny entrance to the station cracked open to reveal the shadowy, elephantine figure of Mambo Jumbo. The DJ switched on his flashlight and stepped out of the station.

"What's goin' on?" Mambo asked the night. He poked the beam of light at the radio tower as if trying to discern if it was still there. Then he noticed the two silhouettes.

"Hey," the disc jockey said. "What're you doing here?" He flashed the light into Smiley's eyes.

Wetzel fired twice.

The DJ's career came to an abrupt end.

Wetzel crunched across the gravel and shells of the parking lot and bent over the body. Carefully he went through the disc jockey's pockets, removing the money and change.

"Give me a cut," Smiley said.

"No way," Wetzel hissed. "I aced him, I get his stuff." He jerked the two gold rings from the dead man's fingers and picked up the flashlight. He and Smiley trudged to the car and squeezed in. Wetzel started the engine and the two mercenaries drove away.

Andrea Todd's third team was led by Eddy Kellerman. The man was in his fifties; the others in the gang believed he had once been with the

CIA. But Kellerman never said anything about his past and no one was crazy enough to ask. It was common knowledge, however, that he had honed his killing skills in Vietnam, Cambodia, and Afghanistan. Two of the other men in Andrea's gang had been there with Kellerman or had friends who had accompanied him.

In Coopersville, Kellerman waited for Andrea's signal.

A nervous tic squeezed his pale face into a grimace. He rested in the shadows—back against a wall—across from the city's police station. There was no military on the tiny island. Only the police.

Kellerman wore old blue slacks, a white bush jacket, and zippered boots. He dragged at the cigarette in his thin lips, waiting for the bored patrolman to torpidly walk past.

Once the black policeman had trudged by, Kellerman hauled his Polish wz 63 "RAK" submachine gun from under his jacket. He yanked out a cylindrical silencer and screwed it in place on the submachine gun. From another pocket, he produced a magazine of subsonic 9mm Parabellum cartridges. He retained it in fingers so skinny they might have belonged to a corpse. Reassured that the magazine was full, he tapped it against his thigh to align the cartridges, then inserted it into the grip of the submachine gun. The soft clack announced the magazine was locked in place. With the stockless firearm prepared for use, he replaced it in its shoulder harness under his jacket.

He took another puff from the cigarette, watching the police station across the street. A pair of drunken tourists sang their way past. A bicyclist shot by, veering at the last moment to miss the tourists.

Kellerman took one last drag on the cigarette, then tossed it in the street. He readjusted his radio's earphone into his left ear.

Three minutes later, the CB hissed, "Roll call."

"Number One. We're in place. It's clear."

"Two is home free," Wetzel growled.

"Three's clear," Kellerman whispered in his New England accent.

"All right," Andrea said. "In three minutes."

Kellerman pocketed the CB, leaving the receiver in his ear in case there were other messages. He paced across the street in long strides, his boots clattering against the paving stones. Once across, he banged his fist on the side of the rusted van sitting in front of the police station. Three thuds, a pause, then two.

With the completion of his signal, the van's side door creaked along its runners. Five men stood inside, dressed in uniforms like those of the local police. They were armed with FN FALs.

"Lock and load," Kellerman commanded.

The five rifles clattered, chambering cartridges from their magazines.

"Follow me," Kellerman said evenly. "No shooting unless I give the word. I plan on doing all the work myself. You're only for backup. Sam?"

The tall black snapped to attention. The nostrils on his wide nose tightened and his brow furrowed.

"You'll guard the entrance once we get in. No one leaves until we're done."

"Yes, sir."

Kellerman wheeled around and pulled the submachine gun from under his jacket. His bony fingers cocked its bolt back as he ascended the limestone steps. He shoved open the heavy mahogany and glass door and stepped into the police station.

"What the hell?" the desk sergeant said in a thick Jamaican accent.

Kellerman expertly tapped the RAK's trigger. A three-round burst cracked from the muzzle of the silenced gun. Bloody flowers blossomed on the sergeant's chest, throat, and cheek. He tumbled behind the desk.

Kellerman's team followed him into the station. Sam closed the door behind him and guarded at the entry as he had been ordered. Kellerman signaled silently with his hands.

You and you, Kellerman's fingers designated the two mercenaries on his left. Stand there, his fingers ordered by pointing. You and you, his finger chose the other two, follow me.

Kellerman knew that unmarried policemen slept in the small barracks at the station. Because of the poor pay, most of the policemen were unmarried. Consequently, all but six of the city's police force were now in the barracks, asleep. Kellerman jostled his way into the lounge branching from the main lobby.

The eleven sleeping policemen inside didn't have a prayer. Kellerman's first volley struck six while they lay on their stained white cots. The bullets danced along the bodies; scarlet gushers of blood and flesh splashed from the impacts of the 9mm bullets.

The six were murdered outright. Another burst; two more cried in pain and two lay still. Kellerman stopped to exchange his empty magazine for a full one. As he reloaded, one man rolled from his cot and frantically crawled into the bathroom, vainly searching for safety.

"Hold your fire," Kellerman yelled as the mercenary on his left lifted a rifle. Kellerman cycled his submachine gun, a smile on his face. The unarmed policeman slammed the door shut.

Kellerman waited a second. Then his finger twitched on the trigger. The gun stitched a neat row of bullets across the width of the door. A muffled scream came from the bathroom. Kellerman answered it with three more rounds. The door swung open and the policeman sprawled onto the floor.

"Find the keys to the jail," Kellerman ordered. "I'll finish here."

His men didn't hesitate. They pivoted on their heels in the manner of those used to taking orders unquestioningly. They shoved through the exit to leave the blood-splattered lounge.

Two officers remained alive. They lay on the floor.

One moaned and tossed onto his side, hand clasping the heavily bleeding wound in his stomach. "Please . . ." he begged through clinched lips.

"Let me free you," Kellerman cooed. He knelt and stroked the black man's head. "I'll take care of you." Kellerman straightened and then placed a precise shot behind the man's ear.

The official sprawled flat onto the bloody floor. His leg twitched and then he was still. Kellerman smiled, then stepped over the body to stand by the last living policeman.

The man had raised himself to a sitting position. He coughed blood and rocked silently back and forth. He stared at the killer, terror in his eyes.

Kellerman fired his RAK. The man choked and fell back onto the floor.

Kellerman shoved his way into the lobby of the station. He crossed it, slamming a new, full magazine into his weapon. "Let's take care of the prisoners."

Sam spoke tersely, "Got trouble."

"What?" Kellerman asked, turning on his heel to face Sam.

"The policeman on foot patrol. He's outside the station. I think he saw or heard us."

"Damn," Kellerman said. "Is he armed?"

A pistol discharge answered his question. The bullet from an old .38 revolver crashed through the window.

Sam toppled to one knee, blinking at the shower of glass fragments. Then he saw the hole in his chest. He gaped at the spurting blood that stained his white uniform. He groaned, then crumpled to the wooden floor.

Kellerman darted his head around the corner of the doorway. He saw the officer in the street. The man was concealed by the van—only his feet showing beneath the van gave him away.

The officer peeped around its edge and aimed an old Smith & Wesson. Kellerman ducked back. Another slug shattered the glass and sprinkled the marble floor with crystal shards.

It was ominously quiet on the street.

"Come out," the policeman yelled in a thick Caribbean accent.

Kellerman laughed as he crouched next to the doorway. "Four shots left in his pistol and he's going to take us prisoners." Kellerman glanced at one of his men crouched under the front window. "Put down your rifle and come here."

"But—"

"Do it!" Kellerman leveled his submachine gun at the man.

"Yes, sir." The black man leaned his FN FAL against the wall and crawled to the edge of the doorway.

"I'm coming out," Kellerman shouted from behind the doorway. He motioned to his hench-man and whispered, "Go. When you get out, stand to one side and distract him. Then I can get an un-obstructed shot."

"Hands on your head!" the policeman or-dered when the unarmed mercenary appeared in the doorway. "Are there more of you in there?"

"Uh, no," the mercenary said, placing his hands on his head. He descended the steps. "Just the two of us."

"You trying to trick me, mon?" the policeman asked, getting behind the van in the street. "That was a white face I saw peeking around the corner a minute ago. An' why're you wearing a police uniform?''

The mercenary said nothing. He hesitated and then sidestepped from the stairs in an attempt to give Kellerman a clear shot at the policeman.

"Stop. Stay right where you are," the officer ordered.

The mercenary froze. Sweat formed on his brow as he recalled Kellerman's orders. The mercenary started to step to one side again.

"Stop!" the officer yelled. "Or I plug you right where you stand."

A metallic ball bounced down the steps. The mercenary recognized the clattering. He dived to the sidewalk with a bone-breaking jar.

"What you do, mon?" the policeman asked, not sure what was happening.

There was silence.

Then the explosion of the hand grenade.

There was little fire or smoke. But the shrapnel riddled the policeman's legs and torso. He dropped to the pavement. Gasoline trickled from the van's punctured gas tank, swiftly forming a pool around the groaning man.

Kellerman stepped outside to inspect his damage. He pulled another cigarette from his pocket, licked its end, and placed it in his lips. Ignoring the pleas for help from the mercenary who had also been wounded by the grenade, Kellerman touched a match to his cigarette and puffed it to life. He tossed the match into the street.

There was a crackling of flame as the match hit the vapors. Then the tank of the van exploded.

The flames engulfed the officer and the mercenary lying on the sidewalk. A hubcap popped from a burning tire and clattered across the street. The hubcap came to a spinning stop. Human flesh crackled in the flames.

"OK, you guys," Kellerman told his men inside the police station. "You're the new policemen for this island. Your first job is to control the crowd that's collecting out there until the sorry excuse for a fire department gets here."

C H A P T E R

4

The alarm hummed at oh-six-hundred. Oz struggled to pull up the collective pitch lever of his chopper. The alarm continued to buzz in his ear. Oz sat in the lead helicopter. The MH-60K behind him was supposed to follow his course exactly, but for some reason, it suddenly veered to the right.

"Eagle Two," Oz called over the radio, "look out for the power line! You're headed for the cables. Change course! Dale—"

His warning went unheeded. As Oz watched in horror, the helicopter below him slashed into the low power line. The lower cable cut into the cabin, instantly killing the pilot and navigator. The strong titanium and fiberglass blades of the MH-60K cut into the upper cable and then become entwined in them. The aircraft fell the short distance separating it from the earth, killing almost everyone aboard when the power cable brushed the skin of the craft.

Oz hovered above the wreckage, the sparks still flying from the cable. The wire hissed and snaked around the damp earth. Three panicked infantrymen jumped clear of the burning aircraft and were fried when the cable brushed against them.

The alarm in Oz's cabin continued to drone.

Oz jerked himself awake, bathed in sweat. The alarm clock hummed on the night table beside him—not in the cabin of his MH-60K. He poked an arm from under his shroud of blankets and hit the alarm button.

There was no doubt in his mind where the terrifying dream had originated. The exact event had happened three weeks before. Oz stared at the ceiling, wide awake and wondering how long it would be before he quit having the nightmare. He unconsciously groped toward Sandy.

There was a cool spot under the blankets where Sandy should have been. Then he remembered. She'd left a week before, the chopper accident being the catalyst that had brought their marriage to an end. Oz pushed the memory of their argument—along with the crash—from his mind.

Time to get going, he told himself. He swung his well-muscled legs over the side of the bed with a groan. Five years ago, staying awake to work at gluing together a lute—or even a night on the town—wouldn't have bothered him the next morning. That wasn't true anymore. These days it took time for him to bounce back.

He wondered if he was getting out of shape or old. Both, he decided glumly as he rubbed the scar tissue at the back of his skull. The plastic plate embedded there reminded him of his own helicopter accident.

It had been near the end of the Vietnam War.

He'd been a newby copilot, flying secret missions into Cambodia in March of 1975 against the Khmer Rouge forces in the area near Prey Veng.

The helicopter Oz sat in was a UH-1 Huey, the chopper that had become the all-purpose work-horse of the US Army during the Vietnam conflict. The side doors of the chopper were open; air streamed through the noisy machine, giving them respite from the intense heat rising from the green jungle they hurtled over.

The six SF troops they'd extracted sat in the passenger compartment of the helicopter, half asleep, their eyes glazed from battle fatigue. One slept sprawled across the swaying floor of the air-craft. Behind the special forces troops, in niches on either side of the passenger compartment, the two door gunners sat behind M-60 machine guns. They had the dark visorlike goggles of their helmets pulled down to protect their eyes from the wind and sun.

The crew was tired. The whopping blades above them, coupled with the heat, almost lulled them all to sleep.

"Look out!" the left gunner's voice abruptly crackled on the intercom, breaking the serenity of the ride.

Instantly alert, Oz leaned in his seat, scanning the jungle below and behind them in an effort to locate any potential dangers. His eye caught a blur of motion.

The young copilot was unable to shout a warn-ing that he'd seen a rocket bolting at them when the blast of its warhead shook the passenger compartment. Oz was thrown forward by the blast and felt shrapnel smacking against the back of his helmet and digging into his scalp. Metal fragments raced past him to pepper the windscreen like buckshot. The pilot next to Oz fell forward, grasping at his neck, his body held upright by his shoulder harness. A jagged hole just below his jawline marked the path of a metal fragment that had severed his jugular vein. Blood spurted from the wound, blotting the six-pack dials in front of him.

The chopper screamed downward, amid cries of terror and pain from those in the smoking passenger compartment.

The near free-fall of the helicopter put a floating feeling in Oz's guts. He frantically jerked at the sluggish collective pitch lever. The controls refused to budge for a moment but then came free. The UH-1's turbine whined, struggling to counter the chopper's plunge.

The tail rotor sliced into a palm and the chopper lurched to the right as Oz shoved the column, avoiding a tall, dead tree in their path. Oz fought the helicopter's crippled controls, lifting the machine upward. He disregarded the bloody dials in front of him that warned of damage to the aircraft, and concentrated on keeping the Huey aloft.

Oz lost track of time. He ignored the dead pilot beside him and forced himself to stay conscious, aware that he was losing blood. His head started to throb and the back of his neck was sticky with it. The rusty smell of blood filled his nostrils and his shirt clung to his back. He struggled to keep the UH-1 on course, crossing the Vietnamese border and heading for the landing strip.

He ignored the throbbing pain, not daring to remove his hands from the controls to assess the damage to his scalp. He didn't bother to try calling ahead as they approached the runway; the radio was obviously out, a piece of jagged metal sticking from its front.

Oz gently set the Huey on the earth, mechanically shutting off its smoking engine and reaching toward the low ceiling to trip the breakers of the electrical systems. The helicopter became deathly quiet, with only a low moan from one of the SF team breaking the silence.

Suddenly the helicopter was swamped with men. Oz fought at the release on his seat belt but found himself too weak to work it. He leaned forward in his harness and passed out.

The dead and injured were pulled from the chopper and hastily carried to the Quonset-hut hospital—or the morgue next to it.

The next thing Oz remembered was riding on a gurney. The medical team expertly lifted him onto an operating table. When they rolled him facedown, he caught a glimpse of the brightly lit green operating room and wondered momentarily why he was there.

"How the hell are we going to get that helmet off?" a doctor growled.

"Don't touch that!" the surgeon warned the orderly. "Extract that chunk of shrapnel and he'll bleed to death before we get the helmet off."

Oz struggled to move and matter-of-factly noticed the pool of sticky blood that was forming under him, too tired and woozy to be frightened by it.

"Hang on, soldier," the doctor said. The pilot felt a squeeze on his shoulder that felt a hundred miles away from his body. "Let's put him under so he doesn't go into shock," the doctor instructed another green-gowned figure.

A plastic mask was fitted over the pilot's face. Oz promptly blacked out, unsure if he'd ever waken.

Now Oz rubbed the scar where the three-inch piece of shrapnel had pierced his helmet and skull. He shuffled into the bathroom and critically studied the face in the mirror.

Almost handsome, masculine features under a shock of wavy, light hair scrutinized him from the glass. Above his lips was a thin scar from an accident in 1989. His jaw was just short of being massive. His ears were plastered close to his skull. This morning, he had blue *and* bloodshot eyes.

X-ray eyes, Oz thought with a grim smile. Sandy had called them X-ray eyes when they'd first met. Because they look right into me, she had said. But now the X-ray eyes had crow's-feet.

You're aging, he told himself, shocked at how much he resembled his father. He opened the medicine cabinet and retrieved two aspirin, turning on the faucet and downing them with a stream of lukewarm water he cupped in his hand.

He closed the medicine cabinet and lethargically turned from the mirror. Thirty-eight wasn't as ancient as it had once seemed. Getting old wasn't so bad—considering the alternative.

He relieved himself and then enjoyed a long steaming shower that drove away the cobwebs of concern about aging and the nightmare of the crash. He brushed his teeth to remove the stale, dry cotton taste of the drinks of the night before. Then he lathered and meticulously shaved the blond stubble from his face.

When he returned to the bedroom to get dressed, sunlight streamed into the window, casting beams of light across the Queen Anne furniture Sandy had saved their money to buy. In the corner was the sole piece of furniture that didn't match: a gun cabinet in which Oz kept his father's hunting rifles. The firearms, cabinet, and a potato-bug mandolin hanging on the wall were among the few things left of Oz's inheritance from his family's estate.

Breakfast was a glass of orange juice and a cup of coffee. He added the empty juice glass to the pile of dirty plates and utensils in the brimming sink, feeling guilty that he hadn't washed them the night before.

Oz remembered to place dry dog food—the cat's favorite meal—into his bowl. The cat was nowhere to be seen—as usual. The animal liked to tomcat around the neighborhood, acquiring numerous battle scars in the process. Sandy had remarked, "That cat looks like hell," and Hell had become his name.

Oz absentmindedly strummed the open strings on the lute sitting atop the kitchen table. He had nearly finished building the instrument. The metal scrapers, calipers, and sandpaper sat around the lute, waiting patiently for him to continue the precise work.

He left the house balancing a second cup of coffee in a mug that read "Chopper Pilots Do It In The Air." He squinted at the sun, then put on his mirrored Gargoyles sunglasses.

He got into his car, an Acura Integra GS that had been modified into a convertible, started the engine, and backed out of the driveway.

The pilot traveled through the checkpoint at the east entrance of Fort Bragg. Leaving the base, he headed up highway twenty-four to Manchester where O.T. lived.

Oz brought the red Acura to the speed limit on the highway. He rode with the top down and the wind gusted through the car; the engine's sixteen valves hummed. The pilot flipped through the radio stations and listened to a news broadcast. He wondered if he might eventually become involved in the newest airline hijacking that was unfolding in the Middle East.

When the announcer turned to the local news, the pilot switched the radio to its tape player mode. The strains of Vivaldi's "Four Seasons" floated from the player. The tape was one of the ones he'd discovered at his father's home and Oz found it magically soothing. The music seemed to blend into the fog that clung to the valley as he sped over the blacktop.

Oz soon reached his destination and he parked the car in the driveway in front of O.T.'s light gray ranch house. Oak trees framed the structure, and as Oz approached the home, a gray squirrel sat in the foliage above the yard, noisily biting into an acorn.

The pilot knocked at the glass storm door; the front door behind it stood open.

"Come in," O.T. yelled from inside.

O.T.'s real name was Harvey Litwin. It was hard for Oz to imagine the man ever having been anything but middle-aged, but O.T. relished his age and referred to Oz and the others in his crew as "youngsters." He was appalled by Luger's and Death Song's ignorance of recent historic events. O.T. knew ways of circumventing regulations and red tape—another definite asset as far as Oz was concerned.

O.T. was a little pudgy and Oz often wondered if he was pushing the Army's maximum weight requirements. The warrant officer was conspicuous in a crowd; he shaved his crown to hide his bald spot and his skin, which burned easily, was sprinkled liberally with freckles.

Oz entered the house, glancing at the TV that entertained the empty living room. The house had a lived-in look; an empty beer can and a pile of magazines sat on the coffee table that was surrounded by a curved modular couch.

"I'm finally ready," O.T. said, clomping into the living room in his Army boots. Like Oz, he wore a battle dress uniform—BOU—with an aviator's blue ascot.

The two men left the house and climbed into the Acura. They journeyed to the base hospital to visit Jack Winter, the sole survivor of the helicopter crash that figured in Oz's nightmares.

"You can only stay a few minutes," the nurse wearing a prim white hat told them.

Oz nodded. She left to attend to a patient in a neighboring bed.

Jack Winter lay there, unrecognizable in the swaddling of gauze bandages that covered oozing burns over almost his entire body. Tubes ran into his arm and the bump that marked his nose. A catheter snaked from under the sheet.

"Jack?" O.T. asked softly.

"Uhh," a voice moaned from the bandages. "Who is it?" the injured man asked in a soft whisper. "The light's not too good in here." He chuckled and then coughed, his limbs twisting with pain.

"It's O.T. and Oz," the pilot said softly.

"Nice of you to come and see me," Winter said. "Frankie and the Savage came by yesterday. But none of my crew's been in. They in here somewhere? Nobody will tell me and I can't see . . ."

O.T. glanced at Oz. They both realized that Winter didn't know the rest of his crew had been killed in the accident.

Oz spoke, "They'll be OK. You worry about yourself for right now."

"Yeah." Winter nodded beneath the bandages. "Guess I've got enough to take care of right here. But you tell them to hurry up and get better and not to worry about me, OK?"

"We will," O.T. lied. "You need anything?"

"A T-bone steak and some baked potatoes, maybe? So far all I've been getting through these tubes is sugar water." He shook an arm, rattling the drip tube against the chromed bar on the side of the bed.

"We'll treat you to a steak when you're mended," Oz promised.

Winter coughed. "Damn," he said in a low voice. "Pain never quits."

"You'd better go now," the nurse said, appearing from nowhere.

"We'll check on you in a couple of days," O.T. said.

"I'm not going anyplace. I'll be right here. Be careful flying the unfriendly skies."

"We will."

O.T. and Oz pushed their way through the double glass doors of the Army hospital. The place jogged Oz's memory as he recalled his own stay in a similar hospital a decade and a half before.

He'd been lucky to ever make it to the hospital. After he'd been brought in from his wrecked Huey, the Army surgeons had been amazed that he was still alive.

They finally sawed his helmet to get it off without disturbing the shrapnel that had ripped through it. They filled his veins with blood as fast as it poured from his wound. They fought to keep the pilot alive and succeeded. Oz had been transported to the States after his condition had stabilized.

In the stateside hospital, he found the pain in the back of his head to be almost unbearable while the bone and skin grew in and around the plastic plate that patched the hole in his skull.

There was mental anguish as well. The TV

news had detailed the chain of events as Cambodia, Laos, and Vietnam fell to the communists. They reported the evacuation of Saigon. The pictures of the helicopters lifting fleeing Americans from the roof of the US Embassy were etched into Oz's mind.

He watched, vowing to do everything he could to prevent his country from ever again suffering such a humiliating defeat.

His wound had healed, though it still hurt with changes in the weather. But the Army doctors had determined he would be able to fly without any problems. Oz had reenlisted, a Silver Star and Purple Heart added to the medals he'd already collected. He worked hard; in the process, he had become one of the best pilots in the Army—a Night Stalker.

5

Except for the crowd attracted to the front of the police station, Andrea's three teams had been successful. And the crowd hadn't been hard to disperse. The dead policeman would lend credence to the story Andrea planned to spread across the island. About the only problem they'd encountered had been the escape of one kitchen boy from the Presidential Palace. And, Andrea thought, he was some spaced-out Rastafarian that no one would believe anyway.

She slinked up the marble stairway to where the President and his family were captive. It's going to be hard to make this dump livable, she said to herself, running a finger along the dirty railing.

Stucky, one of her mercenaries, came stomping down the steps. He looked like a long-necked chicken. His squeaky voice grated on her nerves. She didn't meet his eyes and hoped he'd pass her without speaking.

"Nice shooting," Stucky said, stopping on the steps.

"What?" she said in a tired voice. She paused

on the steps but faced the empty hallway rather than Stucky's ugly face.

"The guards out front. You aced them perfect."

"Like they say, I always get my men," Andrea said, suddenly turning to glance at Stucky's pimply face.

She discovered Stucky gawking impulsively at her full bosom. He glanced at her face and then his eyes darted away. He wanted to scamper down the stairs, but instead found his feet rooted in place.

Andrea lowered her voice, "If I catch you staring at me like that again, you'll be carrying your eyes—and balls—in your pocket."

"Yes, ma'am," Stucky said in a flustered voice. He whirled away and half stumbled down the marble steps.

Andrea topped the stairs and sauntered along the wrought-iron railing. She made a mental note to waste Stucky the first chance she got. She paused at the massive mahogany door, then pushed through it.

The suite inside was like a small house. A petite foyer, a marble bath, large living area, and a giant bedroom beyond an arched walnut portal. In the middle of the foyer the President of the Republic of Palm Island, John Philip Noble, sat in a worn velvet chair.

He was flanked by his wife and two children, an eight-year-old boy and a teenage girl. All were bound by nylon cords to their chairs. Behind the family were four of Andrea's henchmen.

President John Philip Noble sat upright in his

chair, straining at the cords binding him. His un-
blinking eyes glared at Andrea; his black skin glistened in the light. Andrea had learned all she could
about the large man. Educated in England, he was
well versed in law and history; he enjoyed painting
during the little spare time he had.

He was a rarity: a politician who wanted only
what was best for his country. It will be hard to
break his spirit, Andrea thought. But it can be
done. The tough part will be avoiding making him
choose between his family and his country.

"What the hell are you doing?" Noble asked
evenly in a low voice most men wished they pos-
sessed.

Andrea studied the man for a moment, then
spoke in her sensuous voice, "We're going to do
what you've been trying to do." She paused to see
what the president's reaction would be.

Noble clamped his mouth shut. His face became a mask.

"We're going to expand the tourist trade and
make your country prosper. Maybe even bring in
gambling interests. Launder money on the side
through new 'offshore' banks."

"You'll never get away with it," Noble
snapped. "My people won't allow you to—"

"Yes, they will. You'll be helping us."

"Nothing you can do to me will make me cooperate. You'll be—"

Andrea reached behind her back and produced a German Sprengers as if by magic. She
thumbed the button on the ivory-handled switchblade. A stainless blade flicked and gleamed in the

light. Everyone's eyes locked onto the blade as Andrea slashed it threateningly at the president's face.

"Kill me if you want," he said.

"Very *noble*. Living up to your name."

"I'll never help you. Never."

"You politicians," Andrea purred. "Always making rash promises."

The blade floated from the president to his wife. Andrea toyed with it in front of the beautiful black woman, but got no reaction. The blade floated on to the son.

"A married man always has a few extra worries," Andrea said. The blade hovered over the boy's frightened face. He squirmed, fighting the ropes that held his arms to the chair.

Andrea grabbed his hair and pulled back his head. Her blade's tip reached forward and jabbed his forehead. A crimson bead appeared.

"Stop!" President Noble screamed.

"You'll reconsider?" Andrea asked.

The president said nothing.

"No? Your daughter is certainly lovely. Perhaps I could arrange to have her, uh, 'meet' a few of my men. They're not *too* rough, though she is a little young."

"What do you want?" the president asked through clinched lips.

"It won't be bad," Andrea told the president. "You don't have to choose between your family and your country. Not at all. We'll bring prosperity to your island and your family can live in peace. The influx of money will help build schools, modern roads, and raise your people's standard of living. All we require is to be able to pull a few strings behind the scenes. We won't ask much. You'll find we can even help. On occasion we might even eliminate your opposition. We'll help your country and you."

"I need to think. And I don't understand how I can help you . . ."

"I need an agreement, now." Andrea paused, eyeing the president's wife. The woman was perfectly shaped, with jet-black skin and a lovely, graceful neck. Her breasts were firm under her blue nightgown. She had the narrow waist of a young woman, with smooth, sleek legs. Andrea felt a stab of jealousy.

"The problem is, you don't understand how serious I am . . ." Andrea's low voice trailed off.

Without warning the switchblade slashed through the air. It sliced into the first lady's hand. The steel nipped into the base of her left little finger.

The president's wife screamed, writhing in pain.

Andrea bore down on the blade with all her weight until it hit the wooden arm of the chair. The severed finger dropped. Blood spurted from the stump.

"Stop!" the president screamed. "I'll do whatever you want."

Andrea kneeled and speared the bloody finger on the tip of her knife. She dangled it in front of the president's terrified eyes.

"I don't kid around, Mr. President. I'm deadly

serious. How many more fingers before you agree to cooperate?"

"Just stop. I'll help you."

"Good. If you cooperate, this is the last time I'll ever touch any of your family. But if you try anything—anything at all—I'll personally butcher each of you. One tiny piece at a time," she said, flicking the finger onto the man's lap. "If that happens, I promise you, you'll be glad when your family is finally dead. Do you understand?"

"Yes. Completely."

"Good." She wiped the blood on the blade on his sleeve. She flipped the knife shut and replaced it in its sheath, hidden under the waistband of her skirt at the small of her back.

The president's wife was trying to contain her sobbing. The young boy cried quietly. The teenage girl glared at Andrea with unbridled hatred.

Have to watch the daughter, Andrea told herself. She spoke to her men. "Get a bandage on her hand. Then escort the president's family to the guest rooms. I'll be moving in here. Release the president."

The tall mercenary on Andrea's right produced a razor-sharp Bowie knife and quickly cut the president's bonds.

Andrea spoke to the black man as he rose, rubbing his arms where they had been tied. "Mr. President, you'll come with me. You'll be making a special broadcast to your people in a few hours."

A short while later, Noble had been transported by car to the small radio station Andrea's henchmen had taken over. Now Noble found himself trying to ignore a FN FAL pointed at his head. The president sat on an uncomfortable wooden chair and stared blankly at the paper on the scarred wooden desk in front of him.

Is there some way out of this mess? he asked himself for the hundredth time. Surely there must be. But I'll have to play along with these maniacs awhile longer. Otherwise, they'll kill more people, including my family. Unless . . . They're determined to force me to speak on the radio.

What if I simply blurt out the truth?

They would surely kill me, he decided. But perhaps not Victoria and the children. And if my people hear . . . Even if the radio were quickly cut off, the travesty would be revealed.

But would revealing the plot do any good? he wondered. The citizens are so poorly armed. Could they throw these well-armed terrorists out even if they knew? For a moment Noble regretted that his country had banned firearms for everyone but the police force. He swallowed and inspected the armed men standing around him.

Andrea and four of her henchmen surrounded Noble in the cramped, cinder-block studio of the radio station. The room was painted a gaudy orange with crudely stenciled purple flowers along the yellow ceiling. A rattling window air conditioner struggled to keep the room cool, though the sun had risen only hours before.

"About ready?" Andrea asked the runty man working in back of the glass window of the engineer's room.

Kelly McClain glanced up from the radio

transmitter's control console. McClain appeared to be totally out of place with the rest of the gang. The bald crown in his black hair made him look more like a college professor or a monk than a criminal. His eyes were distorted behind thick glasses and seemed not to focus on anyone in the studio.

"About ready," he answered through a microphone. Relayed through the diminutive speaker above the glass window he sat behind, his voice sounded even thinner than usual. "This equipment's old even by third-world standards. But give me a couple more minutes and I'll have it running."

McClain's forehead washboarded and he shoved at his glasses. Then he reached to the panel and twisted a knob. There was a hiss, then silence. "There," he said, a flush of excitement coloring his otherwise bleached complexion. He glanced around furtively, like a cornered animal, and then said, "We should be on the air now. Here." He mounted an LP on a turntable and lowered the needle to the spinning disc. A Sousa march blared from the tiny speakers in the studio.

"I hear it!" Smiley Douglas crowed in his high voice. Over the blare of music coming from the headphones of his transistor radio, he hollered: "It works." He held the radio so all could behold the miracle.

Bruce Wetzel glared at Douglas and shifted his rifle slightly as if to cover his scrawny partner.

"Kill the radio," Andrea ordered. "Mr. President," she purred, placing her hand on his shoulder and giving him a condescending pat. "Time for you to read your speech."

The president licked his lips and stared at the microphone in front of him. He knew he'd be beaten or killed as soon as he deviated from the script. And he felt surprised that his imminent death didn't bother him.

Andrea snatched the microphone from the table and held it to her lips for a moment, then spoke, "McClain, can you fade out the music and bring me in?"

"Sure," McClain answered over the tinny speaker. "Tell me when to fade."

"That would be a nice effect," Andrea said, half to herself. "Mr. President, you should know that any departure from the words I've written will spell the death of your family. As I promised. And it won't accomplish anything. See that tape recorder by McClain?"

President Noble stared at the balding criminal through the glass window of the control console. McClain pointed toward the two spinning reels of the ancient tape recorder.

"We're taping your speech," Andrea said as she lowered the microphone. Her eyes bore into Noble. "So all you'll accomplish is a lot of suffering. We'll just kill you and your family. Then I'll get someone new to play president. We'll turn your island over to someone a whole lot less skilled than you are. Alive, you can still help your people and protect your family. Your death would gain you nothing. Understand?"

The president glared at her and then nodded reluctantly.

Andrea smiled at McClain in the control room. "We're ready."

McClain killed the march and nodded a go-ahead.

"Citizens of the Republic of Palm Island," Andrea said, a smirk on her face. "We have an important message from John Philip Noble, President of the Republic of Palm Island. Ladies and gentlemen, our president." She handed the microphone to the man.

The president cleared his throat. Trapped, he thought. No choice but to read. He clutched the microphone tightly, his hands shaking slightly as he glared at the sheet of paper in front of him. "Citizens of Palm Island," he intoned. "As you may know, the horrendous plot to oust our elected government has been—"

"You can do better than that," Andrea hissed, snatching the mike from the president. "Back it up, McClain. To where he comes in."

Turning to the president once again, she spoke in a low voice, "You'd better use your sonorous campaign voice, my friend. Or I'll make it so your wife won't have enough fingers to play chopsticks on the piano."

The president forced a smile that showed his even, white teeth. "I understand. Completely."

McClain manually rewound the reel with the playback head engaged. There was a mousey squeaking of the president's taped voice run backward at a high speed. McClain adjusted the tape reels and signaled through the window.

The president took the microphone, holding it tightly in both hands. "Citizens of Palm Island," he said with deep, sonorous tones. "As you may know, the horrendous plot to oust our elected government has been thwarted. Today we remain free, despite the work of forces from outside our borders.

"Last night an attack was mounted against our police force. Many of our brave officers gave their lives protecting our country. Additionally, other groups of mercenaries attacked the Presidential Palace and temporarily knocked out our radio station. But we have been victorious. We have repelled and killed most of the invaders, though not without loss of life among those serving our tiny Republic.

"I promise you, those who have died to preserve our freedom have not died in vain. We shall discover who masterminded this coup attempt. They will be punished if it is within the capability of our small country to deal with those who would usurp our sovereignty."

The president stopped for a moment, his throat constricting spasmodically, and then he went on. "Tonight, I'm initiating a curfew that will be in effect for the next ten days. I'm asking all citizens to remain off the streets from dusk to dawn. Tourists and foreign visitors in our country will be compelled to leave during the next three days. No outsiders other than those who will be asked to help us maintain order will be allowed to enter our ports or use our airport for the next ten days.

"Because I had suspected a plot was afoot to depose my government, I had taken the liberty of calling in outside forces to help preserve our liberty. Therefore, do not be alarmed if you see strangers on the streets wearing the uniforms of our police force. These men are under my control and have already helped us defend our freedom.

"I have also brought in special consultants to help us reorganize and modify my administration to prevent another attempt to steal our independence. These consultants also have plans to bolster our economy, making us a stronger, freer people.

"While today is a time of sorrow for those families who have lost loved ones, it is also a time for rejoicing. We continue to be free. And we will expose those responsible for this heinous act. They will feel our wrath and the condemnation of freedom-loving peoples everywhere. Thank you, and good night."

The room was silent a moment.

Andrea spoke, "Got that, McClain?"

He gave her a thumbs-up signal through the window.

"All right, let's get it on the air," Andrea ordered.

McClain rewound the tape, threw several switches, and the message was broadcast to the people of Palm Island.

As Andrea listened, she smiled to herself. Everything is going very smoothly, she thought.

Very, very smoothly. The island is now truly mine. And now it's time to start consolidating my power and bringing some money into my new little kingdom.

6

Oz's crew flew in what had unofficially become known as "Laser Tag." The "dogs" they carried consisted of a platoon of Delta troops, the special antiterrorist force that had been created by the US Army. "Hang on," Oz warned the dogs as he anticipated the sudden climb the APQ-168 TF/TA radar would send them into.

Like the other vehicles in the war game, Oz's helicopter was equipped with detectors that would score "hits" from the enemy team's low-level lasers mounted on their various guns. Each of the dogs wore a detector harness with a built-in alarm that would sound if he was hit by a laser beam. For defending themselves, each of the ACRs—advance combat rifles—the dogs carried fired blanks that activated a laser mounted on the gun's barrel. Lasers also replaced the rockets the MH-60K carried in the maneuvers.

The TF/TA, or terrain following/terrain avoidance, radar automatically hauled the MH-60K SOA helicopter into a tight climb over the maple-covered hill, giving the exhilarating feeling of a roller-coaster ride. Behind the helicopter, the other two MH-60Ks followed the same giddy path. Each chopper held a squad of soldiers to complete the air assault tactical force, or AATF, that was being taken in on an antiterrorist training mission.

The exercise was taking place at Fort Benning, Georgia, the home of the US Army Infantry Center, which included the infantry school and infantry board. The Night Stalkers and Delta teams were pitted against the Rangers who were training at Fort Benning. Oz and his crew found themselves honing their helicopter assault tactics on the post's sprawling 182,000 acres of grassland and trees.

Oz was a member of the Night Stalkers, part of TF160 (Task Force Number 160), which had been created from elements of the US Army 158th Aviation Battalion. The Night Stalkers were based in Fort Bragg, North Carolina, along with the Delta teams they carried. Both organizations' operations were cloaked in secrecy, since they were often called on to aid US antiterrorist or other elite military units.

Now the Night Stalkers demonstrated their deadly efficiency as they ferried the Delta teams during the maneuvers. Oz pushed the lead chopper into another exhilarating dive as they topped a hill and dropped into the valley beyond it.

"Still haven't detected enemy radar," Death Song said as he studied the helicopter's instrument display in front of him and noted they were nearing the start point of their landing route. "We're nearing the SP," he announced.

"OK," Oz said. He triggered on his radio,

"Harpy One to Harpy Two and Three, we're nearing the SP. Switching from TF/TA to manual." The switch was made so that the TF/TA radar would not give them away as they neared the enemy in the hilly countryside.

Oz turned off the radio and spoke into the intercom. "Taking it off TF/TA," he alerted his copilot. Oz held the controls tightly as he disengaged the radar. There was a slight shudder in the vehicle.

The pilot dropped the chopper slightly to adhere to a nap of the earth flight route the AATFC, the commander of the AATF, had created for them. Oz kicked his left rudder pedal slightly and pushed the control column to the left as well. The MH-60K angled a bit to shoot through the small depression in the hillside, throwing a shadow in their wake as they shot forward, the sun to their backs.

The pilot goosed the control column forward to acquire even more speed. The aircraft narrowly cleared the hedge of leafless walnuts ahead of them. The fixed wheels of the helicopter raced past the bare branches, leaving only a few inches between clear flight and a crash. The closeness of the treetops demonstrated just how dangerous a war game could be when the pilots were serious about winning.

"Here's the SP," Death Song said after checking his mission control computer on his CRT.

"Silence, silence, silence," Oz said over the radio. This would alert the two helicopters following Oz that they were to observe radio silence so that an enemy would be less apt to discern their approach. "Arm our weapons," he ordered Death Song.

"Weapons pods armed."

So far so good, Oz thought, watching the terrain ahead of him. He knew that one mistake could spell enemy detection or—worse yet—a fiery crash. He shoved back down on the collective pitch lever. The craft dropped to retain the radar cover offered by the tree-canopied hill ahead of them.

"Got some weak radar signals," Death Song announced. "But they still haven't locked on. No radio traffic."

"Good. If we can sneak in, we'll win," Oz predicted. Everything was silent except for the whooping of the blades and the noise of the helicopter's twin engines as Oz wove over the terrain. "O.T. and Luger," Oz finally said. "Almost there."

"The Miniguns are ready," O.T. announced.

Like the other MH-60Ks in the formation, the helicopter carried its weapons pods in external tank suite struts that had been modified to hold four pods, rather than the standard pair of fuel tanks. The ETS rack held the pods high on the side of the helicopter so the six-barreled Miniguns on each side of the aircraft had a wide field of fire. The GE Miniguns had a high cyclic rate of six thousand rounds per minute. Each held a four thousand linked belt and had an electric motor that powered the Gatlinglike machine gun.

The helicopter zipped over the hill and Oz spied their air control point landmark. "There's the water tower. That the ACP?" he asked as he slid around the obstacle.

"That's it," Death Song answered after a quick glance at his CRT and noted that they were approaching the release point. "RP coming up."

"Sergeant Karr," Jake contacted the Delta squad leader on the intercom. "We're going in."

"We're ready," Karr answered, his greenish brown eyes glinting in the sun that filtered through the side of the chopper.

The pilot pushed forward on the control column, increasing the four main blades' pitch for maximum speed. Simultaneously, the pilot used his left hand to pull up on the collective pitch lever, sending the helicopter into the air, over the hill, and suddenly above the enemy camp. The sun was still at Oz's back.

"Radio activity is still low level," Death Song said. He flipped a switch on his console. "Electronic countermeasures should squelch what they have."

As they swooped above the camp, Oz brought back the collective pitch lever and pushed on the right rudder pedal. "Fire at will," he told his crew.

"Armored personnel carrier next to the barracks," the O.T. yelled from his position at the left side door. "I'll take it," he shouted, knowing it was too close to engage with rockets even if Oz had had the time to maneuver.

O.T. jabbed on the triggers of his dual-gripped machine gun as the MH-60K circled the clearing. The invisible laser beams from the modified Minigun flashed at the target as hot blank casings spewed from the chute below the gun. O.T. watched the armored personnel carrier and stopped firing as soon as his lasers had activated the flashing "hit" light.

"We're taking hits," Death Song warned.

"Ground fire from the barracks," Luger yelled. He fired as they passed the building, his Minigun making a whining explosion from the side door. Six armed men ran from the wooden building, AK47s firing at the helicopter. Luger scoured them with fire and was pleased to see them come to an abrupt halt.

"Still detecting hits. Probably from the barracks," Death Song warned as the war game progressed.

Oz booted a pedal and swung the helicopter to face the rear of the building. He fired three 70mm rockets from their pod, sure an umpire would rule the rocket fragments would not damage the helicopter. The laser beams sent from the MH-60K simulated the launch of the rockets. The detectors in the building scored hits, causing lights on the roof to strobe.

"Anyone see anything?" Oz called as he swung the chopper around in a half circle and then darted over the tiny clearing.

"Enemy radar and radio signals still suppressed," Death Song said. "Unless they have a ground line, I think we succeeded in cutting them off from the main force."

"We're setting down," Oz said. "The terrain is flat, O.T. They can exit from both sides."

Oz brought the control column to its center position so they hovered over the clearing. He pressed on the collective pitch lever with his left hand. The helicopter responded by falling toward the ground.

Sergeant Karr and his men jumped from the chopper and charged toward the barracks building.

"All clear," O.T.'s voice crackled on the headset.

"Enemy on the hill to the south," O.T. advised via the intercom. "Harpy Two and Three are setting down."

"Let's take out the guys on the hill." Oz switched on his radio, "Harpy One is lifting to engage enemy. We'll stick to our primary flight path as closely as possible, but you two better use the alternate path."

"Roger that," the radio answered back.

To the din of O.T.'s Minigun, Oz jerked on the collective pitch lever with his left hand. The helicopter jumped from the ground.

"Got a jam here!" O.T. yelled. "Should have it cleared in a moment."

Oz kicked his right pedal and swung the nose of his craft toward the hill. He fired two more 70mm rockets at the group of men and the BMP infantry combat vehicle he saw hiding among the evergreens on the hill. Then he raked the area with the pod-mounted, dual 7.62mm machine guns. His actions activated the laser alarms of half the enemy soldiers in the group and triggered the strobe on the vehicle as well.

"Taking more hits," Death Song cautioned.

Oz continued his course and the helicopter darted beyond the barracks building to screen their retreat. He nosed the MH-60K over a hill and then shot along a small valley.

"We're past the hill but have encountered a—" Static broke up the radio signal from the platoon leader's radio.

"Say again," Oz ordered.

"We've passed the hill," Lieutenant Ovelar repeated. "But there's a tank. Can you take it or shall we use our Dragon? Over."

"We'll get it," Oz answered, wheeling his vehicle in a low, tight circle to head toward the foot soldiers. He spoke to the radio again, "Harpy Two and Three, Harpy One is going to engage the enemy off our flight path. We'll stay clear of the alternate flight path."

"Roger. Harpy Two is lifting."

"Harpy Three is taking on casualties. We'll be loaded in just a minute."

"My Minigun's cleared," O.T. reported. He fired a short burst to be sure it was working.

"The tank should be just over this hill," Oz told Death Song as they hurtled over the ground.

Death Song readied for their attack on the tank. He retracted the pull-out virtual image display for the TOW missile. As he switched it on, the VID gave a high-resolution "TV" picture that would act as the sight for the antiarmor missile. He depressed a button along the viewscreen and flight information symbols were overlaid on the VID to allow him to check his position in relation to the target. He took the TOW's two small joysticks that were attached to the VID. He was ready to guide the large rocket to its target.

"There it is," Oz announced as they popped over the hill. He dropped the helicopter back below the hill so they wouldn't present a target to the enemy tank. "Got it?"

"We're in range," Death Song said. "Move us to the right about fifty meters."

Oz relocated the MH-60K in the direction Death Song had indicated. The new pop-up point would also help keep the enemy gunner from acquiring them too quickly and would give the TOW time to reach the target.

"All right," Death Song said, grasping the joystick, his eyes riveted on the FLIR screen.

The helicopter leapt.

"Up a little more . . . Hold it right there!" he ordered. A pause. "She's off," Death Song warned. It was impossible for Oz to tell when the firing occurred because the simulator lacked rocket exhaust.

Oz held the controls steady, bucking the breeze that tried to shove them to the side.

"On target," Death Song said. "Got it!"

Oz saw the blinking light on the enemy tank as he lowered the helicopter back under the safety of the hill and pulled the craft around. "How's it look?" he asked Lieutenant Ovelar over the radio.

"Good shooting!" the soldier yelled. "Everything's pretty clear. We'll take it from here. Catch you at the pickup zone. Over and out."

Oz turned the helicopter around. "Harpy Three lifting," the radio told him. "We're following the alternate route."

"Harpy One will come around and take the lead," Oz said. He pushed the control column forward; they darted forward to pick up the other two helicopters. "Over and out."

A short time later, the pickup zone command officer had reported the dogs at the pickup zone were ready. Oz headed his chopper toward the pickup zone. The command officer warned him that the pickup zone was hot; the dogs were taking casualties.

"There's the fork in the road. That's our SP," Death Song announced as they neared the pickup zone. "ETA at the PZ is ten minutes."

Behind Oz's helicopter, the other two MH-60Ks followed the same path. All three hugged the tree line as they followed the lead chopper into the start of the predetermined route toward the pickup zone.

"There's the RP," Death Song said. "We need to shift about five degrees to the north."

Oz kicked his left rudder pedal slightly and pushed the control column to the left as well. His chopper angled onto course and rushed over the reference point leading to the pickup zone. They scooted over the depression and Oz pushed them upward to jump over the hedge blocking the pickup zone.

"Smoke," Death Song pointed out.

"Got it," Oz said, watching the cloud of green smoke that had been set off by the ground troops waiting to be picked up.

"Got some ground fire," Death Song said. "But it isn't too hot. No radio traffic."

"The Miniguns are ready," O.T. informed the captain.

"Fire's coming from that tree row at nine o'clock, O.T.," Death Song warned.

"Got it," O.T. said. His machine gun started firing as they swooped at the clearing. Each pull of the trigger fired a ten-round burst with an exploding hum.

Oz brought back the collective pitch lever and pushed the right rudder pedal. Luger's machine gun joined the din being created by O.T.'s gun.

Death Song caught a glimpse of an armored personnel carrier as they swung around. "We've got an APC across the clearing," he cautioned.

"We'll have to ignore it," Oz said. "We're too close. And I'm not sure where all the dogs are." He brought the control column to the rear and pressed the collective pitch lever with his left hand. The helicopter responded by speeding toward the earth.

As the chopper landed, Sergeant Karr and his men charged into the open and jumped onto the helicopter.

"Almost loaded," O.T.'s voice crackled on the headset.

"The APC's firing on us," Death Song advised the captain.

"Harpy Two down," the radio announced.

"We're loaded," O.T. said.

Oz switched on his radio, "Harpy One is lifting. We'll take our alternate flight path to avoid closing with the APC parked ahead of us. I say again, we will take alternate flight path."

"Harpy Three down. Wilco with alternate path."

"Harpy Two. Wilco."

Oz jerked the collective pitch lever with his left hand. The helicopter jumped from the dirt. Once aloft, he watched his FLIR screen. When the APC aligned with the aiming point on his screen, he fired. Two laser-simulated 70mm rockets went at it as the MH-60K lifted.

"Hit!" O.T. yelled as Oz swung the chopper around in a tight turn and took the alternate flight corridor.

"We're clear of ground fire," Death Song notified the pilot.

Oz continued his course and the helicopter darted past the hillside. He dropped to elude enemy radar. He then headed west and nosed the MH-60K over to travel in the river valley ahead of them.

"Harpy Two aloft," the radio divulged as the second chopper left its pickup zone.

"Now if three can make it," Oz said, half to himself.

The crew waited three tense minutes as they hurtled forward.

"Harpy Three leaving the PZ," the radio disclosed. Several minutes later, it added, "We're clear of enemy fire."

Oz changed his radio frequency from the UHF air battle net to the FM net. "Mother dog," Oz said over the radio, "we're all coming home on our alternate route."

"Good job, Harpies," the AATF commander radioed the MH-60K SOAs. "Come on in."

In his office at the CIA headquarters in Langley, Virginia, Larry Grant finished shaving with his cordless razor. He made a few tentative snips at his dense mustache and then decided to leave well enough alone.

How many people will get killed before the situation is resolved, the agent wondered as he attempted to straighten his tie before inspecting his Sun Microsystem workstation one last time. Satisfied the data in the computer was ready, he lit a cigar and tossed the match into the brimming ashtray, checking to be sure it didn't start a blaze in one of the huge stacks of paper that littered his desk. He chomped on the cigar as he strode out the office door.

"Samantha," he said, entering the pristine waiting room, "if the janitor tries to get in there, shoot him."

His secretary wrinkled her pert nose at the blue haze of smoke he exhaled. "Kill him or just shoot him in the leg?" she asked.

Grant stopped a moment as if he were giving it serious thought. "Just the kneecaps—this time."

"I'll see that he doesn't sneak in and turn off your workstation again."

"That'd be nice. Before, the data wasn't that important. This time, there's a lot riding on it. If anyone needs me, you're unaware that I'm with Maxwell in his conference room."

"OK, I don't know where you are." Samantha sighed, watching him as he shoved his way out the door.

The heels on Grant's polished boots clicked and echoed in the hallway. The boots, his muscular frame, and a jagged scar on his left cheek hinted at his military background. He wore a crumpled blue suit that looked as if it had been slept in— which it had. Grant was oblivious to the greetings of his fellow workers as he stormed down the hall.

"Good morning," Maxwell's secretary said as Grant breezed past the painting of the President of the United States.

Grant growled a reply as he entered Maxwell's conference room and closed the door behind him.

"Go right on in," the secretary said to the closing door.

In the conference room, the director of the CIA, Harold Maxwell, sat at the head of the long walnut table that almost filled the chamber. A row of computer monitors, one for each of the twenty chairs around the table, was nestled into its top.

Maxwell looked like a smiling Buddha, nursing an ulcer and wearing a three-piece suit. Though the man now had an extra layer of fat, his arms and shoulders were still powerful enough to kill a man without the aid of a weapon. He had clawed his way up through the ranks of the CIA, and had squeezed out his opposition in a nasty battle for the directorship.

Like Grant, Maxwell had been up all night. The man's eyes were bloodshot and had dark bags under them. "Good morning," Maxwell said, waving Grant toward a chair next to him. "Gentlemen, this is special agent Larry Grant. Larry, I think you know everyone: Secretary of State Mark Taylor"—he motioned to the weasel-faced man in a gray pinstriped suit—"former Ambassador Michael Sullivan"—the short man blanched at the "former" and nodded toward Grant—"and Ross Calazo, with the NSA." Calazo, a lanky, bearded man, looked more like an artist than a bureaucrat.

Grant sat in his chair, centered the computer keyboard in front of him, and then studied each of the faces at the table as he puffed on his cigar.

"Larry," Maxwell said, eyeing the stinking stogie, "Mr. Sullivan brought back a rather strange impression of how things were going on Palm Island."

"Right," Sullivan said, shifting his short, paunchy frame in his chair. He sat up straight and tried to talk in even tones. "Briefly, President Noble acted like a madman during our last meeting—just before he threw us off the island. And Noble's personal secretary was acting completely out of line for an aide."

"Which is why," Taylor said, "coupled with the cables we've intercepted, we're interested in launching a probe into what's going on down there.''

"Cables?" Maxwell asked.

Calazo cleared his throat, licked his lips, and then spoke, "We intercepted some cables from Noble to the Soviets. Nothing concrete has been set up, but he's requesting some rather heavy armament. Especially for a government that doesn't even have a standing army.''

"Why the hell weren't we informed about these cables?" Maxwell demanded.

"That doesn't matter," Taylor said, leaning forward in his chair. "The main thing is we want to stay on top of this situation before we have another Grenada.''

Taylor was a former academic who had fallen in love with the political infighting on Capitol Hill. During the man's confirmation hearings, Grant had realized that Taylor was politician first and public servant second. The agent was convinced that when the secretary of state made a decision, the well-being of American citizens or even of the country came second to the political implications for Taylor and those he supported. Grant hoped he never had to depend on Taylor for his own safety.

"I'll expect copies of those cables immediately," Maxwell ordered. "Larry, show them what you've got. Why don't you start with the photos you processed.''

Grant punched the keyboard and waited impatiently for the system to come on line. There was a bleep signaling that the computer was ready to go, and then his fingers flew over the keyboard, connecting the machine to the one in his office. "Just a moment while I dump the data from my workstation to this system," he said, noting that Taylor was checking his watch.

In moments the information was transferred into the computer and Grant started his presentation. "Not many photos have come out of the Republic of Palm Island since the coup attempt two weeks ago. But this one was sent to us by one of our news sources."

A photo of Noble appeared on each of the small monitors in front of the men. The president was standing in front of a podium, one arm upraised, apparently making a speech.

"Now," Grant said, "notice the faces of the two people next to the president . . ." Grant hit a button and the computer highlighted the two people standing behind and to the side of the president. The agent depressed two more keys and the section containing the two faces dropped down and expanded to fill each monitor.

"Computer enhancement makes it even more interesting," Grant said and hit another series of keys. The photos quickly sharpened, revealing a clear picture of a man and woman.

"That's Noble's secretary," Sullivan said. "Teresa someone. I don't remember her name."

"She didn't give you her real name, anyway," Grant said. "I spent most of yesterday on a data search through the FBI and CIA computerized photo files. Here's the match the computer pulled on the woman in the photo. On the left's the news photo. On the right's her search-correspond."

Grant pressed six keys and the screen split. The computer-enhanced photo slid to the left of the screen and a new picture appeared on the right. "She's Andrea Todd, according to the FBI."

"I think that's what Noble called her," Sullivan said. "Why would he reveal her name after she'd gone to the trouble of using an alias?"

"What's the FBI got on her?" Calazo asked as he tugged his brown beard and studied the screen.

"Here's her file," Grant said, tapping a button.

Calazo whistled as he looked at the list that spun onto the screen. "Dishonorable discharge from the US Army, bank robbery, drug dealing, weapons violations, outstanding warrants . . . Can the FBI extradite her?"

"Not since the Republic of Palm Island severed diplomatic ties with us," Taylor said.

"So," Calazo said, "that leaves us high and dry unless we want to try to snatch her ourselves. But what's she doing working so close to Noble?"

"We were able to track down the other photo," Maxwell said.

Grant hit several buttons and waited a moment for the screen to clear itself. Two photos appeared on either side of the screen. "This one's not a perfect match. The photo on the left is of the man with Noble. The other is from our own computer files. As you can see, the quality is not too great even with enhancement. And it's about fifteen years old."

"Who is he?" Taylor asked.

"Edward Emerson Kellerman," Maxwell said. "He's—"

"I've heard that name before," Calazo interrupted.

"Quite possibly," Maxwell said. "He's on our rogue list."

"One of ours?" Taylor asked.

"He did contract work for the Company during the mid-seventies. Vietnam. But he went rogue and dropped out of sight before we could snatch him. We believe he's been free-lancing in Cambodia, Angola, and possibly Panama."

"But he's not connected with us now, is he?" the secretary of state inquired hastily. "If President Crane's opposition thought one of our agents was operating out of control, the press . . ."

"No, we're distanced," Maxwell said. "Even with Freedom of Information dumps, we'll be clean."

"So what's Noble doing with a criminal and a rogue agent on the podium with him?" Calazo asked. "Any previous record of such dealings?"

"I thought Noble was a straight arrow," Taylor remarked. "You have dirt on him?"

"No," Maxwell said. "Nothing."

"Maybe he overreacted to the coup attempt," Calazo said. "Hired some muscle."

"Perhaps," Sullivan said. "But Todd appeared just a day or two at the most after the attempt. I was familiar with Noble's staff and never saw her before then."

"It'd be hard for someone without criminal

ties to locate these two and bring them in that quickly," Maxwell said.

Calazo turned toward Sullivan. "Just how much influence did this Todd woman have over Noble?"

"Acted like she owned the place," Sullivan said. "She was putting words into Noble's mouth and refused to let him have a press conference."

"What else have you got?" Calazo asked Maxwell.

"Larry found something that was lost in the chain of command," Maxwell said.

"It never would have surfaced," Grant said, "if it hadn't been filed in the NSA's computer archives." The agent again blanked the screens around the table and retrieved a copy of a letter that appeared on each monitor.

"A report from our ambassador in Venezuela," the secretary of state remarked. "Where does this tie in?"

Grant exhaled a billowing cloud of thick smoke before he spoke, "The gist of the report is that one Babblo Forest, a kitchen boy at the Presidential Palace on the Republic of Palm Island, was washed ashore in a dinghy. He imparted a wild story about a group of foreigners succeeding in taking over the Presidential Palace. But no one thought much of his story since Noble came on the radio and appears to be in power. Besides, the boy's very young and a Rastafarian to boot."

"Rastafarian?" Calazo said. "Don't they believe that Ethiopia is heaven or some such thing?"

"It's hard to imagine Ethiopia being heaven these days!" quipped Taylor.

"So the story was lost instead of being flagged because this young man is a Rastafarian?" Calazo inquired.

"More or less," Maxwell said. "Rastafarians use drugs in their religious ceremonies. Maybe someone saw that as a reason to downgrade his story. We're probably lucky a report was ever filed."

"The date on his story coincides with the attempted coup," Taylor said. "Assuming there's any truth in Forest's tale, does it fall into place?"

"Obviously his idea that Noble was captured during a coup is wrong," Grant said. "But Forest's report that the government was systematically taking any potential troublemakers from their homes at night and jailing or killing them might have an element of fact in it."

"That part jives with rumors I heard while I was there," Sullivan added.

"What else have you got?" Taylor asked, again looking at his wristwatch.

Grant punched up a chart on the monitors. "You'll recall that the Omnibus Drug Act passed in 1988 gave the Drug Enforcement Administration, FBI, and Internal Revenue Service a mandate to create computer files that would track the movements of suspected drug pushers, as well as large sums of money leaving the country."

"Certainly," Taylor said. "The records are also tied into the Department of State and about every other government agency that might be interested in the information."

"This chart was created from it," Grant said. "As you can see, there's been a sudden increase in money flowing to the Republic of Palm Island, following the date of the coup attempt. There's also been a sharp increase in telephone traffic from FBI wiretap numbers to the island."

"So you think Noble's organizing a drug ring?" Taylor queried.

"More than that," Maxwell said. "It looks like offshore banks are being created to launder money. Feelers for a casino are also out. The holding companies contacted are all linked to organized crime. And don't forget the cables to the Soviets . . ."

"How could we forget those," Maxwell remarked sourly.

"Which way do we want to run with it?" Calazo asked.

"I can tell you one thing," Taylor said. "It's got to be quiet. I don't need to remind you that the election is going to be close. The president cannot afford an incident this close to November fourth. And he wants to have some options. Let's have some of our elites ready. The Delta teams and Night Stalkers for sure. Who was that hotshot who worked with Grant? Wizard?"

"Oz," Grant answered with a smile.

"Yeah," Taylor continued. "He's good. Maybe some SEALs, too, since it's an island. Things could deteriorate down there in a hurry. We need to be ready to react quickly."

"They'll be ready," Calazo promised.

"And we need to get a man inside the organization," Taylor added. "Or at least get an agent in to nose around. As far as we know, Noble doesn't have any communist leanings. But you never know."

Maxwell nodded. "We could slip an operative in as a tourist and have him back out without any problems."

"Sounds good." Taylor glanced at his watch.

"In the meantime," Calazo said, "we can keep track of the Soviet situation by monitoring Palm Island's cable traffic."

"Let's put one of your people in, too," Taylor told Calazo. "Maybe one of your antiterrorist guys."

"If we have to take decisive action," Calazo said, "I would like for my people to have some input."

"Wait a minute," Maxwell said. "This isn't a job for the NSA."

"Perhaps," Taylor said. "But we need to know what in the world is going on down there. And the president wants options. I'm going to insist that we have some cooperation on this."

Maxwell frowned and said nothing.

"Besides," Taylor said, "we'll have less interference from the Senate if we could treat this as a terrorist incident rather than as a job for the CIA, if it comes to that. Send in one of your guys," he said to Maxwell, "and have someone from the NSA with him as well."

"Just be sure he stays out of the way," Maxwell said to Calazo. "I don't want my agent burned because some amateur is monkeying around where he doesn't belong."

"I can assure you any man we send won't be in the way," Calazo said evenly.

"I'll leave you people to hash out the details," Taylor said, standing. "Sullivan and I need to run."

"I don't like dealing with Haitians," Kellerman carped, snuffing out a cigarette in the ashtray of the BMW he drove.

"What's this?" Andrea laughed. "Eddy Kellerman afraid? I never thought I'd see the day."

"I'm *not* afraid," he declared as he brought the car to a stop in front of the gate of what had been the American Embassy.

The wrought-iron gate creaked on its hinges as Kellerman's armed guard, Yucheng, opened it to admit the car. Kellerman drove up the short driveway and stopped the BMW in front of the mansion.

Huge palms, their trunks gray-green with moss, surrounded the house and shaded it from the noonday sun. A second guard armed with an Uzi stood in the shade on its wide porch.

"Those stinking Haitians can't be trusted," Kellerman complained as he got out of the car and slammed the door. "One minute they're cozying up to you and the next they're slitting your frigging throat."

Yucheng held the car door for Andrea as she slid out.

"Maybe the problem is they're too much like you," Andrea chided as she squinted at the white columns that stretched past the second story to support the roof of the old residence. She donned her sunglasses and sauntered up the cobblestone pathway surrounded on both sides by burnt Bermuda grass.

"What's that supposed to mean?" Kellerman asked. "You know you can trust me."

"Who said I couldn't?" Andrea asked, climbing the three squat steps that led to the wrought-iron railing surrounding the porch. Though sometimes I wonder, she smirked to herself.

Another of Kellerman's men held the oak and beveled glass door as Andrea slinked through, Kellerman following closely behind. Yucheng trailed them into the house.

"Think of the Haitians as cutthroats with lots of cash," Andrea said, examining the foyer for a moment. "They bring the cash to Palm Island and we skim ten percent off the top with our operation. They accept the risks and we get rich. What could be simpler? No wonder the US Government is stamping out laundering operations anywhere they can. There's a lot of quick money to be made."

She glanced around the room and was surprised to see the room tastefully decorated in pale blue with a white shag carpet that contrasted nicely with the antique furniture and woodwork. "Where'd you get this furniture?"

Through one archway Andrea could see an im-

posing Majorelle dinner table, its rich mahogany
sheen in sharp contrast to the light parquet flooring. A brass chandelier hung from the patterned tin
ceiling with twelve electric light bulbs encircling
the fixture.

"The Americans were renting this place for
their embassy and left everything behind when
they made their hasty departure." Kellerman
laughed. "The landlord has 'disappeared' . . . The
sharks and I both enjoyed his departure."

"You killed him without asking me?" Andrea
hissed.

"He was just some little guy that didn't have
much. Nobody's going to miss—"

"You need to check with me first," Andrea cut
him off. "We've got to be careful. We've gotten
along so far without rousing the suspicions of the
natives, but if you start killing and then are seen
owning what belonged to your victim, the citizens
will put two and two together."

Yucheng stationed himself near the front door
while Andrea strolled through the second archway
to her left, entering the huge living room. Several
overstuffed Queen Anne chairs and a large couch
occupied the chamber. The walls were adorned
with oil paintings depicting ocean-sailing ships.

"So what if they do realize what's happening
here?" Kellerman asked, following her into the
room. "We've got the guns and the skill to put
down a small revolution." He picked up a tiny
brass hand bell from an end table and rang it.

"The 'so what' is that *you'll* be the first to pay
if you mess things up." Andrea swung on him an-

grily. "Don't do any killing unless I give the OK. Is that understood?"

Kellerman nodded reluctantly and started to speak, but then thought better of it and put the hand bell down.

Smiley Douglas came clattering down the winding oak stairway. At the landing, he paused for a moment to paw at a lock of greasy black hair that had dropped into his left eye. Behind him, a stained-glass window blazed with color as it caught the sun.

"Whaddya need, boss?" Douglas asked as he entered the living room and stopped in front of Kellerman.

"I'll have a bourbon," Kellerman said, and he turned toward Andrea, "What about you?"

"Nothing," she said, studying Kellerman's face surreptitiously.

Smiley Douglas departed, nearly knocking over a bronze elephant on an ebony étagère.

"Well, I still say we can't rely on the Haitians not to double-cross us," Kellerman said, motioning Andrea toward one of the Victorian chairs.

"We don't have to trust them," Andrea said, smoothing her tight skirt behind her thighs before sitting. "We only require their cash. We'll have all the angles covered here so—"

"The Haitians are here," Yucheng said, stepping into the living room after glancing out the window.

"I can't believe it," Kellerman said, looking at his wristwatch. "They're actually on time."

"Let's stay seated," Andrea directed him.

Kellerman smiled at the idea. "Make them feel ill at ease while we're sitting and they have to stand." He reached to the end table beside his chair and rang the hand bell again.

Smiley Douglas appeared, lumbering in as quickly as he could. "Yeah?" he asked, tugging at his shirt collar.

"Skip the drink," Kellerman ordered. "Get some of the boys in. We may need some muscle in case these jerks try anything."

"Wait!" Andrea said. "Yucheng will be enough."

Smiley Douglas rocked back and forth, unsure whose orders to follow.

"OK," Kellerman acquiesced, flicking his bony hand to dismiss the man. "But I think we're making a big mistake." He jerked a Browning Hi-Power from under his shirt, checked to be sure it was loaded by jacking the slide back slightly, and then shoved it back inside his waistband.

Andrea unbuttoned the two top buttons of her blouse and threw her long platinum blond hair back with a toss of her head.

Yucheng opened his jacket and unsnapped the fasteners on the two long-bladed knives hidden in a shoulder harness. That accomplished, he stood in the corner, as motionless as a statue.

The guard outside the front door admitted two black men who swaggered into the foyer.

"Come in," Kellerman called, remaining in his chair.

"How can we help you?" Andrea asked as the two swaggered into the living room.

"Cut the crap," the taller man said with a thick French accent. He wore a white pants suit with a black-and-pink shirt. His fingers and ears were adorned with gold rings and a gold and ruby necklace twinkled at his neck.

"You must be Jeremie Saint-Marc," Andrea said, pausing a moment as she inspected his jet-black skin.

The hint of a smile flickered across the man's face.

"You want it straight," Andrea said, recovering, "so here it is. We know the US is finally getting serious about policing its banks. It's pressured most of the offshore banks into giving them names of people who are operating shady accounts."

"Even Switzerland is cooperating with Uncle Sugar," Kellerman added.

"So the bottom line," Andrea continued, "is we're the only game in town. With that in mind, we'll be running our bank with a ten percent share of the funds up front."

"Ten percent!" the Haitian said and then swore in French.

"Take it or leave it," Andrea said.

"We'll take it," said the dwarfish man standing to Saint-Marc's left.

"Ah, another country heard from," Kellerman said.

"You're Bernard Golfe?" Andrea asked.

"At your service," the Haitian said with a delicate bow. "We'll agree to your ten percent. But no more. And we must be able to bring the money in day or night and wire it to other banks on short notice."

"We'll have those capabilities within one week. We'll also be giving you clear entry, with no hassles from customs. No other offshore bank can guarantee that. Our requirement is that you call beforehand and enter unarmed."

"Unarmed?" Saint-Marc swore. "I don't like it. How do we know you won't rip us off?"

"Golfe, I'd suggest you explain the facts of life to your business partner," Andrea said to the other man.

"Maybe he's been sampling too much of your product," Kellerman suggested.

"No one talks about Saint-Marc like that!" Saint-Marc retorted hotly, stepping toward Kellerman.

"I do, you skinny bastard," Kellerman said, rising from his chair. "Either shut up or you and your friends can try your luck elsewhere."

Yucheng's fingers inched under his jacket as Golfe whispered to Saint-Marc in French. Saint-Marc glared silently at Kellerman.

"Save the flash and show for your cronies," Andrea said. "You'll trust us because you have to. We've already got mob connections stateside. Check your sources. We'll be protecting your cash the same as theirs. No one's going to screw around with us."

"And remember," Kellerman added. "You'll be able to enter from the harbor or by plane with no complications getting through customs."

"But how do we know that we won't be ripped off?" Saint-Marc asked again, eyes blazing.

"We run the island," Andrea said in even tones. "No one is armed but us, and we need you as much as you need us."

The tall Haitian blinked.

"OK," Andrea said. "If any of your men come armed, they'll be fish bait within the hour. We're keeping this island clean of cowboys. When you enter our borders, you know you're safe from hits. And your money is protected in a stable country that won't be seeing a change in government for some time. Now either sign on or perform your act elsewhere."

Saint-Marc and Golfe conversed quietly in French for a moment.

"We'll do it," Saint-Marc reluctantly agreed through clenched teeth.

"We'll phone in a couple of weeks," Golfe said. "Can you be ready for several million in US dollars?"

"No problem," Andrea said. "We'll see you then."

Yucheng escorted the two Haitians out of the room.

"Stinking Haitian frogs," Kellerman muttered, pacing the room. "Smelled up the whole house."

"Cash always has a foul smell to it," Andrea purred, getting up and smoothing her skirt. "But I'm sure we'll learn to live with it, won't we. Come here," she invited.

Kellerman turned toward her but stood his ground.

Andrea advanced toward him with hips swaying. When her breasts were almost touching him, she murmured, "You seem a little tense. Perhaps I can help." She smoothed his collar. "Show me the rest of your house," she suggested. "Let me see what's upstairs."

"See we're not disturbed," she told Yucheng. She took Kellerman's arm and they ascended the oak stairway.

Yucheng said nothing.

"Where do you sleep?" Andrea inquired as they reached the second floor. "Through here?" She looked through an open door at a sky-blue dressing compartment with an ivory inlaid vanity stationed at one end of the chamber.

"Yes," Kellerman said huskily.

Andrea stepped in and glanced at her reflection in a brass and copper mirror. On one side of the compartment was a cavernous closet full of expensive men's clothing. On the other side was a sky-blue bath with black marble sinks, toilet, bidet, and bathtub, each with silver fixtures shaped like fish.

"The bedroom's through here," Kellerman said in a low voice as he pushed through the double doors at the end of the chamber.

Andrea followed Kellerman into the white-walled bedroom.

He stopped at the four-pillared bed. Andrea glanced at the garland of leaves carved on the pillars and the pink floral silk canopy that billowed over them.

Kellerman spun her around to face him. She felt Kellerman's strong hands encircling her waist and pulling her against him. Andrea snaked her hand to his belt, pulled the pistol from his waistband, and tossed it onto a chair. She pushed herself away from him and carefully unbuttoned Kellerman's shirt, exposing his skinny chest. Her fingers toyed with three pocked scars left on his skin by a gun battle in Vietnam.

She avoided his lips and whispered into his ear, "Let's see what we can do to get you to relax." Andrea let herself tumble backward onto the bed, drawing Kellerman onto her as she fell.

9

With the military exercise over, the Night Stalkers left their helicopters with the ground crews at Fort Benning. While the helicopter flight teams ate and rested for an hour, three Army work crews of six men apiece disassembled and prepared each of the three helicopters for transportation to Fort Bragg, North Carolina, where the Night Stalkers were based as part of the Special Operations Aviation units.

Sergeant Bruce Marvin supervised the loading team that would spend their next hour preparing Oz's helicopter for shipment in the cargo plane. Marvin had a neckless, bulldog head and a hairy barrel chest. His arms and shoulders were muscled from over a decade of sweating and straining while he repaired, disassembled, or reassembled Army helicopters.

"All right," he told his crew, "you know the drill. First, let's get her cleaned inside and out."

After cleaning the helicopter, Marvin supervised the securing of loose equipment inside the chopper. Larger components were removed from the MH-60K and placed in precisely marked crates to be transported with every chopper. "Be sure we can read your printing this time," the sergeant chided Private Scuro as he marked the label on a crate.

Sergeant Marvin next divided his team into two groups. One folded and secured the main rotor blades while the other did the same with the tail rotor.

The team's subsequent operation was to attach a tow ring to the tiedown plate at the front underside of each of the aircraft; the ring allowed the towing bridle to be coupled to the MH-60K so it could be drawn into the transport cargo bay. A hydraulic cart was then inserted into the helicopter and a steering bar attached to the rear wheel so the chopper could be maneuvered from outside by the loading team.

The sergeant took special pains to double-check as his team marked the helicopter's center of gravity and wrote the chopper's weight on the fuselage so Air Force personnel would be able to find the proper locations for the MH-60Ks on the transport plane and would have accurate figures to compute their course during the flight of the cargo craft. Marvin knew a mistake in measurement of either the center of gravity or weight could spell a crash; he corroborated both marks before going on with the work.

A loading manifest was made by Marvin's team and components that had been removed from the helicopters inventoried. After the tiedown plates and fittings had been added to the individual helicopters, they were guided into their preload positions behind the Lockheed C-5A "Galaxy" cargo plane.

The huge, swept-winged craft sat waiting for the choppers with its rear door open. The plane was almost sixty-eight meters wide and over seventy-five meters long. The upward-hinging nose door of the aircraft was left down since it would be unnecessary to have it up during the loading and securing of the MH-60Ks.

The C-5A rested on its twenty-eight-wheel landing system, close to the runway, its rear cargo hatch lowered to form a ramp. On its camouflaged wings hung four powerful turbofan jet engines.

"She's ready," Sergeant Marvin told the Air Force loadmaster of the C-5A cargo transport plane.

"Good," the loadmaster said. He recognized Marvin and was confident the sergeant and his team had done their jobs. The aircraft loadmaster and his crew members watched over the loading procedure and would offer technical assistance should Sergeant Marvin need it—which he normally didn't.

Marvin's crew did most of the actual work in loading the helicopter into the plane. Finally, the equipment in crates was packed onto the plane and everything secured with tiedown components.

"All finished," Marvin told the aircraft loadmaster with a tired smile. Their job done, Sergeant Marvin and his crew left the area so another team could load a second helicopter into the plane.

Two hours after the disassembly work had begun, all three helicopters were loaded into the cargo plane. The Night Stalkers and their ground crews rode in the pressurized and air-conditioned upper deck. Most of the men catnapped as they headed to their home base along with the MH-60Ks that were stored on the cargo plane's lower deck.

The C-5A cargo plane landed at Fort Bragg late that night. Headquarters of the Special Operations Command, the well-kept post was the home of Army troops formally preparing to deal with terrorism and insurgency around the world. The fort was founded in 1918 and named for Braxton Bragg, a general in the Confederate Army during the US Civil War; it covered 132 acres.

In addition to the two- and three-story brick buildings and barracks that dotted the post, special areas of the fort had been set aside for various types of antiterrorist training. These included automated firing ranges, aircraft fuselages for hijack release practice, and "haunted houses" where various types of urban tactics could be tested and perfected.

The team's work was not over after they arrived at Fort Bragg and disembarked from the transport plane. They still had to check in their small arms. While technically the weapons had not been needed in training, they were carried as they would have been for an actual mission so that the men would become accustomed to carrying and storing the firearms.

Bright lights surrounded the ordnance building. The floodlights turned the darkness into day. As the four members of the helicopter crew reached the guard post in front of the ordnance building, Oz handed his weapon's card to the guard, who inspected it carefully. The second guard held her rifle at the ready as she eyed the PK-15 the helicopter pilot bore.

"Damn," O.T. whispered as he stood behind Oz. "They didn't make guards like that when I was a kid."

"Back when the Army dressed in rusty suits of armor," the guard responded as she looked at O.T.

"Touché," Luger laughed.

One by one, the four crewmen passed the inspection. They filed through the gate of the chain-link fence. The perimeter fence was topped by razor-sharp ribbon wire concertina. The crewmen were careful to stay on the walkway so they didn't set off the sensors buried around the building.

"This place always gives me the creeps," O.T. said in a low voice as he followed Oz down the walkway.

Oz knew what O.T. meant. He felt his muscles tensing as they approached the ordnance building. The bleak cinder-block fortress was hunched close to the earth with dirt and gravel mounded around it. The area was devoid of plants. A yellow sign with a black block "4" warned of a fire and explosive hazard inside. Governed by the ordnance battalion, the building was normally off limits unless a soldier was authorized to enter it to obtain or check in his weapons.

The four trooped through the building's heavy iron doors into its cool interior. The air smelled of CLP gun-cleaning oil. Like the exterior, the interior was brightly lit.

"Where the hell have you guys been?" the duty officer at the window asked. He stood up and spit into a Dixie cup that rested on the counter in front of him. "You look like hell."

O.T. chuckled. "Nothing a twenty-four-hour nap wouldn't cure," he said.

Oz stepped to the window nestled in the chain-link and steel wall. He slid his weapon's card across the counter and set his P-85 pistol and PK-15 beside it.

Duty Officer Harvardson took the card in his tobacco-stained fingers and ran his other hand over his cropped, graying hair. His stomach was flat and a row of campaign ribbons was pinned to his chest. Another smile wrinkled his sunburned face. "I had a feeling you'd be the one to get this baby when she came in," he said as he grasped the PK-15. He cycled the action to be sure it was empty, twisted the knob on the Aimpoint sight to be sure the electric scope was turned off.

The weapon carried an empty forty-five-round magazine and was normally loaded with duplex cartridges, each of which carried two bullets. Capable of being set on a three-round burst mode, the stock-less rifle could fire a swarm of six bullets, any one of which was potentially lethal to a foe.

Harvardson laid the PK-15 on the counter and then checked the Ruger P-85 pistol to be sure its fifteen-round magazine and chamber were empty of 9mm cartridges. Satisfied, he snapped the slide release and the pistol's action clattered shut.

Harvardson scrawled the time and date into the logbook spread over the scarred metal counter, then took the weapon and the pistol from the counter, turned, and lugged them directly to the large rack of rifles stretching across the long wall.

"I don't know how you guys manage to get this exotic shit through TO and E so fast . . ." He slid the submachine gunlike PK-15 into its space, ran a chain through its trigger guard, and locked it. "You must have a guardian angel brown-nosing the chief of staff's fat butt." He tugged at the gun to be sure it was locked into place. He quickly stepped over to a cabinet, unlocked it, and stowed the P-85 automatic in it. He closed the metal door, started to lock it, then thought better of it as he remembered that the other members of the crew would be checking in pistols as well.

"I recognize the Ruger P-85 pistol. Good automatic. But what the hell's that peashooter AR-15-lookin' thing called?" Harvardson asked as he returned to the window. He shoved the logbook at Oz.

"PK-15," Oz answered, signing his name in the logbook.

"You gonna make me beg you to tell what the 'PK' stands for or will you be a gentleman about it."

"Provost Kalashnikov AR-15. A cross between our M16 and their AK47." Oz retrieved his magazines and unused practice ammunition from his flak jacket and handed them to the duty officer.

"I don't know," Harvardson said. "I'll stick with my M9." He patted the holster belted to his narrow hips. "PK-15 take standard 5.56? That's what this training ammo is rated as."

"Standard magazines and ammunition."

Harvardson swore under his breath and shook his head. "And what do you have?" he asked as O.T. stepped to the window.

"That'd be telling," O.T. said as Oz passed him and paced toward the doorway. O.T. handed the duty officer his card. "Haven't you heard? Loose lips sink ships."

"Sorry," Harvardson said. "But I like to know what the hell we're guarding here." He leaned over and made a notation of the time and date in the book, then transported the rifle to the rack and locked it into place.

"Looks like a Shorty Commando," Harvardson finally remarked. "But the stock toe's longer. And that freakin' triangular handguard . . ." He shook his head.

"It's from the Army's ACR program," O.T. said as he signed his name in the logbook.

"Judas Priest, O.T., didn't yer ma teach you how to write?" Harvardson asked, looking at the logbook. "Advanced combat rifle, huh?"

"Yeah," O.T. said. "Colt. We'll probably be carrying those before long. Here's my Colt Double Eagle .45," he added, shoving his stainless-steel pistol over the counter. The pistol resembled the Army's 1911 pistol but had a double-action trigger and lacked any type of manual safety.

"And mine's a Steyr ACR," Death Song added as he advanced to the narrow window. Harvardson swore as he saw the spacey bullpup's plastic body. "Not even American. What's the Army comin' to?" He shook his head, then retrieved a chunk of tobacco and shoved the plug into his mouth.

Minutes later, Luger turned in his Colt ACR and the four crewmen left the ordnance building, enjoying the fresh breeze that swept across the carefully trimmed grass lining the concrete sidewalk. Crickets chirped, oblivious to the sound of a distant "Hummer" that was roaring through the darkness toward them.

"I don't know about you guys," O.T. said. "But I'm looking forward to a hot shower and a nice, long—"

"Captain Jefferson Carson?" a woman called as the jeeplike Hummer pulled to a halt on the pavement alongside them.

Oz turned toward the speaker and stepped toward the curb. "Yes?"

"Commander Warner needs to see you immediately," said the thin brunette sitting in the driver's seat.

"I'll be there as soon as I get cleaned up."

"Sorry, sir," the driver said, "you're to report on the double. I'm to drive you there."

"No rest for the wicked." O.T. laughed as Oz groaned. "We'll be seeing you tomorrow and you can tell us about the fun you had while we were suffering in hot showers and soft beds."

"Is this your flight crew?" the driver asked.

"Uh-oh," O.T. groaned.

"Yes," Oz answered her question.

"You are to be on stand-by alert, ready to leave in three hours," the driver said.

"See you." Oz laughed to his crew as he wearily got into the Hummer and half saluted his crew as the vehicle raced away through the darkness.

The three crewman paced forward without speaking. They knew something was up.

CHAPTER

10

Nikolai Vladimir limped down the ramp of the French passenger plane, nursing the old leg wound he'd acquired ten years before in Angola. He cursed the hot Caribbean sun that bore down on the concrete and made the distant end of the runway dance in heat waves. Vladimir mopped his wide brow with the cotton handkerchief he held in his free hand; that done, he dried his bushy eyebrows that were sopped with sweat. In his other meaty fist, he gripped the handles of a flight bag and a leather briefcase.

Give me Siberia any day, he thought to himself. At least you can dress for the cold. Unless you're willing to walk around naked as a plucked hen, it's impossible to accommodate the warmth and humidity of this island. Especially in a Russian suit that has the lightness of a coarse Army blanket, he chuckled. He made a vow to himself: I must quickly come to terms with the country's president and leave this blazing hell hole as soon as possible.

Only the Americans would enjoy this climate and think of this place as a resort, he thought as he jostled past a group of sightseers babbling in English. He pushed through the double glass doors leading into the building that enclosed the customs port.

Sighing with relief in its cool, air-conditioned interior, Vladimir fell into line behind a heavy European tourist and grinned to himself. Some things are just like home, he thought, as he sidled up to the queue. The only difference is I won't be cajoling some proprietor to sell me his last slab of beef.

The Soviet stood only five feet six inches tall and had wide shoulders and a heavy hairy belly that had caused his wife, Trelinka, to dub him her mastodon. His ruddy countenance was lined and his features looked like they had been hammered in granite with a dull chisel. His hair—dyed black to make him appear younger—was cut short. Despite his love for vodka and the old leg injury, he was in sound health.

He straightened his shoulders and smiled at the customs agent as his turn finally came. The Russian knew that the best way to keep the plastic gun strapped to his leg a secret was to appear friendly and unconcerned.

"Anything to declare?" the black man asked as the Russian paced to the counter. The customs official was dressed in an immaculate white suit and hat, both of which were decorated with yellow braid.

"No." The Soviet slid his passport to the official.

The official studied the passport for only an instant and then pulled a list from under the counter.

"One moment," he said to Vladimir. The official turned and whispered something to an identically dressed official.

Vladimir tried to seem unconcerned as the two glanced over at him. How I wish I weren't covered with sweat, the Soviet told himself. That always makes a man look guilty. But maybe not in a scalding hell hole, he added, attempting to forestall his fear.

The first official returned to the counter. "Mr. Vladimir, if you'd come this way."

From the corner of his eye, the Soviet noted that a constable had observed the unusual activity at the customs counter and was advancing toward them. Although the Soviet felt like a trapped animal, he knew his only hope lay in doing what the official wanted. He'd seen more than one person shot when he ran in the face of arrest.

Besides, he thought as he followed the customs agent, this may be nothing. But Vladimir found that he was again sweating profusely, and not because of the heat.

"Right through here," the official directed, opening a metal door.

Vladimir entered a dark hallway and the door clanged shut behind him.

"Nikolai Vladimir?" a voice asked in accented English.

"Uh, yes," the Soviet answered, trying to regain his composure. He squinted and found there was only the single figure standing in the shadows ahead of him. Vladimir tried to decide if the situa-

tion warranted reaching for the gun strapped to his
ankle.

The slight figure stepped forward from the
shadows. The Soviet relaxed. He recognized the
man's expressionless features.

"I am Yucheng," the man said in a flat tone
that was little louder than a whisper. "We speeded
you through customs so you would not waste your
time. I am to take you directly to the Presidential
Palace."

"Thank you for the consideration," Vladimir
replied, wondering if the whole incident had been
designed to unnerve him. Vladimir, he warned
himself, you're becoming senile. Once you would
have taken this whole thing in stride, enjoying the
tension and the hint of danger.

"Come this way," the Oriental said, directing
Vladimir toward a door at the far end of the room.

Vladimir had recognized Yucheng's features
from his photo. His was one of the few that the
KGB had identified from the snapshots taken by
the operative sent recently to Palm Island. Vladimir had read the file that Soviet intelligence had
prepared on Yucheng, as well as those on President
Noble, Edward Kellerman, and a few public officials who had recently vanished from power. Unfortunately, many of the people the president of
Palm Island had surrounded himself with following
the coup attempt weren't in the KGB computers.
All of them appeared to be Americans, and that
puzzled the Soviets almost as much as the overtures
that had recently been made to obtain military supplies from the USSR.

Vladimir recalled the information he had gleaned from Yucheng's file as he followed him along the dark corridor, through a glass door, and into the bright sunlight. From Nationalist China, Yucheng worked for a period smuggling drugs into the US and had, on several occasions, worked with those connected to the communist effort to make drugs readily available to the decadent West. Yucheng was a skilled pilot and often flew old-vintage seaplanes. Vladimir remembered that his guide often favored long-bladed knives or ice picks and once even dispatched an American drug agent using a large meat cleaver. That undoubtedly left quite a mess for the Americans to clean up, the Soviet thought grimly. What have we gotten ourselves into? Vladimir asked himself as he paused before Yucheng's silver 300-ZX parked to one side of the customs building.

"You may place your bags in here," Yucheng said as the trunk lid of the Nissan swished on hydraulic hinges.

Vladimir complied and stood as the tiny trunk was slammed shut. The Russian limped around to the side of the car, located the recessed door latch, and opened the door. The Soviet marveled at the futuristic interior of the silver vehicle for a second and then slid his short, meaty frame into its cramped passenger seat.

"The seat controls are to the lower right side of your chair, if you wish to adjust it," Yucheng advised as he twisted the key in the ignition. The engine roared to life with a sound that, to Vladimir's ears, was more like that of a jet than an automobile.

"Oh, no. The seat is fine," Vladimir lied, not wanting to fool with the controls and be forced to reveal that he couldn't work them. Vladimir viewed the car's instrument panel and was struck by its resemblance to that of an aircraft.

One thing was sure, Vladimir decided as the car careened away from the curb: If the vehicle was any indication of the money these people had at their disposal, they could certainly pay the going rate for Soviet weapons. With the current economic crisis in the Motherland, a contract for even a relatively modest order of military hardware would be an asset in Vladimir's file.

The Soviet looked through his window at the wooden shacks that fought for space as they neared Coopersville. Here and there, houses were piled atop one another, some on stilts, in a haphazard and often dangerous fashion.

The narrow streets between the houses and shops were like beehives and hummed with the voices of tourists and natives alike. Without warning the buildings gave way to a stretch of beach, and the Soviet caught a glimpse of the ocean. Fishing boats were bobbing on the waves. They trawled nets through the warm water, catching herring and scad to sell in the marketplace. Near the horizon were the silhouettes of tall-sailed yachts. On the beach, children in rags played alongside the rich tourists wearing skimpy bathing suits or—to the Soviet's amazement—nothing but the new "thongs."

Vladimir stared at the sun-darkened, bare-breasted female bodies and shook his head. The West had become so decadent. The embarrassing sight vanished quickly as Yucheng turned down a narrow road and screeched around a tight corner.

The Russian closed his eyes, trying to ignore how narrowly Yucheng had missed a cart of fish. Vladimir hoped the military sales might even lead to a promotion so he wouldn't have to travel to all the warm spots in the world any longer. He loosened his collar and risked tilting an air-conditioning vent on the dashboard of the car. He succeeded in sending a stream of chilled air to his face. The Soviet beamed at his minor achievement as he leaned back in the cramped seat.

The trip was soon over. Vladimir thought it a miracle—or as close to a miracle as was possible in a godless world—that they reached the Presidential Palace without a major accident. The prospect of having his body splattered on the pavement—hot pavement at that—was not a pleasant one.

"Follow me," Yucheng said after opening the trunk to the silver automobile and extracting the two cases from it.

As he was led into the grounds of the Presidential Palace, the Russian was startled by the dilapidated appearance of the building, even though the reports from the Soviet agent should have prepared him for the sight. Had the USSR's contacts inside several drug-smuggling rings not given significant information about the new activities on the island, Vladimir would have asked to be taken back to the airport right then and there, certain there wasn't enough money to buy even a crate of Kalashnikov rifles.

Vladimir found himself sweating again as he limped along the rambling, orchid-lined walkway. For a moment he thought he would gain a respite from the baking temperature when they entered the cool exterior of the building. But Yucheng made a sudden detour and took them over a cobblestone path around the side of the aged colonial mansion.

The Russian was vaguely aware of the fragrance of tropical flowers mixed with cloves and cinnamon. He glanced upward. Toward the east was the thick, lush forest that grew along the side of the volcanic mountains.

Yucheng rounded a gangly hedge and there, sitting in a bleached-white cane chair in front of a mirrorlike pool and sipping an iced drink, sat President Noble. Beside the president was a man who Vladimir was sure was Kellerman. To the president's left sat a shapely blond. At the sight of her, the Soviet felt himself automatically sucking in his stomach and trying to minimize his limp.

"Ah, welcome, Mr. Vladimir," Kellerman said, seeing the Russian. He stood and walked toward him. "Can we get you a drink? Take off your coat. You must be dying of the heat."

Vladimir was sorely tempted to remove his coat. But when he thought of his sweaty shirt he decided it would be better to suffer from the warmth than the humiliation. "I'm fine," he lied. "Though possibly a drink would be in order."

"Vodka?" the blond asked, standing and twisting ever so slightly to force her bosom up and forward. Vladimir felt a tightening in his throat.

"Uh, no," he finally said. "Do you have, perhaps, a Coca-Cola?"

"I'm sure we do," the blond replied. "Yucheng," she said condescendingly, "get our guest a Coke." She shifted toward Vladimir and extended a soft, white palm. "My name is Andrea. If you require anything during your stay here, let me know. And this is—"

"President Noble," the Soviet finished for her, regaining his senses. He strode forward and shook the black's hand.

"Mr. Vladimir," Noble said in a low voice.

"And you must be Edward Kellerman."

"Your knowledge is impressive," Kellerman responded, shaking the Soviet's hand and repressing a wince at the viselike grip. "I thought I had kept a pretty low profile. Soviet intelligence must be as dependable as they say. Do you do that by satellite or do you, in fact, have a spy on our little island?"

Vladimir smiled. "Satellite," he lied.

"Have a seat," Andrea said, motioning to the empty cane chair. "And here's your drink," she said as Yucheng returned with the Coke. "Be a darling and bring that table over here for Mr. Vladimir's drink," she ordered her bodyguard. "That will be all, Yucheng." She dismissed the man after the table was positioned by the Russian's chair.

Vladimir settled into the cushion of the chair, then took a gulp of the beverage.

"We don't have a lot of time," Kellerman said,

returning to his own chair. "So let's get right to the point."

"That would be fine," Vladimir said, startled by the man's bluntness. The Soviet had dealt with third-world leaders for so long, he was surprised not to have to endure endless small talk before getting down to business.

"Just what is it you're interested in?" Vladimir said. "And—if I may be direct—will you be able to pay for it? While we don't exploit developing countries in the manner of the capitalistic tyrants of the world, our revolution is ongoing and requires financing just as any other reformation does."

"No doubt," Kellerman said with a straight face. "But don't worry. We have a steady flow of cash."

Andrea spoke, "Provided your prices are reasonable, we should be capable of meeting them in a short while."

"You'll find our prices very reasonable. And our weapons are simple to operate and have been well tested—unlike most of those offered by the capitalists. Also, unlike the many industrial nations, we value each of our client states and are concerned with helping developing countries free themselves from the chains of the West."

"Thus far," Andrea said. "We've thrown off all the chains that needed throwing. Our big concern is dealing with any, uh, invaders. We don't want our island to suffer the fate of Grenada."

"Ah, yes," Vladimir said. "Such a debacle. And the whole world did nothing and let it happen.

But if they had been armed with greater numbers of our weapons . . . As it was, just a few Cuban construction workers held off the invaders for quite some time, I understand."

"We're already set up with small arms," Kellerman said. "And we're having no problem purchasing ammunition for them. But we could use lightly armored vehicles—APCs, heavy machine guns, and possibly a helicopter."

"Most important," Andrea said. "We need antiaircraft missiles."

The Soviet remained silent but raised his bushy brows. It was amazing how abundant their treasury had become. Or were they simply unaware of how expensive military hardware was? he wondered.

"If you can't deliver the missiles to us," Andrea said, noticing his expression, "we won't do business with you. We require air defense more than anything else."

"I'm sure we can reach an agreement," Vladimir said, carefully laying his glass on the bamboo table beside him. "But it will be expensive. And we'll need to train your men on how to operate them."

"Let us worry about the expense," Kellerman said.

"Let's hear what you have to offer," Andrea added.

11

The Hummer took Oz to the division commander's brick building. The three-story structure had been built recently and had been carefully landscaped with shrubs surrounding it. He made his way through the sparkling halls and entered the entrance to the commander's office. He crossed the empty outer office, the secretary having left an hour before. He paused a moment and then knocked on the blond wood of the inner office door.

"Enter," a tired voice with a Brooklyn accent called through the door.

The pilot entered and immediately saw the two men who sat in front of the commander's walnut and glass desk. One was Larry Grant, a CIA agent whom Oz had met previously when ferrying the man on "company business"—as Grant liked to call it. Oz had hit it off with the agent from the very first and suspected that Grant had requested Oz be brought in for whatever mission was about to come off.

Like Grant, the man next to him was dressed in civilian clothes. He sat erect and had the cropped hair Oz normally associated with the military—or intelligence agents.

Upon entering the room, Oz sharply saluted Captain Louis Warner. Warner was a veteran of Vietnam, where he had flown Huey helicopters on combat missions. The commander was a skilled pilot and justly deserved the respect shown to him by the Night Stalkers and others in Task Force 160, which he led. Warner was rail-thin. He had an acne-scarred face, a bald head, and a weak lower jaw.

Warner returned the salute and motioned toward the empty leather chair next to his desk.

Oz sat down.

"Oz," Warner started, "I'm sorry to cheat you out of your rest, but something big has come up. We have a ferry job. Your—uh—passengers," he blundered, thankful he hadn't labeled the passengers "dogs," "will be these two gentlemen. You know Larry Grant," he motioned to the CIA agent.

Grant blew a cloud of thick smoke from his cigar. "Captain," he nodded toward Oz.

"And," Captain Warner continued, "this is Sid Hamilton."

The NSA staff member gave the helicopter pilot a half salute. The wiry man wore an unhappy, hound-dog face, his mustache drooping. Deep lines extended from the man's eyes, disclosing extensive periods spent outdoors in the wind and sun.

"Information about their mission at the LZ will be on a need-to-know basis," Warner said. "I've designated you as the air mission commander for the operation. As such, I wanted you to have input on the plans we've hashed out while you were en route to Fort Bragg. Succinctly, your operation will entail landing these two on the Republic of Palm Island ASAP."

"I'm sorry," Oz said. "I'm not familiar with the destination."

"I hate to admit it, but neither was I." Warner grinned, shoving a map across his desk. "Here's the chart. It's in the Caribbean, two hundred sixty-eight kilometers north of Venezuela."

"The place with the attempted coup," Oz said, the location of the country jogging his memory of recent news events.

"Exactly," Hamilton sneered. "That's what initiated the whole mess."

"We're not at liberty to discuss why we're headed to the island," Grant cautioned the NSA agent, scowling at him.

"I can keep our little secret," Hamilton replied. He continued to smirk, aware of the fact that the CIA hadn't desired to have the NSA agent along. On a personal level, Hamilton enjoyed irritating the CIA agent.

Oz noted the lack of harmony between the two. He also noticed that Warner's pug nose was getting red, which he knew from experience meant Warner was becoming upset. The pilot suspected that Grant and Hamilton had been bickering before he'd come in. No doubt the commander was sick of hearing it.

Captain Warner tried to ignore the two agents and pointed at the map on his desk. "Unfortunately we have no ships capable of accommodating a MH-

60K in the area of Palm Island. The USS *America* could be diverted, but it would take three days to reach the region. So we'll airlift your MH-60K in a C-141B to here—this short commercial airstrip at St. Croix in the Virgin Islands." He pointed to a location on the map. "It's long enough for the transport to land."

Oz studied the map for a moment. "Palm Island's what? Nearly six hundred kilometers out from St. Croix? Do we refuel en route?"

"We're going to avoid that since you might be picked up on Palm Island's commercial airport radar," Warner answered.

"External fuel tanks to ferry from St. Croix to Palm Island, then?"

"That's correct," Warner answered. "We'll replace your modified ETS—external tank storage," he explained the acronym to Hamilton, "with an ESSS—external storage system suite. Then the plotted range for the round trip is well within your maximum. So we won't have to refuel in the air—or at Palm Island."

"Which would be impossible anyway," Grant said.

"We've been thrown off the island," Hamilton snickered. "Caught with our pants down. No one thought to send an agent there until now."

"OK, then." Warner pulled at his lower lip and then glanced at his watch. "We will have the external fuel tanks detached and the chopper ready to go into the C-141B in an hour since it was already partially disassembled from your last exercise. That'd get you to St. Croix at around oh-nine-hundred tomorrow morning."

"Sightseers won't be a problem," Grant said. "We've cordoned off the small commercial strip we'll be using."

"We're going to say there was a medical emergency," Hamilton explained.

"The ground crew will reassemble the MH-60K in an empty hangar that's been set aside for our operation," Warner said. "After sunset, at twenty-hundred, you'll fly Grant and Hamilton from St. Croix to Palm Island. You'll then return immediately and refuel. That way, if Hamilton or Grant run into difficulties, they can radio and you'll be sent to extract them according to new plans. But if all goes favorably, you'll return for them at twenty-hundred, twenty-four hours later."

"Since the sooner we get there, the better," Grant said, lighting another cigar and puffing it to life, "we need to leave as quickly as we possibly can."

"You'll carry minimal armaments?" Hamilton asked.

Warner nodded. "They'd have to anyway, with the ESSS system. All the slots are filled with fuel tanks. And the fuel tanks block the gunner's ports. The crew will have their sidearms, but nothing else."

"That's good," Hamilton said. *"No* armament will minimize the risk of an incident. We couldn't afford to have a bunch of weapons on the helicopter should it be . . ."

"Especially this close to the election," Grant snorted.

Hamilton clammed up, his smile vanished.

Grant ignored him and turned to Oz. "We don't expect any trouble." He knocked ash from his cigar into the ashtray on the desk as he leaned forward. "You'll sneak us onto the island, here," he pointed as he spoke to Oz. "They don't have any radar except at the commercial airport—and it's clear over here on the other side of the island. The northern beach area where you'll take us is sparsely settled."

"If they aren't there when you go to get them," Warner said, "you're to leave without them and return to St. Croix."

"Hamilton and I can take care of ourselves," Grant explained. "We'll get home another way. We want minimal chances of the helicopter being seen and we certainly don't want you or it to be captured."

"We don't want American troops being paraded in front of cameras so the entire world can watch . . ." Hamilton began, and then stopped, leaving an awkward silence broken only by the hum of the flourescent lights in the office.

"The greatest danger of detection will be during landing," Warner finally spoke, hauling out a second map of Palm Island. "Your LZ will be here, along this strip of beach." He pointed to a section along the northern end of the island. "You'll have little chance of being sighted."

"After you drop us off, we'll travel along this route"—Grant tapped the spot on the map—"and according to our sources, we should be able to acquire a car here." He pointed again. "We'll proceed to Coopersville, collect our information, and be at the pickup zone within a day's time."

"It'll be tight," Warner said.

"But it looks workable." Oz nodded.

"Do you see any problem in the plan as it stands?" Warner asked. "I realize this is short notice and—if you feel we're acting too hastily—you can veto the plan. But time is critical," the commander said as he glanced at Hamilton.

"What about the mission data cartridge?" Oz asked. "Is that going to hold us up?"

"It'll be prepared," Warner said as he scratched his pug nose. "We'll have your mission control computer programmed for the flight by the time your helicopter is stored in the cargo plane."

"All right then . . ." Oz paused to consider everything. "I guess that's it. And it's my understanding that my crew will be permitted to carry personal small arms."

"Yes," Warner nodded. "But only for self-defense."

"And Hamilton and I'll be armed as well," Grant added.

Warner looked at his wristwatch. "You'd better get a move on."

Oz stood. "My crew has been alerted by your messenger. We'll be ready to leave by the time the chopper is."

"Good luck, Oz," Warner called as the pilot left the room.

CHAPTER

12

Each knew the secret meeting was dangerous. The four mercenaries sat in a nearly dark room that was normally occupied by prostitutes and their johns. A neon sign in front of the hotel flashed on and off with a monotonous rhythm, alternately splashing the walls of the room with first a sickly green and then a garish red light.

Hobbs sat on the bed, feeling very self-conscious in the Palm Island police uniform he wore. Like the others, he fretted about what would happen if they were caught by Kellerman or Todd. He fought at the constricting collar of the uniform and then sat immobile on the rickety bed next to Smiley Douglas who, it seemed to Hobbs, spent an inordinate amount of time scratching.

Bruce 'Wetzel sat opposite them. He rested his huge frame on a battered chair, facing its back with his hairy arms sprawled over it.

Yucheng sat cross-legged on the floor. He had outlined his plan to the three other men in the room as he nursed a glass of wine.

"But are you certain we can pull it off?"

Hobbs asked nervously. "If we try and don't succeed . . ."

"Andrea will flail us alive," Smiley finished, saying what none of the four cared to contemplate. *"If* we're lucky," he added, appending a disconcerting afterthought to his original idea.

Yucheng gave Smiley a long, hard stare. "But we won't fail. Kellerman has you running his house and playing servant. I'm acting as Andrea's bodyguard. It's a perfect setup," he said to the others. "We have to be ready to take over when they've been eliminated."

"Yeah," Wetzel growled. "If we do it right, everyone but Kellerman's crew will follow us."

"And you can snuff Kellerman's men easily since you supervise the preparation of their food," Yucheng said.

"The rest of them are only interested in the money," Wetzel reflected aloud. "We pay them, they'll follow us."

"And Noble might even be grateful—if we make our moves wisely," Yucheng said. "We could loosen up on his family. He'd be a pushover for a little kindness. But we'd still keep control."

"I don't know," Hobbs worried. "What about the Russians?"

"They don't care who's in charge, either," Wetzel said. "As long as they're getting cash on the barrel head."

"Hell," Smiley laughed nasally. "They'll probably feel more at home if the government changes hands another time or two." He pulled a cloth bag of marijuana from his pocket and commenced work on rolling a cigarette.

Yucheng sipped from the goblet lying on the floor next to him and spoke, "With the new armaments the Soviets are supposed to divert from Cuba, we'll be set for quite a while. No one will be capable of taking the island from us. The US Government will be afraid of an incident with the Soviets and we'll be too powerful for any of the crime syndicates."

"And we've seen how the money's coming in," Wetzel said. "There's no reason for us to keep getting crumbs when we could be taking the biggest share for ourselves."

"We'd be splitting it four ways?" Hobbs asked.

Yucheng swirled the wine left in his nearly empty glass. "Most of it," he finally answered. "Of course we'd have to pay the men to keep them working for us."

"But that will be small potatoes compared to what we'll keep," Wetzel mused, a burly finger poking at an itch on his head.

There was another silence. Smiley struck a match and lit the reefer he had expertly rolled.

"What do you say?" Yucheng asked. "Are you in?"

"I'm in," Wetzel said without hesitation.

"You're convinced it will work?" Hobbs asked.

"Of course it will," Yucheng reassured him. "As long as we each do our part."

"OK," Hobbs whispered, as if afraid someone might overhear them. "I guess I'm in."

"Me, too," Smiley quickly chimed in, aware that everyone's eyes were on him. He tried to sound as positive as he could since it was probable that Yucheng would cut his throat if he didn't join. Although signing on appeared to be voluntary, Smiley was not naive enough to presume his life would be worth anything if he refused. He took a deep drag on his cigarette.

"It's settled then." Yucheng rose to his feet.

"When?" Hobbs asked.

"Things are falling into a routine with both Kellerman and Todd," Yucheng told them.

"So when everything gets into the groove," Wetzel completed the idea, "that's when we should strike."

"Exactly." Yucheng's eyes glowed red for a moment in the garish neon light. "When the time is suitable, I'll contact each of you. In a few days, a week at the most. Each of you must be prepared to strike at a minute's notice. Understood?"

The three muttered agreement.

13

The men flew in a Lockheed C-141B "Starlifter." The men rode on the passenger deck; below, in the belly of the cargo plane, the partially disassembled MH-60K traveled with them.

Oblivious to the danger they knew they would soon be facing, Oz and most of his bone-weary Night Stalkers slept. The same was true for all but one of his ground crew. Those who remained awake gravitated to the rear of the plane for a mile-high crap game. Luger, who often suffered from insomnia in flight, found himself playing cards with Grant, Hamilton, Sergeant Marvin, and Jim Seaton—one of the five flight crew members manning the C-141B. By the time the transport plane neared St. Croix, Luger had exhausted his pocket money and was into IOUs.

A squad of Air Force security guards also sat in the passenger compartment. Unlike the American agents and Army personnel, they assembled into their own secluded group toward the front of the plane, where they conversed quietly. They wore full combat gear and all but two were armed with M16 rifles. The other two carried an FN Minimi and an M203 grenade launcher.

The C-141B that was transporting the men from Fort Bragg to the Virgin Islands was painted in a green-and-gray camouflage pattern. The aircraft was powered by four turbofan jets pylon-mounted beneath the craft's high wings. The pilot barber-poled the plane, taking it to its maximum speed of 495 kilometers per hour in order to get to their destination as soon as possible.

As they neared the islands, the pilot verified there were no Indians—private planes in the vicinity of the runway—and then "slam dunked" the C-141B to the runway, making those in the passenger compartment of the giant nauseous as the aircraft landed at its maximum safe descent speed. The C-141B's ten wheels screeched onto the runway and then the pilot taxied toward the hangar that was to serve as the assembly point for the helicopter riding in the plane.

A local police car approached the plane as the passengers stiffly disembarked onto the runway. The landing strip had been hastily built in September of 1989 to allow the US Government to airlift supplies following the destruction caused by Hurricane Hugo. It had gone unused since then—until the cargo plane had landed on it.

The squad of Air Force security guards quickly fanned out into the darkness to insure that the area was secure while their sergeant conversed for a moment with the policeman in the car. The conversation with the police officer was short; the official soon got into his vehicle and drove away.

The crew of the C-141B remained with their plane to aid in the unloading of the MH-60K. The members of the Air Force crew knew that once their supervision of the off-loading was finished, they were free to change into "civvies" and head to the town of Kingshill three kilometers south of them. There they could see the sights since they wouldn't be needed again for at least twenty-four hours.

Sergeant Bruce Marvin walked through the darkness that was lit only by strobing blue runway lights and a mercury vapor light hanging on a tall pole near the hangar. The sergeant approached the hangar to inspect it before off-loading the helicopter.

He found the hangar dimly lit but fairly clean with only a few oil stains on the wide concrete floor and three piles of battered tires along one wall. He looked upward at the corrugated steel that made a tin rainbow over the floor.

Six of the bulbs are burnt out, Marvin noted, squinting at the ceiling. Too bad we didn't bring floodlights. He flexed the shoulder muscles that had become stiff during the flight and returned to the runway.

"Look lively," he bellowed to his crew as he neared the C-141B. "You know the drill."

Some of his men smiled indulgently to themselves as they stood at their positions. Marvin's "you know the drill" had become his trademark.

The sergeant stationed Private Samuel Brown in the helicopter. Brown would operate the brakes in the MH-60K so it wouldn't travel down the ramp too fast, once freed of its tiedowns. Brown signaled a "ready" through the Plexiglas window of the helicopter.

"OK," Marvin directed, squeezing around the helicopter in the cramped quarters of the cargo plane. "Remove the tiedowns."

His men quickly released the steel cables anchoring the MH-60K to the interior of the cargo plane. Marvin supervised the connection of the steering bar and towing bridle, then connected the hydraulic cart to the twenty-eight-volt power source in the cargo plane.

"Hold it," Marvin cautioned, locking the winch in place as the tail wheel of the helicopter approached the cargo ramp. "Disconnect the steering bar and lock the tail wheel."

The men utilized the hydraulic cart to lower the shock struts so the helicopter had proper clearance to make it down the ramp without scraping.

"Watch the clearance there at the tail rotor servo, Robel," Sergeant Marvin ordered as they backed the helicopter onto the ramp, using the winch to gauge its descent.

Marvin instructed the men to remove the steering bridle and unlock the tail wheel. After the helicopter was on the runway and clear of the ramp, he spoke.

"Simmons, unhook the winch and be sure it's stowed. The loadmaster's got better things to do than clean up behind us."

Sergeant Marvin helped his men shove the helicopter into the hangar. Then they returned and transported the crates of parts, gear, and tools to the hangar and prepared to unfold the tail pylon along with the main and tail rotors.

While the helicopter was being unloaded, O.T. had found a cool, sandy spot outside the hangar and stretched a camouflaged poncho over it. He lay down on it, positioning his helmet and rifle alongside himself. As Oz strolled by him in the near darkness, O.T. appeared to be asleep. The pilot heard a soft snore from his warrant officer.

The runway lights suddenly blinked out leaving darkness in their wake. A gentle wind blew against Oz's face. The breeze came from the nearby ocean and cooled the dirt and grass along the runway. The moon was setting in the west. That's good, Oz thought. It would make the MH-60K SOA's passengers harder to detect when they landed on the beach. As he strolled in the darkness, careful to stay within the perimeter the Air Force guards had set, Oz's thoughts strayed to Sandy.

Before he'd married her, he'd always managed to kid himself into thinking he'd live forever, especially when he went hurtling through the sky in control of a fighting machine worth over a million dollars. But during the last year, he'd caught her anxiety. He'd come to realize—not in his brain but in his gut—that death could come in the blink of an eye. It might pound him to a pulp, fry him in burning wreckage, or leave him crushed, slowly bleeding to death.

Her fear was why she'd finally left him. She hadn't minded his military career, until he'd transferred to Task Force 160 and became a member of the Night Stalkers. She immediately recognized the danger he would encounter. Little by little her anxiety had forced them apart, causing endless arguments. When Oz refused to transfer out of the task force, Sandy packed her bags.

She stood in front of the door, suitcases at her feet. She wore a tight tangerine-colored sweater that outlined her small breasts. Her eye makeup ran with tears down her face.

"You care more about that damned helicopter than you care about me, don't you?" Her sensuous lips quivered as she tried not to cry.

He didn't answer because he knew he couldn't explain.

She had turned and stormed through the door. And that had been the last he had seen or heard from her.

Oz returned to the hangar to discover that the MH-60K was nearly assembled. Luger, Death Song, and Grant were standing in the pool of light created by the open doors of the hangar. They were inspecting the weapons each of them carried. The CIA agent seemed especially interested in Luger's ACR and the duplex cartridges it used, each round containing two bullets. Death Song was examining the Calico 950A the agent carried. The machine pistol had been modified to fire full automatic. The weapon carried a helical magazine that held fifty cartridges.

As Oz approached, Grant was holding the machine pistol in both hands, talking around his cigar: "It hardly needs lubrication. And the cartridges are ejected out of the lower side, here."

Oz half hid the PK-15 he carried as he strode

toward the three men. The short rifle attracts too much attention from the "gun nuts," he thought. In fact, it might be easier to carry a standard rifle, despite the compactness and power of the PK-15.

The pilot noted Sergeant Marvin had completed the assembly of the helicopter. His crew was wheeling the vehicle from the hangar onto the runway.

"Come on, Death Song," Oz enjoined the navigator as he arrived at the small knot of men, "time to check the instruments. Luger," he added, "put that pistol away before someone confiscates it." He laughed.

Luger smiled sheepishly and put the pistol into his holster. He insisted on carrying the Luger pistol—since it bore his name—more for luck than its serviceability. The battalion commander had thus far chosen to ignore the weapon that had not been approved through the usual TO and E for equipment carried by Army personnel.

Like the other crew members of the MH-60K, Luger carried his pistol in a chest harness under his flak jacket. Oz carried a Ruger P-85 in his holster, Death Song carried the standard Beretta M9 9mm pistol issued by the US Army, while O.T. had chosen to stick with the .45 ACP in Colt's new Double Eagle automatic; he felt the .45 offered superior knockdown capabilities compared to the 9mm cartridges employed in other pistols. O.T.'s assertion of the superiority of this cartridge had caused endless arguments with Luger.

Oz and Death Song ambled toward the assembled aircraft.

"She's ready for you," Sergeant Marvin called as the two men approached him on the runway. "Sorry it took a little longer than usual but we had trouble with the left long-range fuel tanks—they didn't want to mate to the ESSS carrying pylons. But they're fine now."

Oz walked toward the nearest pylon of the helicopter and gave one of the pods a rough shake.

"They're as tight as a hungry tick on a fat dog," Marvin chortled happily to the pilot. He nodded back toward the hangar where his crew was piling empty storage containers. "If you need me, I'll be over there getting things straightened out."

"Thanks," Oz said sincerely. He donned his helmet and opened the door on the pilot's side of the helicopter. He grabbed the handrail next to the pilot's door, stepped onto the bar extending in front of the landing gear support, and swung himself into the MH-60K. He stowed his PK-15 behind his armored bucket seat and then sat down and fastened his shoulder harness.

Death Song entered the helicopter from the navigator's door on the left of the cabin and the two men began a quick preflight check of the helicopter.

14

In the darkness, Oz flew the MH-60K SOA at three hundred feet. This kept the aircraft from being detected by the civilian airport radar on Palm Island by placing them within the "shadow" of Mt. Marshal, the extinct volcano that rose from the north of the island. The helicopter was also covered with "stealth" paint, which would further reduce the chances of detection.

Death Song took a reading of his gyromagnetic compass. "To the left a half degree," he told Oz.

The pilot glanced at a CRT screen and slightly adjusted his course. He looked through his door window to see the calm sea below hurtling past, giving a hint of their speed. Through the dome window above, the stars twinkled radiantly in a cloudless night. The bright points of light seemed to travel with the helicopter as it charged forward.

Behind the pilot, in the crew compartment, O.T. and Luger sat in silence. O.T. eyed the empty spot where his Minigun was normally stowed. The gun wasn't there and the gunner's port was covered by its sliding double window. The warrant officer found the lack of armament disconcerting. Luger stared out the gunner's window on the left side of the helicopter and tried to distinguish the unfamiliar constellations that were filling the southern section of the sky ahead of them.

Grant and Hamilton rode aft of the gunners' stations on the flight deck in the passenger's compartment. Grant sat hunched to the side in his canvas and pipe chair, his shoulder harness holding him upright. His feet were propped on the chair opposite him while he tried to catnap. The camera bag containing his submachine gun, a camera, and other equipment rested on the vacant seat next to him.

Sid Hamilton sat on a seat on the opposite end of the row of chairs. He checked the safety on his Beretta 93R machine pistol, set the gun on its three-round burst mode, then replaced it in its shoulder rig that was concealed beneath the thin jacket he wore.

Everything's fine, Hamilton tried to convince himself. Don't sit here and fret. I know darkness exaggerates problems, so I won't think about any of them.

His resolution made, Hamilton sat wide awake and worried about everything from how he could afford a new car to whether he'd be killed during the upcoming twenty-four hours. Finally, the noise of the MH-60K SOA's twin engines lulled him into a fitful sleep.

Nearly three hours after they had departed St. Croix, Death Song checked the satellite geographical positioning system. The satellites gave the navigator their location.

"We're on course and sixteen kilometers from the northern shore of Palm Island," the navigator announced.

"Good," Oz responded. "Everyone put on their NVG," he ordered his crew. "O.T., alert our passengers, I think they both removed their headsets so they could sleep."

Oz surveyed the rolling waves on the ocean's surface. A gale had picked up and the waves were becoming higher as the water piled into the shallows. "I'm descending to thirty meters," Oz warned his crew. The pilot pushed gently on the collective pitch lever in his left hand and the SOA dropped lower toward the rolling waves that showed in green and white in his NVG. The wind kicked the helicopter for a moment and stirred the waves below.

The pilot switched on his radio. Because theirs was the only helicopter involved in the actual mission, it carried a modified AN/ASC-15B triservice battlefield support system. This radio relayed their messages upward to a military communications satellite. The satellite then transferred their coded signal to their AATF commander, Captain Louis Warner, at Fort Bragg. Warner was connected through a scrambler to Harold Maxwell at the CIA.

"Banshee One with radio check," Oz said over the radio link.

"Banshee One, that's a roger," Warner answered, letting Oz know that the signal was coming in loud and clear.

"We're at checkpoint Alpha one, and await instructions, over," Oz responded.

There was radio silence as Warner double-checked with the CIA whether to continue the mission. Oz sat tensely in the darkness, wondering if the mission was about to be aborted. A tiny bug splattered on the windscreen, leaving a faint phosphorescent smear in front of the pilot.

"You have a go-ahead, I say again, go ahead. Verify."

"I verify," Oz replied. "We have a go-ahead. Over."

"Good luck, Banshee One, over and out."

Death Song analyzed the HSD, then tapped a key on the chopper's computer console. "There's our LZ," Death Song said finally. "We're X ringing it."

Oz studied his glowing HSD that duplicated Death Song's display. "Is the crew ready, O.T.?" the pilot asked.

"We're up and around," Grant's voice answered. "Room service has awakened us."

"When we land," Oz said, "remember to keep your heads down and don't go near the tail rotor." The pilot was always apprehensive about personnel around that weren't familiar with the helicopter's peculiar dangers.

"We'll be careful, Mom," Hamilton chided the pilot over the intercom.

"As soon as we're down, get going, too," Oz said. "The less time around the chopper, the less apt someone is to notice you. We'll search the area for heat signatures as we go in but we won't pick up anyone hidden in the brush."

"Thanks," Grant said.

"Permission to lock and load ACRs," O.T. requested.

"Permission granted," Oz said. "Just remember that we're *not* to fire unless fired on."

"We'll remember," O.T. said.

"Right," Luger added.

The tall darkness of Mt. Marshall loomed ahead of them, a triangular shape surrounded by light green clouds when viewed through night-vision goggles. Oz pulled the control column backward and the MH-60K decelerated as they hurtled forward, skimming above the water that lifted and rolled.

"We're going in," Oz warned the crew as the aircraft neared the beach. The rolling waves kicked white foam over the sand as the aircraft passed above it. The sea surged toward the land and then dropped downward, silently, its sound covered by the thumping of the helicopter above it.

The pilot stomped on the right pedal and cramped the control column to the right. The MH-60K lurched to the right. Oz realized the gust was created by the convection currents near the mountain. He pulled on the control column so the MH-60K hovered over the beach like a giant hummingbird.

Oz checked the FLIR. There was no sign of human beings in the infrared scope. "The area looks clear." He swooped down onto the beach. "O.T., get the door for them."

O.T. pushed the door on the passenger compartment aft on its runners. "Break a leg," O.T. shouted as the two agents stood.

Grant chuckled. "We'll meet you in twenty-four hours," the agent promised. Then he tore off his earphones, grabbed his camera bag, and unfastened his shoulder harness. He jumped from the door into the cool sand. After pausing, Hamilton followed.

"Passengers are clear," O.T. reported to Oz.

Oz observed the two men as they ran up the beach and vanished into the brush.

"Ready for takeoff, O.T.?" Oz asked.

"Secured," O.T. answered.

"I'm taking off," Oz announced. They ascended, overcoming the restraints of gravity, the blades cutting through the cool air of the night. The pilot guided the aircraft over the edge of the beach, an ebbing wave racing him for a moment before being swept toward land by an incoming breaker. Oz pushed at the control column to accelerate clear of the shore.

Death Song tapped the buttons alongside his VSD and again poked a button on the HSD. His fingers stabbed at several keys on the chopper's computer console and it plotted the return course to St. Croix. It would take them westward for thirty kilometers in case they'd been sighted by someone on Palm Island. Once they could no longer be sighted from the shore, they would then head northward toward the Virgin Islands.

In the darkness of the foliage along the beach, an elderly man awoke. He stood, forgetting about his pole and catch of fish and limped to his rusty Pontiac parked by the highway.

They're trying to take the island from us, he warned himself. The police must be alerted. The new people the president has brought here to protect us will know what to do.

He cranked the old engine of the dented car and floored the accelerator, racing down the road toward the capital.

15

Nothing out of the ordinary had happened and Hobbs was sleepy as the night shift drew to a close. The mercenary was manning the duty desk at the police station when the fisherman arrived an hour after he had sighted the American helicopter.

"They're coming! They're coming!" the fisherman cried, storming through the front door of the police station.

Hobbs jumped up behind the desk, grasping the butt of his holstered pistol and wondering what was going on.

"Who's coming?" he asked, blinking himself wide awake.

"Soldiers got off the helicopter," the raggedy-looking man said in a syrupy Caribbean accent. "In the dark. I saw them."

"Soldiers?" Hobbs asked doubtfully. The week before a tourist had come in and nearly convinced Hobbs that aliens had landed in a flying saucer. The man had seemed so sincere. After the UFO fiasco, Hobbs had become a bit dubious about anyone who came in through the door of the police station to make a report.

"Take it easy and tell me what you saw," Hobbs ordered the elderly man standing in front of him.

The mercenary listened to the fisherman's story and then tried to decide what to do. Was the man telling the truth or had he had too much rum? If it was the truth, it was necessary to alert Todd—although two or three men didn't seem like much of a threat. The old geezer didn't even know if the men were armed.

And if Hobbs woke Andrea at four A.M., he knew there'd be hell to pay if the story was only the ravings of a soused fisherman.

Call, Hobbs finally decided. He reached for the phone, fumbled with the notepad he'd scribbled phone numbers on, and finally located Andrea's number. He dialed.

Minutes later, the Presidential Palace was in an uproar. Andrea had taken the story seriously and had raised the alarm throughout the mercenary stronghold. She stormed up and down the hallway, dressed only in a long robe, oblivious to the fact that it had fallen open to her navel.

"Haven't you got Kellerman yet?" she cried as she entered the study.

Yucheng stood with the phone cradled to his ear. He shook his head as he listened to another busy signal bleeping through the earpiece.

She continued to swear under her breath as he redialed. *Why didn't I think about something like this happening? Andrea asked herself. Those stupid*

Americans are eternally meddling in other countries' affairs.

Or is it someone else? she wondered. The mob maybe? Perhaps they'd sent in a hit team. Were they trying to take over her action?

"The phone is still busy," Yucheng said. "Shall I drive over and check on—"

"Damn it," Andrea swore, pacing past him. "Eddy's probably got a bimbo in bed with him and doesn't want to be bothered. Yeah, I bet he's left the goddamned phone off the hook. Get over there," she ordered Yucheng. "And hurry it up. Bring him and his men back as quickly as possible. Be sure he's armed. We've got trouble."

Yucheng sprinted out the door of the study, clattered across the marble floor, and raced through the front door.

Andrea swore to herself and then dialed the police station.

"Hobbs," she shouted as the phone was picked up on the other end.

"Yeah?"

"Do you still have that fisherman down there?"

"Yeah. He's here by—"

"You sure he hasn't been drinking?"

"He smells clean and looks normal. But it's possible . . ." he trailed off, afraid to commit himself one way or the other.

"Keep him there," Andrea ordered. "We'll be needing a description of the men who left the plane."

"Helicopter," Hobbs corrected, immediately wishing he hadn't.

"What the hell! Plane, helicopter, whatever! It doesn't make any difference," she hollered. "The important thing is that those guys who got off it could be anywhere on the island by now. I'll be over there in a minute."

"OK," Hobbs said.

"No wait. On second thought, bring him here. Use the police car. On your way, radio and call out the full police force. We must be prepared in case there's a larger force landing somewhere else on the island. Get here as fast as you can."

Andrea slammed the phone down before Hobbs replied.

She paced the room for several seconds, trying to decide what to do. Then she hurried out the door and climbed the steps, swearing as she went to get dressed.

16

Unaware that the mercenaries on the island were looking for them, Grant and Hamilton had split up after reaching Coopersville an hour prior to dawn. Each man hoped to obtain the bits and pieces of information that could be assembled by the CIA and NSA to gain a picture of what was happening in the Republic of Palm Island.

Hamilton had headed for the docks to try to discover what the Soviet freighters were unloading. Later, he would try to glean rumors and information from talkative natives.

Grant had proceeded to the Presidential Palace. He found himself in the bushes alongside the wall of the tattered mansion when the whole place suddenly appeared to come alive.

Swatting at a mosquito, the CIA agent decided to stay hidden in the brush bordering the high wrought-iron fence that surrounded the Presidential Palace. As he watched, a silver 300ZX screeched to a halt inside the main gate. At the wheel was Yucheng.

"Hurry up and open the gate, you moron," the Oriental roared from the car's open window.

The sleepy guard scurried to the fence and opened the barred gate.

"And be alert," Yucheng added. "There are invaders on the island," he warned the guard. The car's V-6 engine roared to life and the vehicle shot into the street. It screeched around the corner to head for the city that twinkled below on the bay.

Invaders? Grant wondered. What in the world is going on? His immediate fear was that he or Hamilton had been sighted. Grant wished he could smoke without risking being seen. He retrieved his binoculars from his camera bag and scrutinized the palace windows.

More and more lights twinkled on. Shortly, the whole mansion was brightly lit. He glimpsed figures briskly walking—or sometimes running— inside the house.

Although he realized it would be dangerous to do, he had to go into the grounds. So he searched about in an attempt to discover another entrance to the palace grounds. He scrutinized the empty avenue, then cautiously stepped from the foliage onto the sidewalk and made his way along the grounds, out of sight of the guard at the main gate.

He quietly made his way down the worn and cracked sidewalk that was flanked by large palms. He divided his vigil between watching the street for approaching cars and looking through the lush shrubbery for a means to get through the three-meter-high wrought-iron fence that was topped with sharpened spikes.

After traveling a short distance, he finally found what he was searching for—a loose bar that had been inexpertly repaired with only a coil of wire securing it at its top and a pile of stones holding it in position on the ground.

Grant scrutinized the rusty bar, then peered up and down the thoroughfare for cars. Nothing. He unslung the camera bag and hid it in the brush by the fence. Then he got down on his knees.

I hope there aren't any poisonous snakes on this island, he thought only half jokingly. He lifted the first large stone and quietly relocated it. He toiled for ten minutes and then paused and listened.

He could vaguely hear a siren, headed in his direction.

Grant got down behind a large magnolia bush and fumbled with the camera bag. In the humid darkness of the bush, he opened the concealed compartment in the side of the bag. He retrieved the Calico machine pistol and pushed its safety off with his forefinger.

The agent wondered if he'd inadvertently tripped an alarm, even though he'd seen no sign of any such electronic device. And he knew it was doubtful that a sophisticated gadget like that would be employed on the island. So he concluded that he must have been seen.

The siren came nearer, the flashing blue lights making strobing flashes in the darkness. Grant held the machine pistol ready to fire, but the police car hurtled right past him.

As Grant heaved a sigh of relief, he leaned his

back against the iron fence and shut his eyes for a moment.

The police car slowed down, and for a terrible minute, the agent feared the car was going to return. Then he heard the front gates clang open and the police car rumbled through the entrance with its siren now extinguished.

Were they searching the grounds? Grant wondered. He waited. There was nothing.

As he placed his machine pistol into its compartment, the silver 300ZX came careening down the lane, followed by Kellerman's blue BMW. The two cars squealed to a halt in front of the front gate and then chased through it.

Grant quickly returned to the task of painstakingly dislocating each stone. As he quietly removed the last one, he inspected the bar for a second; he grabbed it in both hands and slowly increased the pressure against it. The wires securing it bent and the bar twisted inward with a growl.

Grant waited in the darkness, listening. Nothing. There was just enough room for him to squeeze through. He reached down and picked up his camera bag, then twisted sideways and placed his head and shoulder between the bars, pushing and scraping through the space where the missing bar had been.

Finally within the perimeter of the fence, he held his hand in front of his face and pushed through the overgrown hedge. He crept through the hedge and quietly ran through the shadowy yard, hoping there were no dogs.

When he reached the mansion, he pressed his

back against the outside of the building to catch his breath. He looked upward and there, contrasted against the sky's glow that marked the coming of sunrise, was what he was looking for—the telephone cable. It led from the street, over the yard, and connected to the building. The agent followed the cable's shadowy silhouette down the exterior of the mansion and crept along the side of the house until he located the exact place where the cable entered the wall, half hidden by a tall bush.

Grant squeezed behind the bush whose flowers exuded a cloyingly sweet fragrance. He set his camera bag in the grass. Kneeling, he unzipped a compartment on the bag and extracted a screwdriver and a tool that was similar to a wire cutter. With the tools he quickly installed a petite transmitter onto the telephone line.

Using a tiny earphone that he plugged into the bug, he listened to be sure the device was functioning. There was a brief burst of static, then the signal became quiet. He tapped a small button on the transmitter and switched from the first phone line to the next.

"... I don't care if they are asleep," a woman's voice rasped. "Do it!" She slammed a phone down.

The sound caused Grant to jerk the earphone from his ear. The bug was definitely operational.

The agent snatched a spool of wire with several coils incorporated along its length. He carefully strung it into the bush and then plugged its two ends into the small bug on the telephone line to create an aerial for the transmitter.

With any luck, he reflected, this ought to go

undetected for a few days. He stared upward into the murky sky for a moment, knowing that somewhere high above one of the Signal Intelligence satellites would be receiving any conversations now coming through the phone in the mansion and relaying them to Langley.

As the agent knelt and dropped his tools into the bag, two guards toting Heckler and Koch MP5 submachine guns rounded the corner from the front of the mansion. They were carrying on a heated conversation and approached the place where Grant hid. The CIA agent's fingers snaked toward the Calico hidden in his bag.

C H A P T E R

17

Hamilton snapped another quick photo of the Soviet freighter as he strolled inconspicuously along the dock in the soft light of the evening. After looking around, he focused on the crates on the dock and stole another picture. He couldn't read much Russian, but he recognized the symbols for handheld antiaircraft missiles.

He very quickly hid his tiny camera as one of the dock workers seemed to be scrutinizing him. The NSA agent sneaked the camera into his jacket pocket and turned and casually walked along the wharf toward the center of the town. He had five hours to go.

He was pleased with the information he'd obtained so far. His conversation with a customs official he'd bribed that morning had revealed that drug dealers worldwide were doing business through the island's airport and banks. Money and drugs were passing through customs, provided the person carrying them had his name on a special list that came from the Presidential Palace. A casual conversation in a bar had revealed that people were vanishing from time to time. There were rumors of family members being taken hostage to keep potential troublemakers in line.

Hamilton made his way toward a noisy bar halfway up the street where he could hear a steel band creating a tumult of metallic music. The tourists were coming off the pristine beaches now and out of their air-conditioned hotel rooms with the setting of the sun. Peddlers controlled the boulevard from tiny stands or from the backs of hand-pulled carts. The tourists jostled one another, and laughter rang out. Fish, breads, and drinks abounded along with other wares in the open market, which ranged from hand-painted dishes and straw mats to rare coins and gems and, undoubtedly, counterfeit designer watches and sunglasses.

A Lexus LS 400 sedan honked its horn; the driver sat impatiently behind the wheel until the pedestrians cleared a path. Then the car stormed through the throng.

As Hamilton paused at the entrance to the bar, he noticed a man in a customs uniform speaking to a police officer on the other side of the street. The policeman was glancing in Hamilton's direction but looked away when the American caught his eye. Hamilton lit a cigarette, and when he glanced up again, the two men had melted into the crowd.

The NSA agent strode into the sleazy bar filled with smoke and calypso music. He made his way past the few dancers on the floor, looking for the rear exit.

Feeling panic lodging in his throat, the agent shoved past a couple that staggered in front of him.

Then he glanced back over his shoulder and saw a police officer standing in the open entrance, his hand on his belted pistol.

"One moment please!" the lawman bellowed over the music.

Hamilton slipped into the darkness toward the back of the room, hardly able to discern the outline of a rear door with his sun-blinded eyes.

When he reached the door and grasped the door handle, it creaked open. He ran into the garbage-strewn alley.

His hand groped into his jacket for his 93R. The agent quickly looked in both directions and turned to run when a voice came from behind him at the far end of the alley.

"Hold it!" the voice ordered.

Hamilton's thumb clicked the safety of his machine pistol as he grasped its forward grip with his left hand, hooking his thumb through its oversize trigger guard. He spun to face the policeman who stood spread-legged at the other end of the alley, his revolver pointed toward the American.

The agent's finger tensed on the trigger as he swung his weapon at the officer. Both guns fired at the same instant with deafening roars that echoed through the alley.

The police officer's bullet clipped Hamilton's shoulder, grazing it and sending a sharp pain coursing along the agent's arm.

The bullets from the machine pistol pocked the garbage cans to the side of the police officer with 9mm-sized holes. Hamilton jerked the trigger. The gun cycled through a second burst that stabbed the lawman's jacket with three dark holes. The holes filled and overflowed with blood as the officer tried to keep his balance. The policeman dropped his gun and collapsed onto a pile of brown garbage bags.

Hamilton ignored the clatter of his empty cartridges as they rolled along the pavement. He spun to flee when he saw a flicker of movement on the periphery of his vision.

Before the agent could react, the barrel of a policeman's revolver clipped his skull with a heavy blow. The American experienced a flash of bright light and then blackness. His machine pistol clattered to the cobblestones as it dropped from his hand.

Two and a half hours later, Hamilton was brought back to consciousness for the third time by the harsh fumes of smelling salts. Pain engulfed him. He coughed and spat out blood and clots and discovered with his tongue that two front teeth were missing.

The NSA agent tried to remember what had happened.

He recalled being brought to the basement of the Presidential Palace and being tied to the chair. He remembered the bitch in the white dress who gave orders to the Oriental man. And he remembered with chilling precision the agony of the knife.

"So, our guest has revived," Andrea's voice purred as she entered the room. "Go easier this time," she ordered Yucheng. "We can't afford to lose him before he talks. And get more astringent on those wounds. We don't want him to bleed to death."

Hamilton braced himself. He bit his lower lip and tried not to scream as the stinging astringent was dumped into his deep cuts.

"One more time," Andrea said in a low voice. "Where are the others who came with you?"

Yucheng held his knife in front of Hamilton's remaining eye. The blade had been wiped clean of blood so it glittered in the stark light.

Todd nodded and the blade flicked out of sight. Pain raced up Hamilton's leg. He strained against his bonds. He tried to flex his fingers and discovered four were gone, with only painfully cut ligaments signaling where they had been. He gasped for breath and tried to think.

He had known he was a dead man from the moment they'd strapped him into the chair, so he had vowed to stay silent until Grant had had time to escape the island.

But he had no sense of time. Minutes, hours, or days? He was unsure; the pain stretched time into infinity.

The pain came in another wave. He writhed, trying to jerk his leg away from Yucheng's blade. The blade made a ripping sound as it cut through his flesh and muscle.

The torment in his thigh jerked him alert as it traveled upward with a wet cutting sound toward his groin.

"You'll tell us eventually," she crooned. "Why not do it while there's something left of you?"

Hamilton gasped for breath, sweat and tears rolling down his cheek as he observed the blade coming toward his face. The steel and blood sparkled in the light.

The agent knew they'd kill him once he'd told them about Grant, but death was welcome now.

"All right," he softly gasped as the blade touched his eyebrow and drew a crimson jewel. "I'll tell you."

CHAPTER

18

Grant sat in a parked Corona behind the Hilton Hotel in Coopersville, the rendezvous point he and Hamilton had agreed on. He had hot-wired the car and driven it to the parking lot to wait for the NSA agent.

He looked at his wristwatch. Hamilton was late. Damn him, Grant thought, he's probably drinking somewhere unaware of the time. Grant had little patience with cowboys from the NSA. The CIA agent chomped at the unlit cigar in his mouth, shut his bloodshot eyes, and thought about how close he'd come to being caught at the Presidential Palace. Fortunately, the guards hadn't been too alert and had walked right by him.

He heard footsteps in the parking lot.

The agent sat up in the seat and studied the rearview mirror. Some distance behind the car an Oriental man was walking down the aisles of parked cars, looking to his left and right.

Searching for someone, Grant realized with alarm. He slid down in the seat, hoping to remain hidden in the shadows. He reached up and adjusted the mirror so he could continue to spy on the man.

The man wore a black leather jacket. He stepped into the light falling from the floodlamp on the hotel building and searched the parking lot. Grant observed the man closely and noted the telltale bulge that had to be a weapon hidden under his jacket.

The man gave a signal with his hand, and ahead of Grant's car, two policemen entered the parking lot, blocking the exit.

Shit, Grant thought, where the hell is Hamilton? The agent unsnapped the camera bag lying on the seat beside him and removed the Calico machine pistol. He pushed the gun's selector to its fire position. And then all at once it came to Grant that Hamilton wasn't going to be meeting him.

The man in the leather jacket and the policemen were looking for Grant in the parking lot because Hamilton had been captured and had disclosed their meeting place.

Grant laid the submachine gun on the passenger seat and bent down to tap the two bare starter wires that hung loose beside the ignition of the car. He sparked the wires together and the engine made a chugging sound.

The man in the black jacket whirled around to stare in Grant's direction. His hand snaked into his jacket and pulled out a long-bladed knife.

"Come on, start!" Grant rasped as he tapped the wires together again, creating a spark. The engine turned over and sputtered to life.

The agent floored the accelerator of the car

and sped through the parking lot, nearly hitting the Oriental man, who cursed him as he jumped aside.

The two policemen held their ground at the exit of the parking lot. They brought their FN FAL rifles into position and started firing.

The windshield spalded as the .30-caliber bullets hit the glass, cutting Grant's arms and face as he ducked below the dash. The Corona bumped over one of the policemen with a dull thud.

As Grant sat back up again, he tried to regain control of the careening vehicle as it shot into the street. The car veered across the pavement, smashing into a parked car in the process. Grant straightened the wheel and sped up to the cacophony of grinding metal as he accelerated down the straightaway.

Two bullets clipped through the passenger compartment, narrowly missing Grant as he wheeled around a corner and sped away from the policeman who stood in the street firing his gun, oblivious to his dying companion.

Steam was coming from the radiator of the car and the agent realized he had to get another one. The Corona had had it and would be easy to spot. He eyed the red ZR-1 Corvette coming toward him in the other lane.

"Might as well go in style," he snorted as he cramped the wheel of the Corona, sending it into a screeching skid and blocking the path of the Corvette.

A tall man in an expensive sharkskin suit jumped out of the Corvette and swaggered toward

Grant. Spoiling for a fight, the man reached into his jacket and pulled out a stainless-steel revolver.

Grant slowly climbed out of the Corona, spitting out the remains of his Cuban cigar.

"You looking for trouble, buddy?" the tall man snapped at Grant. "My boss says you either get out of the way or—" The man ceased in mid-sentence and froze in his tracks when he saw that Grant was calmly pointing a submachine gun at his groin.

"Did you say something about looking for trouble?" the agent asked dryly. "You've just bought yourself a whole dunghill full of it."

The man in the sharkskin suit dropped the revolver and placed his hands over his head. Grant aimed the weapon at the passenger sitting in the car. The short man jumped from the vehicle and sprinted down the street without ever looking back.

"You follow your boss," Grant ordered.

The big man whirled and ran like he'd been set on fire.

Grant jerked his camera bag from the wrecked Corona and strode over to the Corvette. He slid into the red cotton-candy interior, thankful the owner of the car hadn't had the presence of mind to take the keys with him. He pushed the stick shift into reverse and skidded backward into a bootlegger's turn, jerking the transmission into first.

The agent raced the car down the narrow route leading to the highway that would take him toward the pickup zone. As he bounded over a hill, he saw the roadblock ahead of him. Two police cars blockaded his route.

Grant swore under his breath and then tried to relax. He knew he had the training. Go around, he advised, as if his instructor were speaking in his ear. And if you can't go around, go through the roadblock.

Since he couldn't go around, the agent smashed the Corvette into the side of the police car on the right, just over its rear wheel. Grant kept the gas pedal down, causing the squad car to whip around the Corvette, letting him pass. He sped on, thankful for the maneuver his instructor had called the "demolition derby revolving door."

Grant shot up the hill as bullets chewed the pavement around him and zinged through the interior of the car.

CHAPTER

19

As Grant raced down the hill toward the pickup zone, he switched on the car's dome light and looked at his watch. It's going to be close, he thought, I should get there right on time. He snapped off the bulb. With the caravan of cars following him, he knew he wouldn't have time to wait around for the helicopter.

He studied the rearview mirror again. Through the bullet-riddled rear windshield he could distinguish five cars—one a police vehicle, judging from the flashing light. They wound down the mountain road behind him. Although they weren't gaining, they weren't falling behind, either.

He looked at the red idiot light on the dashboard. How long can a Corvette run with its oil light on? he wondered. One of the bullets fired at him had clearly punctured the oil pan. And his fuel was low, suggesting another bullet hole somewhere in the fuel line or gas tank.

The question was, if he did make it to the beach, would he be able to find the helicopter in the dark. Unfortunately, Hamilton had carried the radio . . . Grant wondered if the helicopter would even hang around when the crew saw the welcoming party trailing him.

He kicked the accelerator as he hit a patch of straight highway. The engine clanked ominously as the car lurched into fourth gear and gained speed.

He heard the muffled reports of distant rifle shots, but none of the bullets seemed to be coming near him. He slowed to round the last curve at the base of Mt. Marshall, and then he floored the gas pedal as he hit another straight road at the base of the peak.

Suddenly the engine of the Corvette started to clatter and the car began to lurch.

The cottage that Hamilton and he had noted as a reference point on their journey into the city went whizzing by and then vanished into the darkness. "Hang on," he pleaded with the car. "We're almost there."

The car's engine shuddered to a halt and the transmission threatened to bring the car to a quick stop. Grant pushed in the clutch and then shifted into neutral, letting the ruined vehicle coast as long as possible.

While he steered with his left hand, his free hand fumbled in the camera bag. He finally extracted the rolls of film he'd taken. He placed the film in his shirt pocket and glanced in the mirror.

The cars pursuing him were definitely gaining. He twisted the wheel of the Corvette to the shoulder of the road, using the last bit of the car's momentum to cross the shallow embankment along the highway. The Corvette crashed through a wooden fence and came to a standstill on the beach. He shut off the lights, leaned over, and clawed a signal flare and his submachine gun from the bag.

Unlatching the car door and jumping out of the Corvette, he held the Calico 950A firmly in his fist. He raced across the beach, stumbling in the sand and then regaining his footing. As he approached the area that he judged to be the PZ, he looked frantically for the helicopter.

Nothing.

He knelt in the sand and noted that his pursuers were now alongside the Corvette. Flashlights were darting all around the area and a high-intensity spotlight mounted on the lead car was stabbing through the darkness, throwing shadows over the beach as it searched for him.

Grant fumbled with the flare for a moment, unscrewing the protective cap covering its arming mechanism. Once the cover was removed, he grasped the long string inside it and carefully pointed the muzzle of the tube up and away from himself. He jerked the string. There were a few sparks, accompanied by a popping. Then there was a hiss and the flare of a small rocket engine. A second pop, a hundred meters high, and the green star flare hung in the sky on its parachute, signaling his need to be rescued.

His pursuers along the road saw the flare, too, and started firing wildly in his direction. One bullet ricocheted off the sand close by Grant. He hunkered down and gritted his teeth.

He was relieved to hear the gunfire from the

road being directed toward a site about a hundred meters to the west of him. Peering in that direction, he realized his attackers had homed in on a man-size chunk of driftwood.

Grant scanned the night sky.

There! he almost shouted. A black shape near the ocean's horizon was blocking the stars. Suddenly the thump, thumping of helicopter blades filled the air.

The agent slipped a penlight from his pocket and switched it on. He carefully directed the beam of light toward the craft, keeping his body between the flashlight and the men firing from the road. Like the flare, the high-intensity bulb in his flashlight was green.

The helicopter veered toward him, kicking up a storm of dust as it approached and set down fifty yards from him.

A hail of gunfire pelted the area around Grant as the gunmen saw the chopper. He dashed toward the MH-60K as bullets churned plumes of sand around his feet and buzzed through the air.

"I'm coming!" he bellowed, hoping the helicopter would wait. A bullet stabbed into his forearm as he ran. He cried, stumbled, and fell. He got to his knees, then jumped up and continued sprinting toward the MH-60K, still clutching his gun.

As he neared the helicopter, the crew—wearing their NVGs—recognized him. Once Grant was identified, O.T. and Luger started firing their advanced combat rifles at the men pursuing the agent along the beach.

The salvo from the helicopter immediately

shattered the spotlight, which winked out leaving a sputter of electricity behind. The men along the road scrambled for cover and those on the beach dropped onto their faces. Several cried out in pain—the duplex bullets had reached their targets.

O.T. grabbed Grant's free hand as he scrambled aboard. "Where's Hamilton?"

"Captured," Grant gasped, falling onto the floor.

The agent rolled over and fired a long burst from his submachine gun at the attackers on the beach.

"We're secure," O.T. reported to Oz over the intercom. He slid the side door shut.

Luger continued to fire from the gunner's port.

"I'm taking her up," Oz warned as a bullet smashed through the Plexiglas window close to his head. Loud thumps marked the impact of bullets elsewhere in the body of the craft, and the metal fragment detector blinked a warning.

The pilot lifted the helicopter from the earth, guiding the craft toward the sea and sending it forward at full speed. The MH-60K shot through the darkness and vanished from sight as the men on the beach fired wildly at the receding shape.

Oz continued to press the helicopter forward at its top speed. Death Song plotted a flight path and Oz directed the helicopter onto the route for the Virgin Islands.

C H A P T E R

20

Albert Stolle studied the lobby of the Hilton Hotel on Palm Island. A mint-green carpet covered the floor; the white-and-flamingo-pink walls were decorated in Art Deco style with glass sconces and angular patterns molded into the plaster. Potted palms flourished along the walls and weeping fig trees surrounded the main desk.

Stolle ended his inspection by tracing a cigarette burn in the arm of the pale blue couch in which he limply sat. His manicured finger probed the charred fabric for a few seconds. Then he glanced at his watch for the fifth time.

It's going to be tough to get anything done today, the newsman thought as he unconsciously toyed with the suit jacket he'd draped over the couch to hide its burn. Luckily he'd left a month's worth of articles for the papers carrying his column. Also, he'd known this trip would probably be a wild goose chase—he'd come to the island more for a vacation than on the off chance that Noble's people might actually have anything. And he'd already stirred things up enough in Washington to

163

last for a long time. So, he finally ordered himself to just sit back and relax.

He loosened his wide tie and unbuttoned his top shirt button, exposing his white, fat neck inside the collar. The short-sleeved shirt revealed his pudgy arms. The thin hair on his head was dyed black and hung just over the top of his shirt collar. His hair was so black it looked purple in the Caribbean sunlight that streamed in from the wide lobby windows behind him.

"Mr. Stolle?" a female voice asked.

"Yes?" His pale blue eyes shifted upward to inspect the tall blonde in front of him. He quickly stood, unconsciously tightening his tie.

"I'm Andrea Todd," she said, holding out her hand to him. "I'm glad you were kind enough to come."

He sized up the well-built woman as they shook hands. A tall glass of lemonade, he decided.

Andrea continued, "I thought perhaps we could talk over lunch. Have you eaten?"

"No, I haven't," Stolle answered.

"The food here's excellent," she said as she took his arm and led him toward the hotel's restaurant just off the lobby.

Within minutes, they had been seated at a table in the nearly empty restaurant and had placed their orders with a swarthy waiter dressed in a black jacket.

Stolle admired the mural that sprawled across the far wall of the restaurant. The stylized figures revealed the history of Coopersville. It was complete with eighteenth-century sailing ships, slaves, and a colonial settlement. The panorama flowed on to the celebration of the country's independence and the swearing in of President Noble. The painting had been exquisitely detailed by the artist. Stolle turned back to Andrea to discover her looking intently at him with her green eyes.

"I'm impressed with the beauty of your island," he admitted.

She didn't glance away as Stolle met her gaze. Finally, she spoke, "And we have been impressed with your work. Especially your revelations about the Pentagon bomber kickback. And, of course, you were one of the first to break the Mexicgate story involving US Drug Enforcement officials."

"Well," Stolle said modestly, "lots of good sources, good researchers, and some lucky breaks..."

"And lots of writing talent." Andrea flattered him with a broad smile. "And you seem to make your own lucky breaks."

Stolle said nothing but toyed with his ice water.

"I know you're a busy man," Andrea proceeded. "So I'll get right to the point. As we indicated in our cable to you, we have proof that the US Government sneaked two agents into our country in an attempt to stir up a rebellion. One was killed by our people as he attempted to get through a roadblock. The other escaped in an American helicopter that picked him up on the beach. But not before three of our men were killed. Eight more are in the hospital recovering."

"You can prove he worked for the American government?" Stolle asked.

Andrea nodded.

"Do you think this has something to do with the recent coup attempt?" he persisted.

"You're the investigative reporter. We'll let you see if you can make that connection."

The waiter placed a small salad in front of Andrea and its twin was set before Stolle. Neither Andrea nor Stolle spoke until the waiter had left.

The newsman studied Andrea a moment and then spoke, "Even without the connection between the two events, there'd be quite a news story if you have proof that US agents were involved in trying to create trouble for your government . . ." He thought for a moment as he speared a tomato with his fork. "So how are we going to work this out between us?"

"We'll give you access to our evidence," Andrea eagerly replied. "I think you'll find the two events can easily be connected by a little, uh, 'creative reporting.' "

Stolle smiled. "I make no promises there." He tried to hide his enthusiasm as he continued, "But why didn't you call a press conference and contact other journalists? I'm sure they'd have come scampering down here if there were even the hint of some dirt on Uncle Sam."

"We'll do that in time," she answered. "But first we wanted to lend some credibility to our allegations. That's where you come in."

"Well, I'd certainly be interested in seeing what you have," Stolle responded around a mouthful of salad. "But I can't make any promises. And I can't work on the story for long. I have a lot of expenses. Much as I like your beautiful island, I can't stay here for long without exhausting my budget."

"We'd be happy to meet your expenses—if that wouldn't compromise your objectivity," Andrea suggested.

Stolle took a drink of water before speaking. "I'm sure that wouldn't cloud my judgment. However, I do think it'd be good to have any payments made in cash—so some investigative reporter backed by the State Department doesn't try to smear my image. You'd be surprised how many enemies I've made over the years."

"I don't doubt that you've made some enemies in the District of Columbia, Mr. Stolle." Andrea smiled coyly. "Meeting your expenses in cash would be no problem, and we'll also bear in mind that a man with your abilities deserves top dollar for his time. Of course we can supply you with a stipend for equipment, too—fax machine, word processor, whatever you may need in the way of office equipment."

"That'd be great," Stolle replied. "All I brought was a small portable."

"We've also taken the liberty of reserving a small suite for you in this hotel. And I personally will act as your guide while you're here. If you need anything, you can just let me know." She picked up a small tomato with her fork, bit into it, and sucked out its juice.

"You really shouldn't go to any more trouble," Stolle insisted.

"It's no trouble at all." Andrea smiled, reaching across the table and lightly touching his hand. "I've always admired your work. You're a sort of *hero* to me."

Stolle laughed. "I've been called a lot of things . . ."

"I really mean that," she insisted as she gave his hand a gentle squeeze and then let go. "It takes courage to go after sacred cows in high places. I'm really looking forward to our time together."

The waiter arrived and set a steaming plate of crab legs in front of Stolle.

"Will that be all?" the waiter asked.

"Yes," Andrea replied curtly.

Things are certainly looking up, the newsman thought as he helped himself to the seafood.

CHAPTER

21

"I sure hope the CIA discovered something worthwhile down there," President Robert Crane remarked acidly to the group of men seated around his desk, "because we're really getting smeared by the press." The president sat behind his desk in the Oval Office, a middle-aged man who had aged noticeably since he'd been sworn in almost four years earlier. He'd also picked up an ulcer, which had been bothering him all morning.

"Damn it," he continued, "did you see today's *Washington Post*?" He rapped the open newspaper on the desk with his knuckles.

"Yes, Mr. President," Taylor said as he opened his briefcase and passed a pack of photos to the president. He gave identical packs to the director of the CIA, Harold Maxwell, and the National Security Agency's director Ross Calazo, who sat in chairs near the president's desk.

Luis Sanchez, the president's Central American security adviser, took the last identical stack of photos from Taylor and then spoke: "Albert Stolle's column has done more to hurt your reelection campaign than the whole blasted bunch of media experts that Bill Oliver has hired. And now Cuba and Nicaragua are demanding that the UN take action against us for meddling in Palm Island's internal affairs.''

"And Congress has my hands tied since we can't legally intervene in another country's internal affairs,'' the president said, fanning out the pack of pictures on his desk without looking at them. "If we do anything about this mess on Palm Island, it'll have to be after the election. My lead over that stupid jerk is narrowing. That last CBS poll showed we're only sixteen points ahead. I'm getting *killed* by the press.''

No one said anything. They knew that the president was taking the brunt of the attacks from both the opposition presidential candidate as well as late-night comedians.

"So what are we looking at in these photos?'' President Crane asked.

"I'm sorry to report that the situation continues to be about as bad as before,'' Taylor said. "Our satellite photos reinforce the rumors that our agent heard on the island—''

"The agent who got out?'' the president asked.

"Right,'' Taylor said. "Photos ten dash A through ten dash F—those right there''—he pointed to the correct black-and-white pictures in the stack in front of the president—''those photos show that the Soviets have been bringing in a lot of hardware over the last few weeks.''

"You can see their freighters there in the harbor," Maxwell added.

"They're being diverted from Cuba. Our surveilliance on the Soviets shows the cargo came from their arms factories."

"But no sign of bombers or ballistic missiles?" the president asked, a note of apprehension in his voice.

"No," Maxwell said, rubbing his hand over his bald scalp. "Only little stuff. Helicopters, small arms . . . maybe some hand-held antiaircraft rockets. Usual third-world crap that the Soviets like to dole out to the banana republics."

"How about the drug angle?" the president said, putting down the photos. "The FBI and Drug Enforcement have been telling me there's a lot of activity. What have you got on that?"

"Well, our man heard a lot of stories when he was there," Maxwell said. "And the bugs we put on the president's phone lines—"

"Are you sure there's no way those can be traced to us?" the president asked, squirming in his chair. "I can imagine the uproar *that* would cause if . . ."

"No," Maxwell assured President Crane. "It's clean. Jap ICs. Nothing American to it. When it's found, they'll suspect we put it there. But there's no way to prove it."

"It's easily deniable," Taylor said.

"Good." The president nodded, sitting back in his chair for a moment and stroking his chin. "So have the bugs given us anything new?"

"Lots of drug and Mob money is going into

the island," Maxwell said. "The FBI has every reason to be concerned. They're probably losing a lot of tracks at the island's border. So's the IRS."

"Noble's people have set up a bank that wires funds into Europe," Taylor explained. "When the casino gets running—"

"The one the Mob's setting up?" the president asked.

"Right," Taylor answered. "When that becomes operational, the money-laundering process will be more efficient since they'll be able to use the gaming money to cover marked bills."

"And, of course, the Republic refuses to cooperate with us," the president said half to himself. "So where does that leave us? What're your opinions of this mess?" he asked his advisers.

"Well," Maxwell offered. "The good thing is that there isn't a massive buildup of Soviet weapons." The CIA director half grimaced. "We'd be in a spot if the Soviets had supplied them with a couple of bombers."

"Hell of a mess, this close to the election," the president said. "Not to mention from a security standpoint. Drug runners with bombers." He shook his head. "But is there anything critical? Any sign of anything dangerous to our interests—outside the drug and Mob operations?"

"We can let those slide until after the election," Taylor noted. "The public has pretty much lost interest in fighting drugs these days, anyway."

"There are the shoulder-launched missiles," Calazo said. "If they start selling those to terrorists . . ."

"Or to the stateside drug cartel," Maxwell said. "Imagine what would happen if a couple of our border patrol planes were knocked out of the air."

"Damn," the president said. "But that would give us an excuse to go in. Any sign of anything like that going on down there?"

"No," Maxwell said. "But it's hard to track. Those missiles aren't that big."

"And they don't fall under our agreements with the Soviets, either," the president added.

"Right," Maxwell agreed. "The Soviets seem to be selling them equipment rather than giving it to them. As such—"

"So what's the situation with the government of Palm Island?" the president asked.

"Our phone bugs show that Noble has all but withdrawn from actually running the country," Maxwell said. "Todd and Kellerman—"

"The two Americans Noble brought in to help him," Calazo explained, noting the puzzled look on the president's face.

"A photo of them with President Noble is—there." Taylor pointed to a black-and-white picture.

President Crane picked it up and studied it a moment.

"Those two hoods are practically running the country for Noble," Maxwell explained.

"We also have reports of people being rounded up at night," Sanchez added. "And one of Noble's political rivals has vanished."

"So democracy is going to hell in a hand basket," the president summarized, tossing the photo on the desk, "and crime money is flowing into the island. So what can we do? Or can we do anything this close to the election?"

Everyone was silent.

Taylor finally spoke, "Frankly, there isn't anything we can legally do. Since Noble is running the show—"

"And he was elected by popular vote," Sanchez interrupted.

"You hit the nail on the head earlier," Taylor said. "Anything we do would be interfering with the internal affairs of the country. Congress would raise hell."

"And I already have enough of them chewing my tail," the president finished the thought.

"I think our best ploy," Taylor said, "is simply to continue to deny that Hamilton was working for the US Government. And turn up the heat on the drug and money-laundering connections here in the States. But if we take any further action now, we could find ourselves embroiled in another Contragate."

The president rose from his chair, strolled past the American flag, and stood at the window. He was silent a moment as he stared outside. He finally spoke with his back toward the other men in the room, "If we do anything, it'll just look like what Stolle has said about us meddling in the island's affairs is true. And that damned Bill Oliver is making all kinds of allegations in the campaign—that's hurting us, too." He was quiet again for a few seconds. "But if we hunker down and don't do anything . . ."

"But a *covert* response wouldn't have to hurt you," Calazo offered. "A small group like our Delta team could be in and out without ever even being—"

"Look what happened to your man this last go around," Sanchez interrupted. "That's what's gotten us into this mess a week before the convention."

"But suppose," Calazo continued, "we had word that they were selling antiair rockets to the drug cartel. Then we'd be justified—"

"But we don't have any sort of information to indicate that," Sanchez said.

"We could rig some information," Maxwell suggested. "Let it appear to come from non-American sources. Then, if it turned out to be false after we'd acted on it, we could simply say we'd made an honest mistake."

"There's no reason for any covert action," Taylor argued. "Besides, it could backfire and knock us out of the election race. Organized crime gaining a foothold on the island is not a concern to all our voters. That can slide for some time without damaging our position."

"Well, I know I don't want any more Iran-Scams or Contra Affairs," the president said, turning back from the window. "But it bothers me to watch a country in our hemisphere going down the tubes while we just sit by and let it happen."

"The voters—and Congress—won't put up with any more secret operations," Taylor said.

"We got out of this with just one dead agent and a few bad columns from Stolle. Let's not press our luck with any more covert operations. If they had American hostages or the criminals had taken over the island by force, it'd be different."

"But that isn't the case," Sanchez said. "The criminals were invited in and US citizens are flocking down there in droves."

"We'd better stay out of it," the president said. "But it still bothers me to let it go on." The man turned back to the window and stared once more.

The room was again silent.

"Well, I need to get to the Joint Chiefs of Staff in the Situation Room," the president said, turning back to them with his campaign smile. "The usual problems with what's left of NATO." He picked up his jacket and slipped it on.

"So we just sit tight and manage the media?" Taylor asked.

"I think we're pretty much in agreement there," the president said, looking at each man in the room. "The CIA and NSA will keep monitoring the situation to be sure the Soviets don't move in any big hardware. Other than that, we'll table any plans for either covert or overt actions. Let's turn up the pressure with the IRS and FBI, Taylor. Maybe they can figure a way to damage Noble's operation in the pocketbook."

"Yes, sir, I'll get on that," Taylor said, rising to his feet with the others as the president prepared to leave.

"I just wish there were something we could do," President Crane said as he walked toward the door. "It really bothers me to see a democracy fail, especially in this hemisphere."

22

Larry Grant paced around his office. Something about the situation in Palm Island bothered him, but he couldn't quite put his finger on it. It was like a half-forgotten dream. He had tried and tried to jog the thought loose from his subconsciousness, but so far had been unsuccessful.

Earlier that day, he had been called to Maxwell's office where he was informed that the CIA had been ordered to take no further action with the Republic of Palm Island.

"They've discovered the bugs on the Presidential Palace, anyway," Maxwell said, holding his paunch in his hands and looking more like Buddha than ever. "So that's the end of the whole damned affair as far as the Company is concerned."

"What about the Soviet weapons being shipped in?" Grant asked. "I realize they've just been peanuts, but . . ."

"Military intelligence will continue to monitor the weapons being exported from the USSR to Palm Island. But we're to stay out of it. Taylor's got the president wired for the election."

Grant nodded. Although he was surprised that they were abandoning Palm Island, he wasn't surprised that Taylor was worried about the political angle. The administration had been taking a lot of heat from the media.

"Why don't you take the afternoon off?" Maxwell asked. "Go home and enjoy your weekend." Maxwell waved him toward the door. "We'll get started on the raw data from our Libyan surveillance next week. That should give you something to sink your teeth into."

"All right," Grant agreed, but by the time he had returned to his office, he felt ill at ease with the idea of dumping Palm Island.

He continued to pace his office restlessly, chomping at his cigar, and becoming more and more convinced that something had been overlooked. Finally, he decided to stay at the office and review all the data they'd obtained on the situation in Palm Island—if for no other reason than for his own peace of mind.

He yanked open his office door.

"Samantha," he said, standing in the door frame, "I don't want to be disturbed. If anyone asks, I've gone home for the weekend."

"OK. Will you be needing anything?" Samantha asked, pushing a lock of blond hair from her eye.

"No, thanks." He turned, shut the door behind him, and then suddenly opened it again. "On second thought, could you bring in some donuts and coffee before you leave? I'd really appreciate it."

"Sure," she answered. She glanced up from her word processor and looked at his closed door. Then she shook her head and smiled quietly to herself.

Grant walked across his office and stood looking at his computer console. He decided to sift through his data base on Palm Island to see if anything might trigger his memory. He felt certain that whatever he was looking for was waiting for him somewhere in the records, and he knew the secret to locating it would be to search methodically. That meant he'd have to start from the very beginning of the computer files he'd collected and slowly winnow the data, bit by bit.

Wondering whether he might be wasting his time, the agent seated himself at his Sun Microsystem workstation and switched it on. The computer took a few seconds to warm up and run its diagnostics, and then displayed its main menu of operational choices. His fingers danced along the keyboard as he retrieved the file of various Palm Island photos he'd created.

He commenced with the satellite photos and then viewed the news pictures of Noble and the members of his staff taken after the coup attempt. After scrolling through dozens of photos that were stored in his workstation's files, he returned to one.

"Todd, Kellerman, and Noble," he mused to himself. He wondered what it was that disturbed him about the photo. Noble stood behind the podium flanked by the two criminals.

Something looked wrong. Noble was serious; Todd and Kellerman looked almost jovial. Did that mean anything or had the photo simply caught a momentary flicker of emotion that reflected nothing other than a microsecond of confusion. He had so little to go on. He decided not to puzzle over it any longer. The agent tapped the keyboard and dumped the photo into a new file.

He erased the photo file from the computer's temporary memory and called up the records of the transcripts from the bug he'd planted on the Presidential Palace's phone lines. For the next two hours, he read the workstation's screen, wading through reams of transcripts a page at a time. Grant finished by reviewing the report he'd created to present to Secretary Taylor.

Still he had uncovered nothing that really helped scratch the itch in his mind.

"Excuse me," Samantha said, cracking his door open and slipping in. "It's time for me to leave. Here're the donuts and something that resembles coffee—the cafeteria coffee maker is on the blink." She pushed a stack of papers on his desk aside to make room for the plastic tray piled with donuts and a steaming cup filled with murky liquid.

"Oh, uh—thanks." Grant swiveled in his chair distractedly and gazed in her direction. "See you tomorrow," he mumbled distantly.

"No you won't," Samantha responded.

"Pardon?" He blinked.

"Tomorrow's Saturday, and the start of my vacation. That's why I'm here so late. Remember, I'm headed for a scenic desert island in Hawaii."

"Oh, that's right." Grant stood up, finally regaining all his senses. "Be careful scuba diving and have a good trip. I'll see you in a week—if you decide to come back," he jokingly added.

"I'll be back, all right," she assured him, laughing. "I'm no Robinson Crusoe. Desert islands are great for a week or two, then I long for good old Washington, DC, and the joys of civilization."

"Have a great time then, and I'll be seeing you." Grant smiled as he waved to her.

She blew him a kiss and waved back as she closed the door.

Grant slowly walked to his desk and picked up one of the sugar donuts. "Robinson Crusoe," he chuckled to himself, thinking about what she'd said. He briefly examined the liquid purported to be coffee.

When he had finished the donut, he turned back to the computer screen, sat down, and lit a cigar. And then the memory came back to him, slowly enveloping all of his attention. He stared blankly at the screen for a long time, then he suddenly began hammering the keys, and the workstation retrieved the copy of the report from the ambassador in Venczuela. Grant exhaled a dense cloud of smoke as he leaned forward in his chair and studied the screen.

He reread the pertinent facts in the report: Babblo Forest was the kitchen boy at the Presidential Palace on Palm Island the night the coup attempt occurred. He escaped the island in a dinghy that was washed ashore—like a modern-day Robinson Crusoe. He claimed that a group of heavily armed foreigners had succeeded in taking President Noble prisoner.

Suppose the kitchen boy's story was completely true, the agent conjectured. Grant remembered how everyone, including himself, had assumed that the young Rastafarian had simply made a mistake in his panic; that since Noble had addressed his people the following day and reassured them that the coup attempt had failed, the boy had simply escaped too soon to know the outcome of the fighting.

But what if the coup had been successful?

Grant speculated on the possibility for a moment, blowing a smoke ring into the air and closing his eyes.

What if Noble had somehow been forced to make his radio message?

The agent leaned forward and typed on the Sun Microsystem's keyboard to retrieve the computerized transcripts from the Presidential Palace phone bug.

Ninety-five minutes later, he'd located a snippet of conversation that set him to wondering:

> *Todd: The president is bitching again. I'm beginning to think it's time to enlist his wife's help to convince him.*
> *Kellerman: [Laughter] She's not going to like that.*
> *Todd: That's what makes it so effective.*

Does it mean anything? Grant wondered. Is it a veiled threat or just another innocuous conversation?

Four hours later he still had little to go on except for the fact that Noble never talked on the phone and Todd always made arrangements in the president's name, seemingly without consulting him. There was some circumstantial evidence to support his new theory but nothing solid.

The bottom line was that Grant had little besides a gut feeling. He stood and paced the room for nearly an hour, chomping nervously on sugar donuts.

Finally, he reached a decision.

He sat down and dialed Director Maxwell's home telephone number.

"Yeah," Maxwell's tired voice answered.

Grant explained his suspicions to the director.

"This sounds like the break we need," Maxwell said. "You start making plans for a quick trip to Palm Island. Take a Company plane so you can get in and out quickly. You'll need someone to help you fly. Let's see . . ."

"How about Oz?" Grant asked. "He'll be with the Delta team if they get involved later. This would give them a chance to have someone see the island firsthand."

"Good idea," the director agreed. "You make the arrangements and I'll contact the president's people. I'll get in touch with you ASAP."

Grant hung up the phone and then punched up another file on his workstation. He went down the list of names and stopped. "Captain Jeff 'Oz' Carson" was centered on the screen, followed by the man's phone number.

Oz was trustworthy, reliable, and capable. He also was one of the few men Grant considered to be a friend. Grant thought it would be good to have him along on the trip. The agent grasped the receiver of his phone, pressed a button for an outside line, and dialed Oz's number.

A moment later, Oz answered.

After a long talk with the pilot, Grant hung up, retrieved a second number from the workstation, and dialed. When there was no answer, he dialed an alternative number listed after the name.

This time Captain Louis Warner, Oz's division commander, answered. Grant spoke to him for a few minutes to make arrangements for Oz to go on the mission and then hung up the receiver.

The agent dialed one more number, this time from memory.

"Yes," a sleepy voice answered on the other end of the line.

"This is Larry Grant. How soon can you have my plane—"

"Damn it, Grant. Do you know what time it is?"

"Yeah. I'm sorry to bother you this late. But I need my plane in"—Grant looked at his watch—"two hours."

"Two hours?"

"Yeah. Can you have it ready?"

There was a pause. "I guess. I know better than to ask where you're headed." When there was no answer from Grant, the voice conceded, "All right, I'll have it prepared by the time you get here."

"Thanks. I owe you one."

Grant replaced the receiver into its cradle and

deliberated a moment, then punched a set of commands into his workstation and it fed digital photos to the Genicom 6142 laser printer next to it. He watched the printer as a photo of Kellerman slowly appeared on the page. The agent turned away from it knowing that pictures of Todd and Noble would follow.

Grant crossed to the side of his desk, knelt, and shoved his wastebasket out of the way. He pulled up the chunk of carpet that had been under the wastebasket to reveal a floor safe. He carefully tapped the combination into the plastic keyboard of the lock.

There was a hum in the electronic lock and a soft click; the safe was unlatched. Grant pulled the door open and reached in to retrieve a Ruger Government Model .22 pistol with an integral silencer along with a transparent fourteen-round Ram-Line magazine for it. The gun was followed by a Colt 380 Pocketlite automatic chambered for .380 ACP; a little bigger than a small .22 pistol, the Colt was Grant's favorite pocket pistol. The agent carefully extracted several boxes of cartridges and laid them on the floor beside the two pistols, then locked the safe and replaced the carpet and wastebasket.

He opened his briefcase and nestled the two pistols into it. He crossed to the Genicom printer and retrieved the pages in its tray. He studied the photos and, satisfied with the copies, he inserted them into his briefcase and latched it shut, spinning the dial on its lock.

Grant inspected his office, trying to think of

anything he might have forgotten, when the phone rang. He lifted the receiver.

"You have a green light," Maxwell said. "Good luck."

23

Oz surveyed the instruments on the Cessna Model 172 "Skyhawk" plane that he flew. He kept close track of the instruments because he knew failure of the plane or pilot error could easily cause them to miss their destination or even to be forced to ditch the plane at sea.

Oz piloted the plane on the last leg of the journey, flying at two thousand feet above the open ocean. The sky and water glowed in shades of pink, orange, and purple that melted into each other as the sun rose in the thin clouds that lay along the horizon.

The white single-engine Cessna 172 flew near its maximum airspeed of 250 miles per hour. The high-winged airplane had four seats in its cabin. The two rear seats were empty. Grant rested in the passenger seat next to Oz. The CIA agent had reclined his bucket seat and was catching a nap before they reached Palm Island.

Their trip to the Caribbean country had been a series of hops due to the one-thousand-mile maximum range of the airplane. After meeting Oz at a modest civilian airport at Hopkinsville, Kentucky—just north of Fort Campbell—Grant had refueled the plane and flown the two men to Coral Gables, Florida. There the plane was again gassed up and Grant piloted it to Kingston, Jamaica. They had refueled there and Oz had guided the Cessna along the final leg of its journey to the Republic of Palm Island.

Twenty minutes after sunrise, the plane neared Sheep Island which rested four kilometers north of Palm Island. Oz reached over and tugged at Grant's sleeve. "We're almost there."

Grant groaned and brought his seat upright. "How far to go?"

"About ten kilometers. I'm radioing now." Oz flipped the radio's master switch on, set the radio to its COMM (communication) rather than the NAV (navigation) position, and adjusted its volume. He ascertained that the channel selector was set to 122.0 megacycles, the frequency used by private aircraft to radio airport towers. The pilot held the microphone. "Coopersville air traffic control, this is Cessna Delta one twenty-four calling."

There was some static on the radio and then a metallic voice announced, "Cessna Delta one twenty-four, we read you. Go ahead, over."

"Our position is approximately twenty kilometers northwest of Coopersville. We're on a heading of"—Oz glanced at the magnetic compass over the dashboard—"one sixty-two degrees, cruising at"—he inspected the altimeter—"one thousand feet."

The control tower gave its landing instructions to him. A few minutes later, the plane was circling the Coopersville airport for the aircraft's final landing descent.

As with most other airports, the traffic over the Coopersville runway followed a counterclockwise pattern; Oz had checked the air traffic control tower to be sure its amber light wasn't blinking. He had found that it wasn't, indicating that the counterclockwise pattern was in effect.

Oz kept the airplane at one thousand feet and carefully searched for other planes as he entered the airport traffic pattern. Ahead of him was a Lear jet that was also preparing to land. Like the Cessna, it was entering the circular flight pattern that would slowly bring it back to earth. Far beneath them, a DC-9 jet airliner was touching down on the runway.

"When we go through customs," Grant said as Oz approached the airport in the controlled descent, "I want you to hang back and act as if you don't know me. That way, if I get nicked sneaking contraband through the gate, you might still be able to get through and return to the States later."

Oz pulled the throttle back until the tachometer indicated fifteen thousand rounds per minute. The pilot took care to maintain a desirable flight attitude about a half kilometer to the right of the landing field. Then he allowed the speed of the plane to drop to one hundred miles per hour.

"So what's this contraband?" Oz asked.

"Nothing much. Just a couple of pistols. In case we get into any sort of jam."

"You're positive it's worth the risk?" Oz asked as he scrutinized the altimeter.

"If we need them, we'll *really* need them. Don't worry, I've done this before. The airport doesn't have any metal detectors. It'll be a piece of cake. But I want you out of the way when I go through customs just to be on the safe side."

"And you're certain no one will recognize you?"

"Pretty confident. No one got a very good look at me last time I was in Palm Island. And if they did, they won't be expecting me to return. So it's practically definite I'll get through."

" 'Practically definite' isn't too reassuring."

Grant laughed. "I've been in Washington too long. I am positive I *am* going to get through the gate without getting nabbed."

Oz checked the altimeter, which registered five hundred feet. The pilot established a straight and level path over the runway by powering the engine back to its cruise RPM. As the plane hung alongside the center of the airport, still half a kilometer parallel to it, Oz pulled the carburetor heat control full-out. He passed the boundary of the airport and reduced his power.

The nose of the aircraft dropped slightly. Oz pulled back on the wheel to maintain his five-hundred-foot altitude. When he reached a point two kilometers beyond the runway, he activated the flap control, bucking the plane up slightly and diminishing its airspeed. At this point, Oz headed the plane into a ninety-degree turn. After traveling the full distance of the airport's northern length, he executed a second turn that brought him onto his final approach to the landing strip.

The plane hung at five hundred feet above the ground; Oz reduced its power to drop its speed gradually, making the plane start a slow descent. As he came to within one fourth of a kilometer from the runway, the pilot placed the flaps in their second position and fought a cross wind from the ocean that rocked the aircraft.

As suddenly as the gust of wind had come up, it stopped. Oz recovered from the gale as the runway rushed toward the plane. He throttled the engine to keep the plane on course.

They reached the runway. Oz reduced power so the airspeed dropped to eighty-five miles per hour, then brought the power all the way back. The plane hurtled only a few feet above the runway, the concrete surface blurring below the aircraft's three wheels.

Oz eased the steering wheel back to hold altitude until his airspeed dropped below seventy miles per hour and eased the steering wheel forward. The wheels gently contacted the runway with a squeal. He maintained his directional heading on the runway with the rudder pedals under each of his feet.

With the plane firmly on the runway, the pilot taxied to the hangar tiedown area and stopped. He then pulled the mixture control to its lean setting, turned the magnetos off along with the master switch, and closed the fuel selector. The engine sputtered to a stop.

"Nice job," Grant remarked as Oz pushed the carburetor heat control all the way in. The CIA

agent was once again impressed with Oz's skill as
a pilot.

The two men opened their doors and were
greeted by a wave of hot, humid air. Oz used the
footrest on the side wheel to step to the runway.
He slipped off his red windbreaker and threw it
into the plane before retrieving his flight bag and
slamming the door shut. Standing in the tropical
sunlight, he was glad he'd only worn a short-
sleeved shirt and light dress pants.

Grant got the plane squared away with the
hangar crew, being sure to give them a healthy tip.
The two Americans then slowly walked along the
tarmac and joined a crowd of dozens of tourists and
businessmen who had disembarked from the DC-
9 that had recently landed.

The crowd milled at the gate leading to customs. As Grant had suggested, Oz hung back in the
crowd so the two men didn't appear to be together.
The group of Americans jostled its way through the
double glass doors leading into the building.

They entered the cool, air-conditioned interior of the building and everyone quieted down,
with only an occasional wisecrack or whispered
conference breaking the silence as they formed a
line in front of the single customs agent.

A flight was announced over the tinny PA and
then equally tinny Musak echoed in the lobby. Oz
watched the head of the line where Grant was approaching the customs official's desk.

Grant's cool, Oz noted to himself. The pilot
decided that if Grant hadn't been working for the
CIA, he could have collected a fortune as a smug-

gler. Oz watched the agent as he clutched his flight bag in one hand, grinned at the surly customs comptroller, and slid his passport to the official. Oz couldn't hear what was being said, but he watched as the customs official, dressed in a white suit and hat, asked Grant a question.

Grant shook his head and spoke.

The customs comptroller studied the American's passport intently and then verified that it wasn't one of the names on the list atop the counter. Although the four tourists ahead of Grant had gone through customs without having their luggage inspected, the official now pointed to Grant's blue bag.

Oh, no, Oz thought as he stood in line and watched. It seemed doubtful to Oz that the customs official would not find the two pistols.

The comptroller unzipped the middle compartment of the bag and dug around inside it. He glared at Grant and then zipped the bag shut. The official then unfastened the side compartment of the bag. He poked a finger into the bag and then, quite obviously agitated, he spoke to Grant.

Oz couldn't hear what Grant was saying, but the agent was no longer smiling.

The customs official motioned to a man stationed across the room.

The fat man waddled over to stand by the customs agent and muttered something to him. The official pointed to the bag and talked heatedly. A uniformed policeman walking the hall stopped and strode to the two men arguing behind the customs desk.

Oz searched about the room, wondering what he could do to aid Grant in escaping from the three government workers. He glanced back toward the customs desk.

There was a brief discussion among the three and then the customs official extracted a box of cigars from the bag, placed the package under the counter, and waved Grant through the line with a harsh warning. Grant shrugged without replying. He retrieved his passport and bag and slowly walked through the waiting room and pushed through the double glass doors of the front of the building.

The people ahead of Oz finally made their way by the customs official and the pilot stepped to the counter and forced himself to relax.

"Anything to declare?" the black comptroller asked.

"No," Oz answered, sliding his passport to the official.

The man behind the counter studied the passport intently for what seemed to Oz to be a long time and then checked it against his list of names. The official glanced at the flight bag slung over the pilot's shoulder and in a flat voice said, "Enjoy your visit to the Republic of Palm Island. Next."

Oz hoisted the strap of the bag higher on his shoulder, retrieved his passport, and strode through the nearly empty waiting room lined with rickety metal chairs and vinyl couches.

After crossing the lobby, he bulldozed through the front doors of the building into the hot sun. Grant was leaning against a rusty taxicab waiting at the curb.

Grant gave Oz a crafty smile, then laughed at the puzzled look on Oz's face. "Right this way for the ten-cent tour of Coopersville."

"How the hell did you get through . . ." Oz whispered, glancing around to be certain no one was within earshot of them. "I thought for sure they'd find the guns in your bag."

"The guns are *on* me," Grant confided, "not in my bag. Old trick: Let them find one bit of minor contraband and they think that's all you're trying to sneak through. The hard part was deciding between sacrificing the guns or the cigars." He then spoke in his normal voice, "Fortunately, they sell very good Cuban cigars on the island. The trick will be sneaking *those* back through American customs!"

"Next time let me know the game plan so I don't have a coronary, OK?" Oz griped.

"Fair enough. Now come on, we've got some serious sight-seeing to get done."

The two piled into the moth-eaten cab and it drove off.

As the cab left, a tall man in an expensive sharkskin suit was standing on the sidewalk, staring at the departing cab. He turned to the short sullen man standing beside him and asked passionately, "That's him, ain't it? The guy that swiped your Corvette?"

"Yeah," the short man answered. "Let's get a cop. That sucker's gonna pay for what he did to my car."

CHAPTER

24

Grant and Oz spent the day holed up in a seedy hotel to minimize their chances of being detected. Their room was painted a sickening pink and decorated in "Early American bargain basement," according to Grant. They spent most of the day trying to sleep.

At dusk, the men left their room and ate a greasy meal in a sweaty dive. The two meticulously avoided conversation with talkative natives and tourists since they were interested only in keeping a low profile until nightfall. At eight o'clock, both left the bar and proceeded on foot in the direction of the Presidential Palace.

Grant hoisted his flight bag onto his shoulder and elbowed through a crowd collecting around a juggler. As they neared the center of Coopersville, there were more and more tourists, vendors, and musicians crowding the sidewalks and spilling into the narrow streets. In the distance, Grant could hear firecrackers popping.

"Is it always like this?" Oz asked him.

"No. This is the perfect time to be here."

Grant stepped aside for a nearly naked woman wearing a tall headdress composed of flowers. "The Jouvert festival is beginning this weekend. It's purely for the entertainment of the tourists these days. But traditionally the natives dressed like demons. According to local legend, they then mock the devil and his host and drive them out of the city."

"Looks like it's bringing more devils in than it's chasing out," Oz observed dryly.

The two men traveled beyond the center of the city and the numbers of costumed villagers and bizarrely dressed tourists thinned. The sounds of dancing, singing, and calypso bands faded into the distance as they ascended the hilly street leading to the Presidential Palace.

"You're giving your military background away," Grant chided as they climbed the incline.

"What?" Oz asked, puzzled.

"You're staying in step with me," Grant answered. "If you want to spot a bunch of guys who are really soldiers in civvies, just watch them walk. Before long, they're marching in step."

The two Americans studied a goup of jab-jab players approaching them. The women had smeared their bodies with black grease and wore horned hats. They promenaded down the narrow sidewalk, each carrying a plastic snake in her mouth with red, bloodlike liquid painted below her lips.

"Now that *would* scare a demon," Grant observed quietly after they had passed.

Oz and Grant were within a block of the Presidential Palace. By now they had the street nearly to themselves. The agent glanced back toward the city that lay below them. Above the bay a skyrocket exploded into a fiery pinwheel of blue and green; it faded, and the dull thud of its explosion barely reached Grant's ears.

A few moments later, they had reached the perimeter of the dilapidated Presidential Palace.

"How are we going to get over that?" Oz whispered, tipping his head to indicate the barbed iron fence surrounding the old mansion.

"Hopefully we can go through the gap I used before—if it's still there," Grant responded.

They paced along the cracked sidewalk until Grant slowed down. "This is the spot," he said as he glanced over his shoulder to check for cars or pedestrians. Observing no one, he motioned to Oz to follow and they cautiously stepped from the sidewalk into the damp foliage under a large, untrimmed magnolia bush whose pink flowers and leaves had folded for the night.

The agent scrutinized the rusty bar. The large stones that he had piled at its base were still in place. He rolled them out of the way with the toe of his shoe. After he'd finished moving the stones, he wondered if anyone had had the good sense to place a booby trap on the fence. He knelt and probed with his hand for any telltale wires or strings, but detected none. He stood and peeked through the brush for any sign of cars or pedestrians, but the street was still deserted. "Ready?" he asked Oz.

Oz nodded, removing the Colt pistol from his pocket and thumbing off its safety.

Grant grasped the loose bar and again shoved and twisted it to one side. The two men squeezed between the rusty bars and shouldered their way through the overgrown hedge beyond it.

They then crept quietly across the dimly lit yard, avoiding the front grounds of the mansion that were brightly illuminated. They cautiously slipped toward the shadow-covered rear of the building, where they hid in an unkempt hedge of mock oranges.

As soon as they were settled, Grant removed a pair of binoculars from the flight bag he'd been carrying. "Take these and watch for Noble in the windows along the second story," he directed Oz. He then retrieved a second, tiny pair from the bag. "I'll watch the ground floor."

The two maintained their vigil for an hour and a half. The moon rose, filling the yard with its pale white light and creating pitch-black shadows beneath the brush and trees. The illumination was dangerous for the two men.

Suddenly Oz pulled Grant down into the brush.

As the agent recovered from his surprise, he heard two guards approaching, talking loudly as they came. Grant's fingers grasped the Ruger pistol in his belt.

"Todd's going to be sending for him before too long," the fat guard said. He slung his FN FAL rifle over his shoulder as he and his companion sauntered along the path.

"I wonder what Yucheng's up to," the other said as they passed.

"Who knows," the fat mercenary said, lighting a reefer. The two continued to talk as they went along the back of the mansion and rounded its corner.

Grant and Oz returned to their vigil. Shutters concealed several of the windows in the mansion, allowing only a few cracks of light to escape through them. Other windows were completely dark. Grant feared they had missed seeing which room the president was occupying when Oz suddenly whispered, "There he is! Second story, third window from the left end."

Grant raised his binoculars.

Noble was standing at the window. As the agent watched, the man reached to the side of the window and unfolded a shutter, blocking the view to the interior.

Grant lowered his binoculars. "At least we know he's still alive. Now the next trick is to get in there and see whether or not he's in charge. Any ideas how to do it?"

Oz studied the structure for a few minutes. "It seems like a lot of the rooms aren't being used," he responded. "Have you ever seen the light go on in that window down on the left end of the ground floor?"

Grant thought about it for a second and then answered that he hadn't.

"We could break into an empty room and then go from there . . ."

"It might work," Grant answered, "*if* we can get through the bars on the outside. First, let's try the drain spout. If it's cast iron, we might be able to climb it. Let's check it out."

The two men crouched in the brush, holding their pistols and listening for the guards. When it appeared to be clear, they darted across the yard to the drain pipe at the rear of the mansion.

After carefully examining the pipe, Grant said disgustedly, "Scratch that idea." The pipe was so rusted he could jab his finger into it. "Let's try the window."

They inched their way along the dark back wall of the mansion until they had come to within a few yards of the darkened window.

"Did you hear something?" Grant whispered, his eyes straining in the darkness. Like Oz, he tried to view things from the corners of his eyes, improving his night vision.

Oz listened for a long time, then said he didn't hear anything. The two men crept the remaining few feet to the window.

Grant felt along the edge and found what he was hoping for: an exposed screw. He studied the top of the window. It would be a stretch, but if he stood on Oz's shoulders, it would just be possible to loosen the top screws. He jammed his Ruger into his belt, then knelt on the grass and searched for the screwdriver kit he carried in his bag. He located the tool, felt around for the proper blade in it, placed it into the screwdriver handle, and stood.

"I don't think we're going to need that," Oz whispered. "Look." He gave a sharp tug on the grillwork as quietly as he could and it jerked out a half inch. "Wood's rotten," he explained. "Will it make any difference if they discover where we entered?"

"No. Let's see if we can pull the grill off." Grant dropped the screwdriver into the flight bag that hung over his shoulder. Then he grasped one end of the window grill and Oz clutched the other.

The two men strained until the bars vibrated and their muscles shook from the effort. Then there was an abrupt rending of the rotten wood and the bars came loose.

Grant and Oz stood silently, listening for any sounds of alarm. When, after a few minutes, they had still heard nothing, they carefully laid the heavy metal grill beside the window.

Oz nudged the window sash. The window rose.

The window isn't even locked, Grant realized. He wondered whether it had been carelessly left unlocked or if the two of them were stumbling into a trap.

25

The two Americans found themselves in a storage room in the Presidential Palace after entering through the window. They immediately left the cubicle through a creaky door that—it seemed to Oz—was noisy enough to alert the whole household. In fact, no one seemed to notice.

Oz studied the cavernous, nearly empty hallway they had entered. It was eerily lit by dim, bare bulbs whose light filtered through dust that coated them. Empty, dusty couches and chairs lined the wide hallway, throwing shadows across the walls and floor. The silhouette of an armed guard passed the window by Oz, giving the pilot a start. He glanced out the window to see the guard stroll past outdoors, unaware of the intruders inside.

Grant pointed toward the curving stairs at the end of the hall, hoping the stairs would convey them to the room they'd spotted the president in earlier.

Oz let the agent lead the way since he had the silenced Ruger. If they met anyone, Grant would be able to deal with them with less chance of attracting attention.

The two men topped the creaking stairs and opened a door. They found themselves on the balcony overlooking the grand foyer that looked out onto the front of the Presidential Palace. The huge hall was dark and empty.

The two men crept along the balcony rail until Grant paused at a massive mahogany door that the two judged from its location to be the room Noble was in. The agent gingerly turned the doorknob and discovered it was locked—but the key was in the lock below the knob. The agent twisted the key. The lock opened with a sharp metallic clank.

Oz glanced down the dark hallway. Still no one.

Grant opened the door on its squeaking hinges. The two men entered and found themselves in a dusty foyer, dimly lit by a tiny Tiffany lamp. Grant removed the key from outside the door, closed it behind them, and locked it.

Oz pointed to the closed door on the other side of the foyer. Light was streaming from under it.

Grant nodded and the two men eased their way toward the door. The agent took ahold of the knob and slowly rotated it. He opened it a crack, saw no one, then swung it wide open and strode in, pistol at the ready. Without warning, a heavy metal lamp clipped his temple, knocking him almost senseless. Grant fell to the floor.

Oz sprang forward, catching Noble's arm as he stepped from behind the door and prepared for another blow to Grant's head. The pilot shoved the president to the floor and covered him with his pistol.

"You can kill me if you want," Noble hissed, rising to his feet. "But you'll not get any more help from us." He crouched to renew his attack, his hands like claws in front of his body.

"No, wait," Oz ordered. "We're Americans."

"Don't try your stupid tricks on me," Noble sneered. "You're all Americans."

"We're with the US Government," Grant said, getting to his feet, holding his hand over the freely bleeding wound on his temple.

For a moment Noble seemed almost convinced. Then his eyes narrowed. "If you're with the US Government, you'll free us. Right now."

Grant reached into his pocket. "Here's the key to the door." He handed the key to the black man. The two Americans put their firearms away.

"Damn," Noble swore.

"These aren't Todd's men," Victoria Noble said to her husband as she peered out from behind the curtain where she'd been hidden.

"I don't recognize them, either," Noble admitted. "Can you get us out of here?" the president asked as he put his arm around his wife. Their two children stepped out from the closet to stand by their parents.

"It's not that simple," Grant explained. He sat in a tattered chair next to the bed.

"We came in a plane that only seats four," Oz said as Mrs. Noble turned and ripped a strip of material from the crumpled bedding next to her.

"Even if we could steal a larger one," Grant continued, "just getting you off the island without getting you killed wouldn't be that simple. They'll be guarding the airport. Thanks," Grant told Victoria as she handed him the improvised bandage. He noticed that one of her fingers was missing.

Grant dabbed at his wound and then held the cloth tightly against it to stop the bleeding. "Kellerman is running the island, right?"

"Todd," Noble said. "Andrea Todd is running things. But Kellerman does a lot of her dirty work and controls the police force."

Grant eyed Victoria's hand again. "Maybe we could get your family out tonight, if I stay behind on the island. The children don't look like they weigh much." He glanced toward Oz.

The pilot shook his head in agreement.

"I don't know . . ." Noble said.

"But she said she'd kill one of us tomorrow!" Victoria Noble cried and then the distraught woman broke down and started to weep.

"We will not save our lives by having this man give up his," Noble vowed. "Just get us out of this building. We can hide on the island. There are plenty of loyal citizens who'll shelter us." Noble tried to comfort his wife.

"I had only planned on speaking to you and bringing in a force to rescue you in a few days if you weren't in power," Grant said. "But if you're in danger, the first order of business is to get you out. We'll sort out the particulars of who rides and who hides later."

"Are Todd and Kellerman here in the mansion?" Oz asked. "Maybe a surprise attack to-night—"

"No," Noble answered. "They left a while ago . . ."

"Then we're going to have to live to fight an-other day," Grant said. "How soon can you four be ready to leave?"

"In just—"

"Shhh," Oz hissed, holding a finger to his lips.

The six were quiet. Oz listened intently as a noisy group of men climbed the stairs. They stopped at the door leading to the foyer.

"Where the hell's the key," a muffled voice yelled at the door. "Todd'll have our hides if we don't get 'em downtown pronto."

"She said it'd be in the door," a second voice said.

"Get down," Grant whispered to the presi-dent's family. "Quick, give me the key," he or-dered Noble.

The president handed the key to Grant. The agent followed Oz, who rushed to the door leading to the hallway.

There was a loud argument outside as Grant slipped the key into the door. "Ready?" he whis-pered to Oz.

Oz again clicked the safety off his Colt pistol and nodded.

"Let me do the shooting," Grant directed as he held his Ruger next to the door. "I've got twelve rounds. After that, you'll have to take over." The agent twisted the key, unlocking the door. He raised his pistol and fired five rapid shots. He yanked the door open to inspect the damage.

In the hallway were five guards dressed in police uniforms. Two lay on the floor dead. A third rolled on the floor moaning, clutching a wound on his arm. Two stood, one armed with an unsheathed knife, the other with a rifle in his hands and his mouth open in surprise.

Grant pulled the trigger as fast as he could. The man with the knife dropped to one knee as a bullet clipped his scalp and another smashed his hand so his knife dropped from his fingers. He rose to his feet and ran down the stairs, screaming as blood spurted from his wounds.

The rifleman lunged toward Grant as the agent shot at him. The tiny .22 bullet had no effect on the man, who butt-stroked the Ruger from the agent's hands.

Oz hurtled forward and bowled the off-balanced rifleman over before he could fire. The pilot jumped over the fallen rifleman, intent on keeping the escaping guard from reaching the front entrance, where he could spread a warning.

The American reached the balcony rail and leaned over it. He aimed and fired at the man as he neared the front door of the mansion. The man was instantly silent as he sprawled like a rag doll in the entrance, a hole in his neck.

There were two cracking sounds behind Oz. He spun around to see that Grant had retrieved his pistol and shot the two remaining men. They lay still on the floor.

Oz looked all around him. Seeing no immediate danger, he engaged the safety on his pistol and pocketed it. He knelt and collected one of the FN FALs that lay by one of the dead men, then removed a spare magazine from the pouch on the man's belt. Oz shoved the magazine into his rear pants pocket as Grant picked up a rifle for himself.

"Come on," Oz yelled at the president's family as he cycled a round into the rifle's chamber.

Grant and the Noble family stepped over the bodies on the balcony. Below them, two more men raced through the entrance of the mansion.

Oz shouldered his rifle and expertly fired it from the balcony. Both dropped with the two snap shots.

A third mercenary peeked through the doorway. Grant fired at the man, lacing him with a bullet. The man fell forward over the two bodies in front of him.

Racing down the stairs, Oz reached the doorway first. He peered out of it quickly, then pulled his head back in. A moment later, a rifle bullet cracked through the door where his head had been. Three more quick shots stitched the area alongside the door.

"How many guards are there?" Grant asked Noble as the two knelt beside Oz, well back from the entrance.

The president, who now carried a rifle, deliberated and then spoke, "There shouldn't be more than one. But I'm not sure . . . I thought most of the men left with Andrea."

There was another burst of gunfire outside. It shattered the window near Oz. As the glass tinkled across the marble floor, the phone in the study started to ring.

"Damn," Grant said. "I bet that's Todd calling to find out what's going on. Bet they could hear the rifle shots from outside clear into town."

"And they'll be coming to find out what's wrong," Victoria warned.

No time to waste, Oz thought. He stood and vaulted over the bodies in the doorway, then dashed out the door. He plastered himself against one of the chipped marble pillars as a burst of fire came from the brush.

Oz dashed to a second pillar, then knelt and peered from behind it. He detected the muzzle flash a fraction of a second before the bullet struck the pillar above his head.

He quickly shouldered his FN FAL, leaned out from behind the pillar, and blanketed the small bush where he'd seen the muzzle flash with his salvo.

There was a long scream in the darkness, then nothing. Oz waited, watching the bush. There was no more shooting.

"I think we've got them all," Grant said from behind another pillar. "See their truck over there—near the fountain?"

"Yeah," Oz said. "Cover me." Holding the FN FAL in one hand, he placed the palm of his free hand on the marble railing and vaulted over the side. He hit the ground running, zigzagging to the truck at a fast trot. He quickly opened the door and slid into the vehicle.

The key was in the ignition. He twisted it. The

engine turned over and started with a cough and sputter. Oz thrust in the clutch of the old Ford and put it into first gear and guided it to the Presidential Palace.

"Hop in," he yelled as he slammed the truck to a stop in front of the wide marble porch.

Grant and Noble piled onto the bed along with Noble's son. Victoria and her daughter, still dressed in their nightgowns, slid into the cab next to Oz. Oz floored the accelerator and they raced out of the grounds of the Presidential Palace.

At Victoria's suggestion, they selected a roundabout route toward the airport to avoid meeting Todd's people who they knew would be racing toward the Presidential Palace.

Once in Coopersville, their progress was slowed because of the huge crowds. The truck tediously crept through the thronging street toward the airport. They had nearly reached the airport without incident when, a block from the customs building, Oz stopped the truck and sprang out.

"Time for a council of war," he announced, jostling past a pair of singing drunks to stand next to the pickup bed by Grant. "My vote is for trying to carry all six of us on your Cessna. We don't have any luggage. We might even dump a couple of the seats."

"Sounds good," Grant agreed.

"I'm sure we'd be safer off the island," Noble yelled over the music of a small band strolling by them.

"But is there any way we can get you and your family through customs?" Oz asked.

"No," Noble replied. "The officials working there are in Todd's pocket. They'll never let us through."

"Then we'll have to use caveman tactics," Grant said, taking a cigar out of his shirt pocket. He thought a moment as he lit it. "Will this old crate get through a chain-link fence?"

Oz eyed the dented truck a moment, weighing the odds. "It depends . . . If we can get up enough speed, yes. But we don't have a choice, do we?"

"No," Grant conceded. "Let's go. The longer we wait the better Todd's chances of getting organized."

Oz dodged a devil carrying a pitchfork, then leapt back into the cab of the truck, slamming its rusty door shut behind him.

In order to ram the fence, Oz knew he'd need to be running at high speed. The throngs filling the streets would make accelerating difficult, if not dangerous. He honked his horn and drove as fast as he dared. Finally, the crowd thinned out slightly and he swerved around the corner onto the street leading toward the airport.

"What are all those police doing?" Victoria asked, pointing to the armed men standing behind a sawhorse barricade at the end of the street.

"Looks like they're expecting us," Oz replied. "But at least the crowd has shied away from them. Now maybe I can gain some speed."

Oz honked at a thin man who staggered from the curb, too drunk to realize what he was doing. He nearly fell in front of the truck. Oz veered to miss the man, then floored the accelerator pedal.

The truck lurched, its motor refusing to labor any harder than it had been. Then suddenly it revved up, whipping them forward. Oz watched the needle of the speedometer climb as they approached the roadblock.

The police saw the truck hurtling toward them and scattered, firing their pistols as they ran.

Their gunshots were answered by the sounds of rifles from the bed of the truck as Grant and Noble fired back. Then everyone prepared for the crash against the fence. "Hang on!" Grant yelled to Noble's son over the noise of the engine.

Oz sped toward the blockade as several bullets fired from the street shattered the windshield, showering him and the two women beside him with glass. There was a thud and splintering of the lumber comprising the roadblock as he smashed into it. The truck raced on through the intersection and bounced over the curb so that they half flew against the chain-link fence.

The metal fence resisted them, bringing the truck to a complete stop. Almost instantly, the fence sprang back, shoving the truck rearward. Oz continued to depress the accelerator and the tires sang against the pavement, generating a cloud of smoke.

Without warning, the fence tore away along its seam. The truck mashed through the opening, threatening to tip over on its side. Oz whipped the wheel around as the fence tore at the wheels and threatened to flip the vehicle. From behind the truck, gunfire erupted as police revolvers and the deep thumping of the FN FALs resumed.

Oz guided the truck down the tarmac toward the hangar that held their plane. As they neared the building, a Soviet BRDM came out of the shadows to block their way.

The American slammed on the brakes of the truck as the tanklike BRDM swung its turret-mounted machine gun toward them. Oz swore under his breath and cramped the wheel of the truck, flooring the accelerator to launch into a screeching turn.

Oz straightened the wheel on the fishtailing vehicle and burst across the field. He whipped the wheel into another turn to position a Cessna Citation between himself and the armored car.

The truck rushed along the concrete toward a Gulfstream II that Oz had spotted as it sat in the darkness beyond the Cessna. The jet appeared nearly ready for takeoff with its door ramp down, waiting for the pilot and navigator to board. As Oz sped toward the plane, he noticed the pilot and co-pilot walking toward the plane, staring over their shoulders trying to determine what was causing the commotion behind them.

Oz passed the pair, who started to run toward their plane as the old truck wheezed by. As he passed the two men, the BRDM fired a long blast of machine-gun fire toward the truck, but it hit the jet instead. The Cessna burst into flames with a sudden explosion. The wreckage fell all around the tarmac, blocking the passage of the BRDM.

As he reached the Gulfstream, the American slammed on his brakes, sliding to a stop alongside the plane. Flames leapt from the wreckage of the burning Cessna, making his shadow dance along the runway as he jumped out.

"Can you fly one of these mothers?" Grant yelled as he leapt from the truck.

"I certainly hope so," Oz yelled over his shoulder as he raced toward the loading ramp.

"Let's move!" Grant hollered as he herded the president's family toward the loading ramp.

Oz entered the brightly lit interior of the Gulfstream only to be confronted by a bearded man wearing a blue warmup suit and Nike jogging shoes. He waved a stainless-steel revolver in his hand. "Drop it," he said to Oz.

Oz dropped his rifle to the floor as the president's wife and daughter entered the plane behind him.

"I don't know what's going on," the bearded man said. "But Todd gave us the go-ahead on this drug run and you clowns aren't on the passenger list." He aimed the revolver at Oz.

The president's FN FAL flashed, filling the small plane with the thunder of its report. A volcano of flesh and blood burst in the gunman's chest and the white wall behind him was splattered with blood. The man dropped to the floor without uttering a sound.

A giant of a man came charging down the aisle, a Mini-Uzi in his hand. He cycled the bolt and fumbled with its safety.

Oz drew the Colt from his pocket. The giant brought the submachine gun into position. Oz and the president simultaneously fired their weapons.

The two explosions reverberated and the giant dropped at the president's feet.

"Stay right there," Noble ordered, covering a third man who was now cowering behind one of the passenger seats.

The man raised his hands. "Our pilot's not here," he offered, incomprehensibly.

"I'm hoping you're wrong," Oz said as he pocketed his Colt, strode to the pilot's chair, and sat in it.

"Sit still!" Noble ordered the drug runner. "And keep your hands over your head."

Oz studied the instruments for only a moment, then powered up the twin engines of the Gulfstream. He switched on the radio of the plane so he could listen to the control tower. There was a clatter of noise as various pilots and the air traffic controller tried to find out what was happening on the field.

As the jet engines of the Gulfstream hummed to life, Grant worked furiously outside the plane. He drove the nearly wrecked truck in a tight circle so it pointed toward the approaching BRDM; the armored car was now lumbering through the burning wreckage scattered over the runway. Several of the wheels on the armored car burned as its machine gun fired a salvo that sent bullets ricocheting from the pavement beside the Gulfstream II.

The BRDM rotated its turret slightly and fired toward Grant, missing by a wide margin, suggesting to Grant that the people firing from inside must have been unfamiliar with the weapons in their vehicle.

The agent kicked the clutch of the truck, then grabbed his rifle and jammed its butt against the accelerator, hooking the magazine under the edge of the seat so it revved the engine. Free of the transmission, the motor climbed to its peak RPM, raising such a racket that Grant wondered if the engine would throw a rod.

The agent unlatched the door of the truck, took a deep breath, then released the clutch. The transmission clanked and the truck spun out, tires smoking and leaving a trail of rubber.

Grant steered the vehicle at the BRDM, then leapt from the truck. The vehicle bolted toward the BRDM while the armored car's machine gun rattled nonstop, lacing the passenger compartment of the truck with bullets. The truck continued forward, gaining speed as it went. At the last minute, the BRDM tried to avoid the driverless truck, but the two vehicles slammed together with a crash of metal and glass.

Not waiting to see what the results of the wreck might be, Grant rose gingerly on the ankle he had twisted and half limped, half hopped toward the Gulfstream II. He knew a Soviet armored car was too tough to be severely damaged by the collision, but he hoped the driver would be confused enough by the wreck to buy them some needed time.

Grant hopped up the ramp and hauled in the Gulfstream's door as its twin jets whined to full power. He glanced at the BRDM and was surprised to see that it sat motionless in a pool of burning gasoline. The agent pulled the door shut and carefully latched it. Then he turned and eyed the bloody mark on the wall of the cabin and the two bodies lying in the aisles.

The short man holding his hands over his head frowned from the back of the plane. "Just wait until Sammy Cassebona hears that you've stolen a plane-load of his drugs."

Grant eyed the packages of white powder sitting in a half-opened package. "The plane's full of drugs," Noble informed Grant.

"Sammy will give you a Panamanian necktie," the little man warned as Grant drew his Ruger.

"You know what that is?" the short man continued as the agent limped down the aisle toward him. "That's when they take a knife and cut your—"

Grant slapped the short man on the side of the head with the heavy pistol. The man crumpled unconscious in his seat. "Sorry," the agent said to the president who was staring at him. "But I'm too tired to listen to that kind of crap. I'll tie him up later."

The agent turned toward the nose of the plane as it started to move forward. Through a window, Grant could see a police car chasing alongside the plane as they taxied down the field. An Oriental man rode with his head and torso half out of the passenger side, firing a pistol at the plane. His bullets zinged through the thin skin of the aircraft.

The plane attained greater speed and left the car behind.

"Gulfstream II, you are not, repeat not,

cleared for takeoff!'' the radio warned Oz as Grant
entered the cockpit.

The pilot ignored the radio as he scanned the
sky ahead of him. "Gulfstream II taking off," Oz
warned the tower over the radio. "I'm taking off.
Give me a clear runway."

"You are not cleared for takeoff!'' the air traffic controller yelled.

Oz scanned the sky again as the plane taxied
forward. "See anything?'' he yelled at Grant as the
agent strapped himself into the navigator's seat.

"Looks clear," Grant answered.

The pilot inspected the gauges of the plane
and throttled the engines to a higher pitch. He kept
the speed building, holding the plane straight on
the runway. He eased the wheel back slowly; the
plane lifted smoothly into the air.

Oz kept the plane very low to avoid traffic over
the airport. He guided the jet through a steep turn
and headed toward the ocean, maintaining his
minimum height.

"Hang on!" the pilot warned.

Grant stared through the windscreen as the
plane went into a dive. In the moonlight, he could
barely discern the silhouette of a Soviet Hind-D attack helicopter as it hurtled over them, its landing
gear nearly scraping the roof of the jet as they
passed under it.

Oz lifted the plane from its dive at the last moment so that it almost skimmed the ocean below
them.

"Can you outdistance that chopper?" Grant
asked.

"If we have time to get some speed," the pilot answered. "It'll take them a while to recover and turn to pursue us. I didn't see any rockets on it."

Grant was silent as Oz took them out over the ocean.

C H A P T E R

26

Andrea soaked in a tub of bubbly hot water, trying to relax.

I can't believe the fools working for me let Noble and his bitch get away, she thought angrily. She was sure the Americans would try some kind of operation now that they had Noble. But she'd already started making plans to keep them off the island. The antiaircraft missiles, APCs, and Hind-Ds would help. The trump card, however, would be the American hostages Kellerman was rounding up as she sat in the tub.

But she was still angry that the Americans had managed to get in and out. Adding to her frustration was the story Smiley had told her.

She sat up and twisted a wing on the golden swan that perched on the edge of the black marble tub; luxuriant hot water flowed from the bird's mouth. She mounded bubbles over her chest, admired herself in the mirrored wall, and then leaned back into the perfumed water and closed her eyes. Was Smiley telling the truth? she wondered.

A knock at the door interrupted her thoughts.

"What?" she asked in an irritated voice.

Yucheng entered the opulent marble-and-gold bathroom, locking the door behind him. He stopped next to the white marble toilet and smiled at her.

"What the hell are you doing in here?" she demanded.

He said nothing but took another step forward.

"Who the hell do you think you are that you just waltz right in here?" She reached for a towel.

"I'm the man," Yucheng said as he drew a long dagger from under his jacket, "who's going to dispose of the shrew who's been trying to run my life. I'm the man who's going to be running this island."

He took another step toward her, the knife even with her eyes.

There were two small explosions.

Yucheng stopped, a shocked expression on his face. The dagger fell from his hand, which suddenly spurted blood from a tiny hole that had appeared in it. With his uninjured hand, he grasped the small opening in his belly, trying to stem the stream of blood that leaked out of it and splattered onto the marble floor.

Andrea took careful aim with the Minx pistol that had been hidden in her towel. There was another pop. The bullet drilled through Yucheng's white suit, piercing his kneecap. He tumbled onto the floor.

Andrea laughed as he struggled, trying to rise.

"So, you're the man who's going to take over the island," Andrea said, rising from the bath. She stepped onto the white fur rug, soaking it with the water that cascaded from her naked body. "You're the one that's going to kill the shrew who's running your life? You pathetic little coolie," she snickered, taking a stride toward Yucheng.

Yucheng stretched out his hand, reaching for the knife that had slid against the base of the marble bidet.

Another bullet snapped from Andrea's gun.

Yucheng moaned, jerking his arm. A flower of red grew from his elbow, staining his white jacket.

"Have you taken over yet?" she asked.

He ignored the pain and extended his arm toward the dagger. His fingers nearly brushed its hilt when she kicked the blade across the room. Refusing to acknowledge that all was lost, Yucheng crawled toward the bathroom entrance.

"Don't want to stay and talk?" Andrea snickered as she followed him. The water dripped from her nude body onto the floor and mixed with the pools of blood that marked his passage.

As he neared the entrance, she took careful aim and pulled the trigger.

"Oh, God!" he moaned as the bullet crashed into his spine. He lost all sensation below his waist. Still he crawled, pulling himself with his hands, his legs dragging uselessly behind him.

Andrea ignored his struggle and wrapped a terry-cloth towel around herself. Then she opened a gold filigreed box on the vanity that stretched along the wall and extracted a phone from inside it. "You're almost there, fearless master of the island," she derided Yucheng.

Yucheng's fingers clawed at the edge of the door.

"Ah. Too bad you locked it when you came in. Looks like you're trapped until I let you out." She ignored him as she dialed Kellerman's number.

Yucheng continued to claw in panic at the door, his fingernails digging into the wood, breaking and leaving bloody smears on the white enamel paint.

"Eddy," she said as Kellerman answered the phone. "Smiley was telling the truth."

Kellerman swore at the other end of the line. "Guess I'll have to let him out of his room then. Are you all right?" he asked.

"Yeah. Yucheng made the attempt just like Smiley said he would. So I was ready for him."

"Want me to send some guys over to—"

"No rush. I'll take care of him. Send your boys around later."

"The crabs will have plenty to eat tonight." Kellerman laughed. "Shall I round up Hobbs and Wetzel now? Smiley said they were involved in the plans, too."

"Yeah. And add Stucky to your list."

"Stucky? Did he have anything to do with this?"

"No. But I'm sick of looking at his pimply face and having him stare at my boobs. Tell him that before you snuff him. And let's line the bodies up in the courtyard before we dump them. It might help the others to stay in line if they see what happens to traitors."

"Good idea. See you later."

She hung up the phone and turned back to study Yucheng. He was still clawing frantically at the door frame. Andrea knelt and collected his knife from the floor.

"You know," she purred, advancing toward him, "I learned a lot when you worked on that American agent. I think I'll try out a few of your tricks. You can see what it's like to be on the receiving end—I'll bet you've always wondered about that. How does that sound?"

Yucheng turned his head and watched her as she stalked him. A low groan of terror escaped from his lips as the stainless blade neared his eyes.

27

President Robert Crane had been surprised but pleased to discover that Grant and Oz had managed to rescue Noble and his family—while returning with a huge shipment of cocaine and cash. The president's mood was dampened, however, when a cable arrived from Todd, warning that she'd taken American hostages—including Stolle; any more US interference, she promised the president, and the hostages would be executed.

Todd further protected her control of the island by broadcasting a radio message warning the citizens of Palm Island that the CIA had kidnapped Noble. With the populace supporting her, she fortified the police station, harbor, and Presidential Palace. Sandbagged machine-gun nests dotted key intersections of Coopersville.

After a hasty consultation with the other members of the National Security Council, President Crane ordered the cancellation of all flights departing for Palm Island; the State Department prepared a statement advising all US citizens to avoid traveling to the tiny nation. The secretary of defense was ordered by Crane to set in motion plans to liberate the island.

"She's made a tactical blunder in taking hostages," President Crane explained to his staff as they sat in the Oval Office. "Her actions give us the opening we need to legally send in our special units trained to rescue hostages."

"She probably thought having hostages would help her position," NSA director Calazo said. "If anything, it worsens it."

"And if we act quickly," Secretary Taylor added, "we can get this cleared up before our enemies in the press and Congress can get things stirred up."

"Keep it lean and mean," President Crane ordered his secretary of defense as the meeting closed. "Not like Grenada or Panama."

The president's directive quickly went to Fort Bragg where a small contingent of Delta troops and Night Stalkers were activated; one helicopter and squad of SEALs based on the USS *America* were also assigned to the mission. The huge aircraft carrier now lay within striking distance of Palm Island and would serve as the base from which the final assault would be launched. The operation to free the American hostages, along with the citizens of Palm Island, received the code name of Banshee Tempest.

The Joint Chiefs of Staff decided that the USS *America* would engage in the Israeli ploy of sending fighters over enemy positions at irregular intervals to create false alarms of an imminent attack. It was hoped that these mock bombing runs would lull

Todd's troops into complacency by the time of the actual assault on the island.

In the meantime, the CIA directed their RF-19 COSJRS spy plane over Palm Island to obtain detailed photos of the defenses the island's forces were placing along the beaches, airport, and Presidential Palace. The NSA stepped up its interception of messages going to and from the island.

The director of the CIA had warned President Crane that it would be hard if not impossible to locate the position of the hostages with either the US KH-11 reconnaissance satellite or the RF-19 spy plane. Therefore, the decision was tentatively made to place Grant and a small CIA team on Palm Island to locate the American hostages if necessary.

Oz, Grant, and the four men in the CIA team left for St. Croix at once, catching a ride on an Air Force VC-140B "Jet Star." As they rode, the roar of the turbofan jets mounted on the fuselage of the VC-140B soon lulled the tired men to sleep. The transport plane delivered them to the Virgin Islands airstrip, which had again been commandeered for the new mission.

After landing in St. Croix, Oz found that the rest of his team had already reached the island along with three other helicopter crews and their ground support personnel, including the three MH-60K SOAs and an AH-64 "Apache" attack helicopter. The entire contingent had been flown in on a Lockheed C-5 Galaxy transport plane.

"Captain Carson and Mr. Grant?" Warner's blond secretary asked as Oz and Grant stepped off the transport.

"Yes," Oz said, trying not to stare at the secretary's chest; the tight olive-green T-shirt she wore left little to the imagination.

"Captain Warner asked that you come to his tent ASAP," the secretary said. "If you'll follow me."

The two men followed the trim secretary across the airstrip. Oz noted that an Air Force security squad had spread out around the transport plane and dug in since it was possible, though not probable, that the mercenaries on Palm Island might hijack a passenger jet and use it to reach St. Croix. A second Air Force security team was staking down the barbed ribbon concertina they'd strung around the perimeter of the airstrip.

As Grant and Oz passed the old hangar alongside the runway, the VC-140B "Jet Star" that had brought the men to the island thundered off the far end of the airstrip. Moments after the small jet had taken off, an enormous C-151B transport came in for a landing. It carried the Delta Platoon from Ft. Bragg, plus a second detachment of Army troops to relieve the Air Force security team guarding the runway. The transport plane also carried additional personnel and equipment for support services.

Oz glanced at the helicopter maintenance crew working meticulously in the scorching midday sun to assemble his helicopter, then followed the secretary into Captain Warner's huge canvas tent. Inside, Warner's four staff members were busily setting up his temporary Main Command Post/Tactical Operations Center. They scurried around setting up computer consoles on a large metal table and sorted through surveillance photos that had just been flown in from Washington.

"Oz, Grant, have a seat," Warner motioned to the folding chairs sitting across the table from him. "I believe you both know Lieutenant Perry Ovelar." The captain nodded toward the thin man sitting next to him. "He'll be leading the Delta platoon that will be engaged in the fighting on the ground. Kathy."

"Yes, sir," Warner's secretary answered.

"Get these guys some rations. They look like they could use some food." He turned back to Oz, Grant, and Ovelar and immediately started the discussion of various tactics that might be employed to carry out Operation Banshee Tempest.

As air assault tactical force commander, Warner was in charge of planning the actual details of airlifting the Delta teams to rescue the hostages as well as overseeing the assault of Todd and Kellerman's positions on Palm Island.

Oz had been designated the air mission commander. As the AMC, Oz would be responsible for receiving and executing Warner's guidance and directives during battle. At that time, Oz would command the three MH-60K SOAs transporting the Delta troops as well as the AH-64 attack helicopter that would accompany them. Oz was to insure the unity of their efforts as well as those of the Delta group.

Sitting in the hot tent, the four men plotted a simple but effective strategy to carry out the objectives of Banshee Tempest. After several hours of hashing out several possible routes of attack, Oz outlined his idea for mounting it.

"I think that would be the best solution," Warner agreed. "Let's see if this plots out correctly. First, you'll take Grant and his team in to locate the hostages. Once the hostages are found, Grant will send a message back alerting us to their position. He will then move to be ready to take out the island's radio station since it's too powerful for our equipment to jam it.

"We'll use the USS *America* as our home base; that will allow the choppers to arrive with enough fuel for maneuvering and still be able to return to the carrier. Just after the helicopters arrive at Palm Island, Grant will cut the radio station and telephone system—they're both together on the hill above Coopersville. At that same time, the Navy's bombers from the *America* will act as a joint air attack team for surgical strikes against this row of residential houses and this corner—right here—of the civilian airfield on Palm Island."

"And you're sure there won't be any danger of civilian casualties with air strikes?" Grant asked, waving his ever-present cigar.

"Should be safe," Warner answered, retrieving some reconnaissance photos from a pile at his elbow. "Noble informed us that the houses had been owned by a group of investors in England. The buildings were vacant until Todd's people turned them into barracks. Noble said he thinks Kellerman stays in one of them."

"So we might get lucky and snuff him in the

process." Grant smiled. "Sounds better and better."

"These recon photos don't show any sign that they've transported the hostages to the mansions," Warner said. "But if the hostages are there, then no strikes on the houses."

"It's more likely they've put the hostages in a populated area of town," Oz said. "That would make them hard to free without endangering civilians in the area."

"Yeah, that's just what they'd do," Grant agreed.

"OK, then." Warner continued, "The second prong of the bombing run will knock out this corner of the airport. As you can see in this photo, the area is surrounded by new fences and guarded by three APCs, probably some of the old Soviet BRDMs they've been buying. There's little danger of hitting civilians here, either, and with any luck we'll take out most of their Hind-Ds.

"Our advantages are surprise and the ability to hit a large number of Todd's men and equipment there in those two positions before they know what's coming. That will leave the police station, wherever the hostages are, and the Presidential Palace, which will all have small contingents of troops. And also any Hind-Ds, men, or APCs on patrol—and that last part may be the main concern. They have anywhere from one to four Hind-Ds in the air at any given time."

"All right then." Ovelar continued summarizing the plan, "The air strikes, jamming, and Grant's attack on the radio station and telephone system will act as a diversion while Delta Team Charlie comes in to secure the hostages and the other two teams take the palace and police station."

"Right," Oz agreed. "All four of our helicopters will come in behind the mountain just prior to the bombing strikes. That will keep us off their radar until we knock out and jam their communications. The SEALS will also have just enough time to get into position to cover the harbor."

"Once the hostages are secured by the Charlie team," Warner continued, "we can mop up the remaining enemy forces with our choppers and the Delta teams. And when the air is secure, we'll have transports coming in with Rangers from Fort Benning. They'll get things sorted out and the island will belong to Noble and his crowd again. Quick in, quick out—just the way Washington wants it."

"What about that civilian runway?" Grant asked. "Todd could commandeer a jet and take more hostages. We'd have one hell of a mess."

"We'll be using a 'Prowler' from the *America* to shut down all the radio transmissions but our own," Warner said. "That should get things so snarled up they'll keep all the planes on the ground. We'll warn off incoming air traffic. They can be diverted to Venezuela or Grenada. And the SEAL team and their chopper will be patrolling the harbor area to keep them from leaving via boat."

Grant nodded.

Warner rubbed his smooth chin. "Anyone see any problems with this plan?" he asked, studying the men's faces.

"All right then," Warner said. "I'll radio

Washington and inform them of our plans. Meanwhile, Lieutenant Ovelar, Grant, and Oz, you will brief your men and give them a rough idea of what our plans are; they may have some good input. My staff will get the timing of the air assault worked out, prepare maps, and get the air movement table for the final assault rounded out—we'll get those to you when we regroup on the *America*. After your briefings, Oz and his crew will initiate the first phase of the operation by ferrying Grant's team to Palm Island ASAP. Any questions?"

No one spoke.

"Good luck, then," Warner said, rising to his feet. Ovelar and Oz gave sharp salutes to Warner and left the tent, followed by Grant.

While the plans for Banshee Tempest had been finalized, Sergeant Bruce Marvin and his crew had readied Oz's MH-60K. After the briefings of the Delta, Night Stalker, and CIA teams, Oz's crew was soon aboard their helicopter, ready for carrying Grant's CIA team to Palm Island in the first leg of Banshee Tempest.

Since it was possible the helicopter might engage one or more of the Hind-Ds on Palm Island, the MH-60K SOA Oz piloted was fitted with a full complement of weapons. The armament was carried on the modified ETS-style external stores suite that had positions for four pods rather than the standard two.

The helicopter's right weapons pod contained a double 7.62mm machine-gun assembly. The dual machine guns were designed principally as antipersonnel weapons, though they would do damage to many types of vehicles.

The inside right pod contained a twelve-tube 2.75-inch rocket launcher. Like the double machine-gun assembly, the unguided rockets were aimed by positioning the helicopter's body as it pointed toward the target. The rockets were designed to attack personnel, bunkers, or lightly armored vehicles.

Installed on the left pylon, in the inside position, was a 532 countermeasure dispenser, which could launch flares and chaff to defeat heat-seeking missiles. The outer left pod contained a pair of TOW missiles capable of downing a Hind-D or destroying armored ground targets including tanks.

Additional armament included Luger and O.T.'s pintle-mounted 7.62mm Miniguns mounted on either side of the helicopter and the crew's personal small arms. With their assortment of armament, the Night Stalker crew was ready to take on almost any type of vehicle that they might encounter on land or in the air.

Since the helicopter carried weapons pods rather than fuel tanks, which greatly diminished the fuel range of the MH-60K, it was necessary for them to refuel en route to the island. Once the mission was completed, Oz was to head for the USS *America* positioned off Palm Island. There he would be joined by the other two MH-60K SOAs and the AH-64 Apache involved in Banshee Tempest.

Forty miles north of Palm Island, Oz's chopper was met by a KC-10A "Extender" fuel tanker plane. As the MH-60K approached the tanker, the two aircraft initiated their refueling procedure.

"Banshee One, this is Mother Bird," the KC-10A radioed to Ox on the VHF refueling frequency. "We see you and have deployed our drogue."

"Roger," Oz answered. "We see your drogue." The pilot pushed his helicopter toward the three-engined jet plane that seemed to hang in the sky in front of them. The plane's boom, used for refueling Air Force aircraft, was in its up position since the drogue would be used with the MH-60K's self-extending fuel probe.

The boom operator in the rear of the KC-10A observed the SOA through his port. "Please go to precontact position, with caution."

"Roger, Mother Bird," Oz said. "Proceeding to precontact position." He carefully eased the helicopter toward the targetlike drogue that floated on its long hose in the airstream tailing the jet. Oz continued to press the helicopter forward until the cannonlike probe on its nose was seven meters behind and three meters below the drogue. The pilot matched the speed of the jet so the two aircraft were stationary to each other.

"Stabilized precontact and ready," Oz radioed.

"Cleared to contact position. Mother Bird is ready."

Oz narrowed the space between the helicopter's probe and the drogue, mating them together. "We show contact."

"We have contact." The operator started the

fuel pumps and examined the pressure gauges on his console.

When the pumping of fuel to the SOA helicopter had begun, Oz radioed the jet, "Taking fuel, no leaks." The pilot held his helicopter steady as the fuel was pumped into the MH-60K's tanks.

In a short time, Death Song reported, "Our tanks are approaching full."

The pilot radioed the tanker, "We're juiced up. Request disconnect."

The boom operator worked at his panel a moment. "Disconnect complete," he told Oz.

"We're descending to three hundred feet," Oz said. "Thank you, Mother Bird."

"Good luck, Banshee One. Over and out."

Refueled, Oz descended until they were hurtling above the surface of the water, their TF/TA radar allowing them to travel safely without risk of crashing. They headed for the northwestern shore of Palm Island, their route carefully calculated to put the sun at their backs as they reached the land. The LZ was also precisely selected through the use of surveillance photos taken weeks before by a KH-12 Imaging Reconnaissance Satellite. The location was away from population centers and far from the area they'd ferried Grant and Hamilton into before.

The MH-60K had traveled for nearly an hour when Palm Island came into view on the horizon. The calm ocean below them slowly became splotched with lighter blue areas that marked shallows in the water. As they neared the beach, white-headed waves formed and the sand became tinted in shades of pink and orange by the sun that sank behind the chopper.

While the MH-60K approached the shore from the west, two F-14D "Tomcat" interceptors from the USS *America* streaked over Coopersville as a diversion. The two jets flew at maximum speed, their wings racked in their rearward position, making the aircraft look like flying wedges as they cut through the dense air.

The Tomcats flew low to minimize their chances of being hit by missiles. Coopersville rocked with the twin sonic booms of their passing. The planes circled and overflew the city three times, their twin turbofan jet engines roaring. Citizens in the city scurried into their homes and businesses, fearful of a bombing attack; Todd's men nearly panicked thinking an attack had been launched. Instead, the planes wheeled and vanished into the distance as quickly as they'd appeared.

Meanwhile, far to the north of the city, Oz spoke on the MH-60K's intercom, "We're headed in. Luger and O.T., keep your eyes peeled for anybody along the beach. Grant, are you and your guys set?"

"Ready and waiting," Grant said. After arriving at the Virgin Islands, he had altered his appearance by dyeing his hair blond and donning red-rimmed glasses. Grant and the crew had been amused when O.T. had failed to recognize the agent. The changes in his appearance would protect his identity should he encounter someone who had seen him on his previous trips to the island.

Like Grant, the four CIA agents sitting next to him in the helicopter wore civilian clothes that made them appear to be tourists. As they waited to land, all five held the canvas camera bags containing their equipment. Grant's bag carried a tiny transmitter, his silenced Government Model Ruger pistol, and his Calico 950A machine pistol with two magazines of spare ammunition. Three of his team members carried Micro-Uzis and spare magazines of ammunition in their bags; the fourth agent, a thin, bearded man, would wield a TEC-9, modified to fire in the automatic mode. All had hand grenades and night-vision goggles as well.

O.T. and Luger each manned a Minigun on the helicopter. The machine guns had been removed from their storage compartments to point out the open gunners' windows. Each weapon was switched on, primed to fire. The two men rode with their helmet visors down, their bodies half out of the aircraft.

Oz surveyed the beach ahead of them. Waves were crashing in on the fine white sand. No one was in sight. "We're going in," Oz warned. The pilot pushed gently on the collective pitch lever in his left hand and the MH-60K dived like a mechanical bird.

As they neared land, Oz pulled the control column backward and the MH-60K decelerated. It passed the edge of the water to skim the beach; the pilot continued to pull on the control column until the chopper hovered. There were still no signs of anyone in the area so Oz set the helicopter onto the beach, the chopper casting a long shadow over the sand.

Grant and the other agents immediately jumped through the open side door, crouching to avoid the dangerous blades whirling above their heads. Clear of the helicopter, they turned and jogged up the beach. Within minutes, they pushed their way through the ponytail palms that grew next to the ocean-side road leading to Coopersville. The men didn't look back as the chopper lifted with a whooping sound into the evening sky.

As the MH-60K ascended, Death Song spoke, "I'm getting radar signals. They're coming from the south."

"Civilian?" Oz asked.

"Negative. They're at seven o'clock and closing."

"You see anything back there, O.T.?" Oz asked over the intercom.

"Negative."

"Still closing," Death Song said. "They're moving slowly; must be a helicopter. It's only traveling one hundred kilometers per hour. We could outrun it."

"No," Oz replied. "We need to distract whoever it is so they don't locate Grant and his team."

"I see it," O.T. warned. "It's a chopper. Pretty far off and pretty big. Looks like a Hind-D."

"Keep watching," Oz ordered. "I'm going to keep our speed down to decoy it away from Grant and his men. But I'm taking us up to get some maneuvering room. Let's see if we can get them to follow us out over the ocean." He lifted the helicopter skyward and guided it toward the west, aiming at the orange orb of the sun that hung above the rolling waves.

Death Song tapped a button alongside his VSD. "They're still on our tail and gaining. Are you going to call in support from the carrier?"

"No," Oz answered. "Let's string them out some more and take them."

The Mi-24 Hind-D helicopter continued to follow them until they were above the open sea.

"Missile launch!" O.T. yelled over the intercom.

With the warning, Oz sent the helicopter into a sharp turn to the right. At the same time, Death Song activated the 532 countermeasure dispenser, even though the missile probably was a TOW rather than a heat-seeking rocket. A flare shot out from the pod. The missile passed them, then exploded, its blast rocking the helicopter, despite its distance.

Oz continued the long giddy loop of his turn, bringing the MH-60K around so it pointed toward the Hind-D while the pilot in the awkward Mi-24 slowed and tried to rotate his craft to face the Americans.

Luger fired his machine gun from the port door. His tracers marked hot paths that laced the side of the Mi-24 Hind-D.

"We're too close for the TOW," Death Song warned, straining to keep his balance in the tight turn Oz used to gain speed and place them behind the Hind-D.

"And too close for the 2.75-inch?" Oz asked.

"Right."

"Then I'll aim to miss," Oz said, studying his FLIR screen a moment before firing two of his unguided rockets.

The rockets hissed from their pod, sending a fiery arc past the Hind-D. Though the missiles went wide of their mark, they had the desired effect of causing the Mi-24 to break to the left to avoid getting into the path of the rockets.

Oz continued his wide turn and was finally directly behind his enemy. The US chopper was still so close they'd risk damage to it if they hit the Hind-D with rockets. Instead, Oz hit the firing button for his machine guns. The twin guns in the weapons pod to his right hummed and spewed empty brass cartridges as the bullets went cracking toward the Soviet-made helicopter.

Knowing that the damage caused to the heavily armored Hind-D would be light, Oz fired only a few short bursts to intimidate the pilot of the other chopper.

The enemy pilot banked to the right to escape the persuing American MH-60K. Oz slowed his chopper and took it higher, allowing the Hind-D to increase the space between them. He kicked the rudders as he went upward to keep the nose of the MH-60K pointed toward the fleeing aircraft.

"They're far enough to use the TOW," Death Song informed Oz as they dropped two kilometers behind the Hind-D.

"Fire when ready," Oz ordered.

Death Song pulled the TOW controls and

viewscreen toward himself. Oz kept the nose of the helicopter headed toward the fleeing Hind-D while maintaining a constant altitude and a nearly nonexistent airspeed.

The navigator fired the TOW. The rocket shot from its pod with a loud hiss, its body barely discernible ahead of its flaming tail and the ultra-fine control wire that spindled out behind it.

Death Song scrutinized the high-resolution VID in front of him, guiding the missile with its joystick controls connected to the VID. The missile neared its target and then smashed into the Hind-D.

A fraction of a second later, the explosive charge of the missile ignited, rupturing the Mi-24's fuel tanks. Oz watched the second explosion as it threw debris from the engine of the Hind-D. The ship seemed to stumble and fall apart in the air as the distant thunder of the double explosion reached the Americans. Bits of metal, glass, and plastic rained into the salt water.

"Good shooting," Oz told his navigator. He dived toward the wreckage, which they circled for several minutes, searching for survivors. There were none.

Oz wheeled the helicopter about and aimed the powerful machine on a westward heading, dropping in altitude so he'd leave the screen of anyone observing them by radar. He checked the navigational reference points on his screen and then looked at the other CRT for his horizontal situation display of their flight plan.

"Engage our IFF mission squawk," Oz ordered Death Song. With the mission's IFF—interrogate, friend or foe—beacon on, the helicopter would be recognized by the USS *America* as a US aircraft as the MH-60K approached the ship.

"IFF engaged," Death Song announced.

Oz then used the information he'd gleaned from the CRT screens to set them onto their course for the American aircraft carrier.

28

The four-acre flight deck of the USS *America* rolled under Oz's feet as the dark ocean buoyed it upward. Some of the flattop's crew members scurried across the deck, the multihued colors of their uniforms indicating their various jobs. They were lugging fuel lines, removing chocks and chains, and relaying signals.

Oz's eyes were drawn to an F-14A Tomcat as it went streaking off the end of the runway into the twilight, assisted by a steam-powered catapult that hurled the plane from zero to 180 miles per hour in just 260 yards of deck space.

The Tomcat shot from the aircraft carrier, dropped a few yards, its jet engines blazing in the darkness, and then thundered away as the lift of its wings overcame gravity. The F-14A, armed with long-range Sidewinder missiles, wheeled through the air starting the first leg of its patrol, equipped to deal with any aircraft that might threaten the carrier.

Combat preparations were nothing new for the USS *America* (CV-66). A conventionally powered aircraft carrier in the Kitty Hawk class, it had first seen combat operations in 1965 and had engaged in warfare in the Gulf of Tonkin; in 1986, the huge carrier had joined in the USS *Coral Sea* battle group during the US strike against Muammar Qaddafi.

Oz and his men, along with the crews from the choppers parked beside his MH-60K, briskly crossed the flight deck to prepare their helicopters for the assault on Palm Island. Oz reviewed the hectic twenty-four hours he'd put in.

After his crew had delivered Grant and his team to Palm Island and successfully defeated the Hind-D, they had returned to the carrier where the pilot had gotten a much-needed rest. Captain Warner and the Army helicopter crews had arrived on the USS *America* while Oz and his men slept.

As the mission's air assault task force commander, Warner worked through the night and into the morning with his four-member staff, setting up his temporary Main Command Post/Tactical Operations Center on the ship and finalizing the plans for the assault on Palm Island. When the actual attack occurred on the ground, Warner and his staff would be aboard the Grumman E-2 "Hawkeye," which would become the main command post during the actual fighting.

The Hawkeye's APS-125 radar would enable Warner to keep his team abreast of the positions of Hind-Ds and commercial aircraft through the use of an onboard 1553A communications and data-handling computer. This system would help interpret the complex aerial configurations of up to

250 aircraft as they were detected by the Hawk-eye's large rotodome radar.

Through the 1553A's communications links and displays, Warner and his people would be able to oversee the deployment of the helicopters, advise and coordinate the Delta and SEAL teams, or call in air support from the USS *America* if it should be needed. Warner would also be able to keep the NSC in Washington informed as the various stages of the battle were unfolding.

An EA-6B "Prowler" had also been incorporated into the Banshee Tempest group. The plane would deal with the Hind-D and keep civilian air traffic from leaving the island's airport by jamming its radio and radar once the assault was started.

After waking, Oz joined Lieutenant Perry Ovelar and the two soldiers reported to Warner. The commander and his staff were meticulously double-checking their plans in a small, windowless room in the bowels of the USS *America,* two stories below the flight deck, when Oz and Ovelar arrived.

"Come on in," Warner said over a cup of steaming coffee. "Kathy, get them something to drink. You two will be glad to know that everything looks good. Weather's cooperating. But we still don't have any word from Grant's team."

Warner's blond secretary, who was dressed in BDUs that looked like she'd starched them, handed Oz a cup of hot coffee.

"Thanks," Oz said, noting the brief smile that flickered across her face as he caught her eye.

"Did you remember to—" Warner started.

He was interrupted by a knock at the hatchlike

door to the small compartment. Army Lieutenant Matlock, a member of Warner's staff who was black and had the physique of a professional weight lifter, opened the heavy door and entered the steel-lined, windowless room without waiting for an answer. "Just received an encrypted message from Grant. Here's the decoded copy."

Warner took the message. He unfolded the paper and studied it for a few seconds. "Good news," Warner announced. "Grant has located the hostages. They're locked in the jail downtown . . . He reports that the roof is clear and appears to have an entrance on it. The hostages are in the south wing of the building. Where's that map, Kathy?"

Warner's secretary handed him a large sheet of paper. "This it?" she asked.

"Yeah." Warner surveyed the map and tapped the red-circled position of the police station. "Right there. But Grant found some obstacles. There's *only* the front entrance to the building. The back is blocked off and there are machine-gun nests at these two corners. APCs are patrolling the blocks surrounding the police station. As we've discussed before, the streets are too narrow to safely land a helicopter. But most important, Grant believes Todd will be moving the prisoners tomorrow."

"So we don't have much time," Oz said. "If we don't strike tonight we may not have another chance to rescue all of the hostages at once."

Lieutenant Ovelar raised one of his bushy eyebrows and spoke, "Is there any reason we can't launch our offensive tonight?"

"It would be tight," Warner said, glancing at

his watch. "But it's possible. Our plans are just about finalized. The catch is whether or not I can convince Washington. The secretary of state seems to be concerned about rushing in too fast. Let's go ahead and get everything mapped out right now. Then, if I can get them to commit to tonight, we can initiate the actual attack without delay."

The three men spent twenty minutes finalizing and plotting the routes for the assault on the police station. They had agreed that the Navy's bombing attack on the Presidential Palace would act as a diversion and knock out most of Todd's forces while the Delta troops rescued the hostages. Then the helicopters and Delta troops would mop up the last of Todd's people.

After the three had finished studying the air movement tables, Warner looked intently at Oz and Ovelar. "Do either of you have any doubts about our plans?"

"None," Oz said.

"Looks doable to me," Ovelar agreed.

"OK." Warner stood up and flexed his stiff muscles. "Kathy, get me Washington."

"Yes, sir."

"I'll try to fast-talk Washington into mounting the strike tonight," Warner told the two soldiers. "When's sunset?" he asked Lieutenant Matlock.

"Sunset will come in an hour and"—the black lieutenant checked his watch—"seventeen minutes."

Warner turned toward Oz and Ovelar. "Assemble your people for their final briefing now and I'll get in touch with Washington. Then we'll either have a go or we'll scrub the mission if Washington puts us on hold."

Minutes later, Warner's call on a scrambled line had connected. After speaking to a National Security adviser, the captain was informed there was no resistance to immediately launching the mission. As Warner finished the conversation, he was told to stay on the line for a moment.

"Captain Warner?" a familiar voice asked.

"Mr. President?" Warner asked, shocked to hear the commander-in-chief's voice at the other end of the line.

"Yes, Captain," President Crane said. "I know I don't need to remind you of the importance of this mission. But I wanted you to know that I've been waiting for your call and will now go down to the Situation Room to see how your mission unfolds. We're all behind you. God protect you all."

Warner thanked the president and hung up the phone. For a moment he was left with a nervous feeling in the pit of his stomach as the importance of the mission sunk home.

He thought of the president, waiting beneath the White House in the bunkerlike Situation Room, surrounded by aides and the secretaries of state and defense as well as National Security advisers and the director of the CIA. The men would monitor the progress of the raid as the battle information was encrypted on the Grumman E-2 "Hawkeye" and relayed to them.

The few seconds of worry passed as Warner put the whole picture out of his mind. I have a job to do, he thought. There's no time to worry now. "Matlock."

"Yes, sir."

"Tell Ovelar that we're going tonight. I'll tell Oz when I see him in the air briefing meeting."

"Yes, sir!"

"Kathy, get these maps packed and aboard our Hawkeye. I'll meet you there."

Warner left the room.

Soon after the briefings had been completed, Oz and the other members of the helicopter flight crews were prepared to board their helicopters. Oz glanced at the helicopters lined up on the deck. As the air mission commander, Oz would command the three MH-60K SOAs, the AH-64 attack helicopter, and the SEALs' chopper to insure the unity of their efforts as well as those of the Delta group.

The choppers rested on the edge of the USS *America*, nearly ready for takeoff. The sun had already set into the gently rolling ocean, leaving only a few dark clouds tinted in yellow and orange to mark its passing.

Oz used the last of the daylight to inspect the exterior of his MH-60K, then donned his helmet, opened the SOA's door, and climbed in beside Death Song. Like the others in his crew, he also carefully stored his rifle in the rack mounted behind his seat, securing it so it wouldn't shift position during any abrupt maneuvers they might engage in during combat.

Since there was every chance the strike force might encounter Hind-Ds, O.T. and Luger readied their six-barreled GE Miniguns. The two gunners slid the motor-cycled weapons into their outer positions on the mounting rails, taking care that the brass and link shoots were clear of the lower edge of the port.

Lieutenant Ovelar climbed into Oz's helicopter along with a squad of soldiers. Like the others in the Delta force, Ovelar wore a Kevlar "Fritz" helmet and a camouflaged vest with a wealth of pockets and Kevlar armor sewn into it. Over his combat vest he wore a "float coat"; the life vest would improve his chances of survival if they were forced to ditch at sea.

Each of his team was armed with stun, tear gas, and conventional fragmentation grenades. Every man carried an M16-A2 rifle except for the M203 grenadier and the machine gunner who carried a Minimi machine gun. Each had a fighting knife of his own choosing. Half the men were equipped with night-vision goggles; each soldier had a gas mask strapped to his leg.

As with the other two squads in the MH-60Ks beside them, one man in the chopper carried a Dragon antitank rocket capable of bringing down a Hind-D or destroying an armored vehicle. Several others had LAW rockets that were also effective against lightly armored ground vehicles or bunkers. Each soldier sat in one of the folding chairs in the passenger section of the SOA and secured a shoulder harness around himself.

Ovelar removed his helmet and checked the miniature radio attached to it. He wasn't yet accustomed to having the device on his helmet, but he enjoyed having the luxury of being able to communicate with support aircraft without needing a radioman. He held the helmet on his lap and put on an intercom headset that O.T. plugged into the ceiling of the chopper. The headset enabled him to communicate with Oz en route. He closed his eyes and listened to Oz and Death Song complete their final preflight check.

All the MH-60Ks wore ETS struts that had been modified to carry four pods. The fourteen-inch, NATO-standard rack system bore a variety of weapons. On the right side the rack was a pod containing double 7.62mm machine guns. Next to it, a twelve-tube 2.75-inch rocket launcher pod. To the left of each helicopter was a 532 countermeasure dispenser to defeat heat-seeking missiles. Its sister pod contained a pair of TOW missiles. The door gunners on each MH-60K SOA manned 7.62mm Miniguns.

To the left of Oz's helicopter sat the AH-64 "Apache." The gunner sitting in the nose of the AH-64 tested the FLIR that was slaved to the M230 30mm chain gun that was mounted to the underside of the chopper. When the gunner rotated his head, infrared beams and detectors mounted on his helmet and in the cockpit fed into a computer and servo-motor system causing the gun and FLIR camera to mimic his head movements. The gun and camera acted as if they were part of the gunner's body. A belt of twelve hundred 30mm cartridges fed into the chain gun's lockless bolt, giving it the ability to riddle any targets it might face.

Below the AH-64's pylons hung a quartet of weapons pods. They consisted of twenty-four ballistic 2.75-inch rockets similar to those on the MH-60K helicopters and eight Hellfire missiles that could be guided to target with a laser designator located in the FLIR assemblage.

Beyond the Army helicopters, an HH-60H (HCS) Navy helicopter waited with its crew and a SEAL "Team 6" antiterrorist unit. The helicopter was similar in appearance to the SOAs but had slightly different instrumentation in its cockpit and had been designed specifically to meet the needs of the SEALs.

The aircraft was devoid of weapons pods and wore the Navy gray exterior paint rather than the antiradar green finish of the Army planes. It contained an AN/ALQ-144 infrared countermeasures system along with an AN/ALE-39 dual chaff and flare dispenser and sequencer, both of which would enable it to counter heat-seeking missiles. Its armament included a MK 46 torpedo, which it carried under a pylon, and two M60 machine guns mounted on either side of the chopper.

The eight-member SEAL team had often trained at Fort Bragg with the Delta troops and now were armed in a similar fashion to the Army personnel. Each of the SEALs was dressed in black and wore a special ballistic vest holding a rifle magazine, a knife, grenades, and an M-9 Beretta 9mm pistol or silenced Ruger .22 pistol. Four carried M16-A2 rifles; two had Heckler & Koch MP5SD silenced submachine guns; one man carried an M60 machine gun; and another, an M203 grenade launcher.

Soon the preflight checks were finished. Oz

spoke over the radio, "Banshee Pack, this is Banshee One. Status report."

The pilot of the AH-64 answered Oz, "Banshee One, Banshee Two is set for takeoff, over."

"Banshee Three's prepared," the MH-60K pilot to Oz's right told him.

"Banshee Four is ready and waiting."

"Banshee Five's set," the pilot on the HH-60H said as the SEAL team sat patiently in the passenger compartment behind him.

As acting AMC, Oz switched his radio to the CAN frequency and contacted the "air boss" of the USS *America* to receive flight clearance for the five helicopters. The air boss gave his OK; Oz switched to his ABN frequency and radioed to the AH-64.

"Banshee Two," Oz said. "You're cleared for takeoff. You'll lead out."

The engines of all the helicopters started, their rotors increasing in speed with a low-pitched, furious thumping. The AH-64 rose from the deck like an angry insect and wheeled above the rose-tinted ocean toward Palm Island, its strobe lights flashing.

"Banshee One lifting," Oz warned, raising his helicopter. "Banshee Three and Four, take off and fall into position," Oz ordered. He wheeled across the dark ocean. The other choppers lifted and gracefully came into their positions in the diamond formation behind the AH-64 Apache, leaving it at the forward point.

"Banshee Five," Oz radioed to the Navy chopper, "give us a five-minute lead, then lift off."

"Roger that, Banshee One," the HH-60H pilot said. The Navy chopper would trail the Army helicopters from several kilometers and act as a reserve force if it was needed, patrolling the harbor while it stood by.

The helicopters had switched to TF/TA radar so that they coasted in a tight formation just above the water, their strobe lights extinguished. Oz switched his radio to Warner's AATF command net frequency. "Mother Banshee, your little Banshees One, Two, Three, Four, are up," he told Warner. "Banshee Five will be lifting shortly."

"Mother Banshee is on schedule and will be rendezvousing according to plans," Warner said from the Hawkeye. With that, he gave the "silence, silence, silence" command to Oz, informing the helicopters to maintain radio silence until they reached Palm Island.

Warner had Matlock send an encrypted message to the White House to let his superiors know that the helicopters were airborne. The captain then settled into the blue-padded seat on the Hawkeye as it cruised toward Palm Island. He studied the computer keyboard and banks of switches surrounding the large CRT display that was tied into the screen operated by the sergeant, who sat next to him for a moment. The helicopters flying from the USS *America* were represented on the green screen as five keyed blimps; slowly they made their way toward Palm Island.

So far everything's going as planned, Warner thought as he closed his eyes to rest for a few minutes. Soon his Hawkeye would be circling over Palm Island at thirty thousand feet and the real fun would begin.

On the flight deck of the USS *America,* the Grumman EA-6B Prowler, propelled by one of the ship's steam catapults, was launched into the air. The four-seat jet banked toward the tiny island where it would perform electronic warfare support for the helicopters and Hawkeye, detecting and jamming enemy radar and radio communications.

Warner opened his eyes and watched the screen. The EA-6B Prowler's blip appeared as it left the USS *America* and became airborne; the aircraft received an ID number that followed its representation as it traveled on the screen. Warner glanced at the time display on the console. The seconds ticked away as all the American aircraft followed meticulously plotted courses that would enable them to converge on Palm Island at the same moment.

"Kathy, get the frequency reserved for Larry Grant's portable radio," he ordered.

C H A P T E R

29

"Banshee Golf is in position," Warner told Oz over the AATF command net. The cryptic message let Oz know that Grant was in place to knock out the island's radio station and telephone transmitter.

"Banshee One and Two, proceed to Golf-Zero-Nine," Warner continued, telling Oz's chopper and Delta squad as well as the AH-64 Apache attack helicopter to go to their point as designated by its map coordinates. "Banshee Three and Four, proceed to Tango-Zero-Four," he ordered the two remaining Army helicopters, giving them the map coordinates for the police station. "Banshee Five, go to Zebra-Zero-One," he finished, telling the Navy chopper with its SEAL team to secure the harbor. "Proceed with plan one. Do not answer. Over and out."

Oz switched to his ABN UHF channel and spoke to the helicopters flying in single line behind him as he neared the island, "This is Banshee One, little birds. You've got your orders, proceed according to plan. Over and out."

High above the island, Warner radioed the

Grumman EA-6B Prowler, "Banshee Six, this is
Mother Banshee, stand by to do your magic. Verify."

"I verify we are on standby," the radioman on
the Grumman EA-6B Prowler answered over the
radio. "Over and out."

Our timing will decide whether we fail or succeed, Warner thought as he circled the island in the
Hawkeye watching the aircraft on the screen in
front of him. The A-6 Intruders were headed in for
their bombing run, the helicopters were almost
over the beach. If the helicopters arrived at the police station too late, the A-6 Intruders' bombing
runs would alert the island that an attack was under
way and the hostages might be transported elsewhere or even killed. If the helicopters arrived too
early, word might get out and Todd's troops would
be called out before the bombers could catch them
in their barracks.

It was going to be tricky. Warner unconsciously reached out and touched the green CRT
for a moment as if trying to shove the blips into
place.

Below Warner, Oz followed the AH-64
Apache into a tight climb above the dark beach and
around the mountainside on the northeast side of
the island. The other two MH-60Ks and the Navy's
HH-60H trailed behind Oz. The pilots all hauled
their helicopters into a tight, giddy turn, circling
the thickly forested Mt. Marshall. After four minutes of travel, the choppers shot over a ridge and
hurtled in near weightlessness down the hill toward

Coopersville. The city's lights shone like bright spotlights in the pilot's NVGs.

"Still no sign of the Hind-Ds," Warner radioed. "Banshee Three, Four, and Five, start your runs. Do not answer."

The pilots behind Oz broke off from the formation and cut down the steep hill, skimming as close to the earth as was humanly possible. The two Army helicopters went directly toward the city, the pilot in the Navy HH-60H slid out of the snakelike formation to circle toward the harbor.

Minutes after the AH-64 and Oz's MH-60K had headed toward the Presidential Palace, Death Song announced, "We're nearing our first SP."

Oz nodded and flipped on his radio, "Banshee Mother, this is Banshee One. We're nearing first SP."

The pilots dropped their choppers slightly to follow the nap of the earth flight route that had been plotted for them. Oz guided his MH-60K through a depression in the hillside, hurtling past a tall palm that rose out of the dark foliage beneath them.

Death Song checked his mission control computer on his CRT. "Here's the LZ."

"Banshee Mother," Oz called on the radio. "We have reached our LZ and it looks clear."

"Banshee One and Two, go in," Warner ordered.

The two choppers dropped into the dark parking lot that sat beside a burnt-grass soccer field. As the helicopters dropped, the crew carefully inspected the area around them. Luger and O.T.

pointed their Miniguns into the darkness that was painted as bright as day by their NVGs.

"We won't be sitting here for long," Oz reassured his crew. "But keep a sharp lookout."

30

After the AH-64 and Oz's helicopter wheeled to the north, Banshee Three and Four continued toward the city for their rendezvous over the police station. The pilots in the helicopters each called their Delta team sergeants to alert the troops that they were going in; the sergeants relayed the message to their men. The men prayed and worried and checked their equipment one last time.

"Banshee Two to Banshee Three," the pilot of the lead MH-60K radioed to the chopper behind him. "We've got a BRDM at eleven o'clock."

"I see it," Banshee Three said, looking down the nearly empty street heading south. "It's headed toward the LZ."

"Banshee Two to Mother Banshee. We have a BRDM. Permission to—"

"No targets of opportunity," Warner cautioned.

The pilot swore under his breath as the BRDM fired a brief burst at the rear chopper. Several of the bullets from the BRDM glanced across the bottom of the fuselage with angry thumps.

The pilot of Banshee Four pushed forward on the control column, increasing the four main blades' pitch for maximum speed. Simultaneously, the pilot used his left hand to push down on the collective pitch lever, dropping the helicopter nearly to the roof of a tall building in his path.

He jerked the helicopter to the side in a violent turn as a second burst of bullets glanced off the side of the building, splattering bits of sand and concrete into the windscreen of the chopper. As the aircraft cleared the building, its tail rotor blades rattled against the tile edge of the roof that they barely cleared. The pilot pulled on the control column and placed the building between him and the BRDM.

"There," the pilot said with a nervous laugh as he leveled his MH-60K.

"Banshee Three to Mother Banshee, ETA five seconds to our LZ."

"Roger Banshee Three," Warner acknowledged.

"There it is," Banshee Three radioed to the helicopter following him. "Good luck."

"Thanks. I'll buy the drinks tomorrow."

"That's a Roger."

The two helicopters got into position. Dark lines snaked out of the sides of the hovering aircraft and uncoiled below them. The Delta troops quickly slid down the lines. One group of soldiers raced through the street toward the entrance of the police station, dodging around the few people who had been on the street and were now running for shelter. The second Delta team dropped on the roof of the old building.

31

As the Night Stalkers had neared their landing zones, Grant and his team members had crouched in the thick foliage along a grove of rubber trees. The night-vision goggles Grant wore painted everything around him in tones of green and black. Even though he had practically soaked his clothing in insect repellent, a swarm of mosquitoes hummed about his head and made him miserable.

The agent unconsciously gripped the Calico that hung from a strap over his shoulder as he eyed the BRDM parked nearby. The armored vehicle had chugged along the road and had parked in front of the cinder-block building less than an hour earlier as if the mercenaries had anticipated an attack on the radio station. Now the vehicle's green frame partially blocked the sign on the building that announced that it was the "Voice of the Island." The radio station's meager antenna stretched above the building, a single warning light blinking monotonously in the black sky.

"Banshee Golf," Warner intoned in Grant's ear. The agent adjusted the earphone of the CIA radio. "This is Mother Banshee. You have a go," Warner's voice told him. "I say again, you have a go. Verify."

Grant flipped the tiny transmit switch on his radio and held its mike to his mouth and whispered, "Mother Banshee, I verify that I have a go. Banshee Golf over and out."

The agent left the tiny receiver in his ear in case there were further messages and crammed the radio into his pocket. He stood, gingerly patting the grenade pouch he'd slipped onto his leather belt. He spit out the stub of a cigar he'd been chewing, took a deep breath, and signaled the men spaced out around him. They pushed their way through the brush, taking care to stay in the shadows as they crept.

They stalked through the undergrowth to get as close as was feasible to the BRDM without entering the clearing. At the edge of the brush, Grant released his machine pistol so it hung on its strap over his shoulder and drew his suppressed Ruger .22 from its shoulder harness.

Clutching the pistol in his hand, he warily gave the signal and they all charged across the narrow blacktop road and into the parking lot at once. By crossing at once, they minimized their chances of detection or being shot if they were seen. The loose paving of gravel and sea shells crunched loudly under their tennis shoes. Grant gripped his pistol at the ready, half expecting an alert guard inside the BRDM to peer out.

Instead, Grant reached the side of the tanklike vehicle undetected. One of his men stood next to him, Micro-Uzi at the ready. The other men stationed themselves in the shadows next to the radio station.

Ducking below one of its narrow viewing ports, Grant heard the music that blared through its turret hatch. "You're full of it," a husky voice yelled and a head popped out of the turret above Grant. "I'll be back in a minute and prove it to you."

Grant motioned to his man to hold his fire.

"Where you think you're going?" a muffled voice from inside the BRDM asked.

"I've got to take a leak." The man climbed through the turret, a holstered Walther P-88 strapped to his waist. He jumped onto the gravel, landing beside Grant. The man cringed, reaching for his pistol as he realized he wasn't alone in the darkness. "What the—"

Grant's silenced Ruger coughed twice. The man fell before he could release the strap on the holster.

The agent replaced the Ruger in its chest rig and climbed onto the BRDM.

"Frank, get in here!" a mercenary shouted from inside the vehicle. The music abruptly stopped. "Frank, what are you doing up there, anyway?"

Grant pulled the pin from the fragmentation grenade. He held it a second, and then dropped it into the open turret, slammed the hatch a fraction of a second later, then stood clear.

There was a low, walloping explosion that blew the hatch open. A thin cloud of smoke rose through the port in the turret. Grant leapt from the top of the smoking vehicle, extracting his Ruger from its holster as he ran toward the radio station. As he neared the brightly lit entrance, he flipped his night-vision goggles up.

"What's going on?" a bored guard asked as he pushed through the front door to silhouette himself in the entrance of the radio station.

Grant's pistol cracked twice and the man sank without a murmur. The agent jumped over the body in the doorway and ran into the empty waiting room. He quickly looked at the unoccupied desk and chairs in the room, then reholstered his pistol and grabbed his Calico submachine gun. His finger automatically checked its safety as he ran toward the frosted glass door through which a barrage of rock music flowed. The door crashed open as the agent stiff-armed his way through it.

"Don't move!" he ordered the four men playing cards at a rickety table. "Just sit tight. You"— he brandished the muzzle of his submachine gun at Kelly McClain who sat in the engineer's booth, his eyes bugging behind thick glasses—"come out with your hands up. Now!"

McClain stood behind the window, looking like a trapped animal. He lifted his hands above his head and warily stepped toward the door of the booth, his eyes darting from side to side.

As ordered, three of Grant's men stayed outside the building to make sure no one else entered. The fourth stood behind Grant, covering his back.

Grant saw the flicker of motion in the periphery of his vision just as the CIA agent behind him hollered a warning.

Grant whirled, mashing the trigger of the Calico.

The large mercenary standing by the table with his FN FAL raised caught the burst of fire. Bloody holes riveted the man as he tried to aim the rifle.

The criminal next to him dived for his rifle an instant before Grant had fired. The agent swung about and fired another stream of slugs, stitching the henchman's chest and throat and then his spine as he sprawled on the floor reaching for an HK-94, half hidden by a couch.

The third man who had sat at the table managed to scoot across the room in the opposite direction. As Grant turned toward him, the thug brought his rifle up and fired.

The shot went wide of Grant but smashed into the face of the CIA agent behind him. The bullet tore through his skull and tumbled into the ceiling, producing a shower of sparks and dust as it hit the aging light fixture over the agent's head.

Grant tapped the Calico's trigger before the mercenary could recover from the recoil of his rifle. Five slugs made the man dance spasmodically before dropping his rifle and sprawling onto the floor.

The agent whirled toward the table. The fingers of the fourth man were touching his rifle as the muzzle of the Calico pointed at him.

"You don't want to do that," the CIA agent

whispered, a thin line of smoke rising from his gun's barrel.

His opponent said nothing. Instead, he raised his hands high above his head and tightly closed his eyes as his body trembled.

"Now get out here!" the agent again ordered McClain who stood in the booth with his hands raised. The man stumbled through the soundproofed door into the studio.

"Sit at the table," Grant ordered him, warily covering him with the weapon. The agent glanced at his fallen comrade and saw that there was nothing that could be done to help him. The man was obviously dead.

The two criminals sat still behind the table. In the silence of the room they could hear Warner's muffled voice in the earphone of Grant's radio.

Grant pointed his weapon toward them, took careful aim, and fired a salvo. The bullets cracked past the criminals' heads and shattered the window of the booth behind them. As the two men gasped, there was a crackle of electricity and the smell of ozone.

"I'm not going to hurt either of you if you sit tight," Grant told the two who now both had their faces plastered against the surface of the table. A sob of relief escaped McClain's lips.

The sputtering of the wiring in the transmitter came to an end and the lights in the engineering booth winked out. Palm Island's radio station was off the air. A few moments later, Grant's men placed an explosive charge next to the phone relay station and effectively removed it from service as well.

C H A P T E R

32

At the Presidential Palace, Smiley knocked once at the door leading to Andrea Todd's suite. He opened the door and raced into the blue foyer without waiting for an answer. He dashed to the bedroom door, throwing it wide ahead of him.

Kellerman rolled off Todd, jumped from the bed, and grabbed a Hi-Power pistol from the carved lamp table.

"Smiley, you'd better have a good reason for breaking in here like this!" Kellerman sputtered. He spun around and switched on the table lamp, picked up his Hi-Power, then whirled around and released the safety on the cocked handgun he clutched in his bony hand. The safety clicked ominously in the otherwise quiet bedroom.

Smiley tried to swallow and was totally oblivious to Kellerman's and Todd's nakedness. Instead, his eyes were riveted on the muzzle of the 9mm pistol that pointed at his face. He licked his lips and spoke in a shaky voice, "The radio's off the air and—"

Kellerman swore and his hand tightened on

the firearm. "That damned station's always breaking down. You interrupted us for that! You'll be
sorry you ever—"

"No, wait!" Smiley pleaded. "I tried to phone
the station and no one answered. It rang twice and
then quit. I called back and got a weird busy signal.
I tried the operator and . . . Nothing. All the
phones are out of order."

"Just a minute, Eddy." Andrea pulled the bed
sheet around her as she climbed from the four-
poster bed. "Let me try the CB." She picked up the
transmitter from the end table, selected the channel
her men used, and flipped it on.

A high-pitched squeal came from the radio.
Andrea swore, attenuating the volume control,
then tried another channel. Again she got the static
and noise. "Damned thing's broken."

"The hell it is," Kellerman said. "It's being
jammed. Listen—"

"I hear machine-gun fire," Kellerman whispered. "Smiley, try the phone again. If it works, call
the guys at the police station and tell them we're
about to be—" Kellerman paused as the low, thundering sound of a jet reached his ears. A flash lit
the nighttime sky. A moment later, a muffled explosion rattled the house.

"Never mind the call," Kellerman said to Smiley, slipping into his pants as a jet thundered over
the city. "Get the car and meet us out front. The
airport is under attack."

"Eddy, I hear another jet," Andrea said.

The room was quiet. There was another flash
of light, another low thundering of bombs.

"The airport," Andrea whispered. "Damn those Americans."

"We're next," Kellerman yelled, pulling on his shirt.

Andrea nodded. "Smiley, get the men roused and have them bring up the BRDMs on either side of the grounds. Maybe we still have a chance."

In the distance, the thumping of helicopter blades could be heard. The noise become louder as the aircraft approached the Presidential Palace.

33

There had been a sonic boom that was barely audible to the Delta troops dropping from the ropes hanging beneath the helicopters. Then the sky had lit up as the first Grumman A-6F "Intruder" dropped its load of bombs, which were guided to their target by a TV camera mounted in the nose of the MK 118, three-thousand-pound bombs. The explosions wrecked the single Hind-D that sat at the edge of the airport.

"Banshee Mother, this is Banshee Intruder," the pilot of the lead A-6F called. "There was only one sitting duck on the runway, over."

Warner was disappointed that only one Hind-D had been located. That meant the enemy helicopters would be a problem later on. But if they weren't there that was that, he decided. "Can't be helped, Banshee Intruder. Start your second run."

Warner watched his screen as the two attack aircraft wheeled over the island to begin their second bombing run.

Far below Warner, there was a slight pause as the A-6F Intruders wheeled above the island to get into position for their second bombing run, quiet as their jet exhausts angled away from the town, then another terrific blast as first one and then the second plane dropped its load of bombs that tore through the air at the row of mansions being used as barracks.

On the street in front of the police station, the American soldiers who'd raveled from the Banshee Three helicopter to the pavement below were racing toward the entrance of the police station. Without warning, a BRDM pulled onto the pavement ahead of them from an alleyway and started firing its 7.62mm machine gun at the Americans.

Sergeant Miller, the leader of the Delta troops on the street, pushed a woman in a bright skirt and blouse behind a beat-up Ford as bullets streaked by, narrowly missing her. "Stay there!" he warned her, then hollered into his helmet's radio, "Banshee Three, can you get that damned APC?"

"We're on it," the pilot's voice yelled over the din of its Miniguns.

Miller peered around the Ford. Another burst from the BRDM racked the three Delta troops lying in the street. Damn them, Miller thought. The men were wounded, and couldn't have continued the fighting. Now the bastards in the BRDM were butchering them with the vehicle's machine gun. His knuckles turned white as he gripped his M16-A2, anger welling in his throat as another burst was fired at the fallen men.

Above the street, Banshee Three suddenly appeared, hanging in midair, its right Minigun flashing.

Plumes of concrete were kicked up around the BRDM as the Minigun bathed it in .30-caliber armor-piercing bullets. Then the machine seemed to expand like a balloon before it burst open with a blast of fire as a TOW rocket from the helicopter split through its armor and ignited its gas tank.

The helicopter darted away, narrowly avoiding a rocket that seemed to come out of nowhere.

Miller had ducked behind the car as the BRDM exploded. He stayed there momentarily as bits of metal from the vehicle rattled down the street. He pulled a smoke grenade, ripped out its pin, and tossed it toward the police station.

"Let's go!" he shouted to his men as he stood. He shouldered his rifle, centering its aiming dot on a policeman who was standing in a window, an FN FAL aimed toward the American troops on the street below.

Without thinking, Miller felt his finger squeeze the weapon's trigger. The M16 sent six bullets to stitch the form of his adversary. Three empty cartridges ejected from his firearm tinkled on the pavement as Miller and his men ran forward.

All was quiet for a moment except for the sound of their boots, then a .50-caliber machine gun thundered from inside the police station. Despite the screen of smoke that filled the street, the three American soldiers beside Miller fell as the heavy barrage caught them in the open.

Miller dodged behind a small Fiat parked alongside the street, hoping the machine gunner wouldn't train his weapon on the small car before the Americans could knock out the gun. He retrieved another smoke grenade from his vest, activated the grenade, and tossed it toward the station.

The street was again silent and Miller peered around the car he hid behind. Where was that machine gun? He couldn't discern it for a moment through the smoke; then he spotted its flash as it fired a short burst through a loop hole that had been cut into the brick wall beside the front entrance of the station.

The islanders are better prepared than we thought, he told himself. The Americans had made a classic error: Never underestimate the enemy. He thumbed on his helmet radio, "Banshee Three, this is Delta Three. Can you put a rocket in the front of the station?" he called to the helicopter that darted above the street.

"That's a negative," the pilot's voice replied. "Too steep an angle for these narrow streets."

Sergeant Miller turned off his radio and signaled his Minimi man, trying to get the soldier to come forward with his machine gun. It wasn't much of a match for the .50-caliber in the police station, but it was better than nothing.

The soldier with the Minimi dashed forward, flanked by three other Delta troopers. As the four approached, the station opened up again. The soldier with the Minimi staggered, his chest exploding as a heavy slug tore through him. He dropped, the momentum of his run causing him to tumble forward with joints that had gone completely limp.

Miller glanced back toward the station. Five more shapes sprang from the front door, raced across the smoky street, and cowered behind a white Toyota pickup, their AK rifles sticking out from behind it.

"Heads up!" Miller yelled to the three members of his squad as they raced toward his position. "Next to the police station's entrance and behind the pickup."

One of the soldiers had scooped up the Minimi as he ran forward. Now he lifted the weapon and fired a long, clattering burst at the pickup. The bullets ricocheted off the pavement, clipping the mercenaries' ankles. The men rolled and screamed as a second burst riddled them.

"Good!" Miller yelled. "Now hit the station."

Four more mercenaries sprang from the front door of the police station and the .50-caliber machine gun fired again to cover their charge. Bullets from the machine gun splattered against the pavement around Miller and made angry humming sounds as they tumbled off the cobblestones and through the air above the street.

Sergeant Miller lifted his gun, throttling the trigger as he centered the scope's aiming dot on one of the running figures in front of him. Bullets erupted from the duplex cartridges in his weapon. Without waiting for his foe to drop, Miller shifted his aim. Six more projectiles crashed into his target as the guns of the soldiers beside him barked. The four shapes fell to the pavement like bundles of bones dressed in rags.

"Don't bunch up," Miller ordered as more of his men approached from behind. "Get over on that side of the street. Give them cover," he ordered the Minimi gunner.

As the Minimi pulled belted ammunition into its side and spit 5.56mm bullets from its barrel, Miller knelt and punched the magazine release of his rifle. Watching the police station, he jerked a plastic forty-five-round magazine out of his combat vest and jammed it into the M16's well. The magazine snapped into its locked position. Miller blinked the sweat from his greenish brown eyes as he stood and faced the station.

A thin cloud of smoke hung in the air. The police station was ominously quiet. An MH-60K hovered over the street, then darted off after an unseen target. Silence again.

Miller was ready to launch his assault of the station when another BRDM appeared at the end of the street, a group of twelve mercenaries surrounding it.

The Americans all opened fire on the men and armored personnel carrier. A grenade launched from an M203 exploded next to the vehicle, throwing shrapnel across the street and peppering the mercenaries. In moments, the criminals were raked by American fire; the dead or dying mercenaries flopped about the street like fish out of water.

The BRDM and .50-caliber machine gun returned the soldiers' fire with deadly effect.

Miller dropped behind the Fiat, the cries of his men ringing out along the street as the deadly fire cut into them. "Banshee Three," he radioed as he grabbed the Minimi from the fallen soldier next to him. "We need some air support."

"We're having some troubles, Delta," the pilot radioed back. "Got some Hind-Ds headed our way. Hold on for a couple of minutes if you can."

Where's the Dragon and LAWs? Miller wondered as he turned. He couldn't see the men who carried them. What a mess, he told himself as he crouched behind the car. He turned toward the BRDM and squeezed the trigger of the Minimi in a long burst. The bullets chipped at the gunner's port and ricocheted off the armored vehicle.

Miller dropped back behind the car as the BRDM trained its gun at him. The Minimi was exhausted of ammunition so he tossed it aside. The BRDM fired its guns at the Fiat, shredding its thin metal body.

By the time Banshee Three circled around and launched its rockets at the BRDM, Sergeant Miller lay dead in a pool of blood.

34

The Delta troops' attack of the police station's entrance from the street had been launched as a diversion. As their attack started, Banshee Four and the Delta squad it carried were hovering over the roof of the police station.

As the MH-60K that was code named Banshee Four hovered above the roof of the building, Sergeant Karr and his eleven-man Delta squad raveled from the helicopter to the roof of the building using the "fast rope" bar attached over the door of the chopper. The soldiers hit the roof, then raced across its surface to the access door. O'Conner was the first one to reach it; he fired his M16 into the door's lock, then kicked the entrance open.

The men on the roof raced down the creaking wooden stairway beyond the door, their boots raising a din as they ran. O'Conner led the charge downward; a white-jacketed mercenary jumped into the bottom of the stairwell, blocking their path with his FN-FAL blazing.

The bullets struck O'Conner. He clutched his chest and stumbled. Dexter, the soldier behind him, triggered a three-round burst from his M16. The six bullets from his weapon cracked over O'Conner and cut an ugly pattern into the policeman's face. The officer's head exploded and he fell to the floor.

Dexter hurdled his fallen companion, trampled the policeman's body, and grabbed a stun grenade as he hit the landing.

"Fire in the hole," Dexter hollered as he tossed the grenade through the doorway.

The explosion in the room shook the stairs. Dexter pulled the pin to arm a second grenade and threw it as two of his team members pressed their backs to the wall on either side of the door. The second explosion rocked the room beyond.

The three American soldiers didn't wait for the smoke and dust to clear in the room but sprinted into it, guns blazing. Trained to shoot anyone who held a weapon to oppose them, the Delta troops cut down the four armed mercenaries who stood dazed in the center of the room. The American troops spread out and the rest of the squad entered the room through the archway behind them.

Sergeant Karr took only a second to gain his bearings inside the smoke-filled chamber. With hand signals he directed three of his men to secure the door to their left. The others he ordered down the hallway toward the holding rooms where the American hostages were.

Karr followed his men as they unfastened the iron-plated door leading to the prison section. The soldiers entered with their M16s at the ready. They found themselves in a dirty hallway lined on both sides with crude iron bars.

A bare bulb dimly lit the hall; prisoners were huddled in the murky cells. A guard at the end of the hall had dropped his pistol and now stood with his arms stretched above his head, nervously watching the Delta troops enter the hallway.

"Help us," one of the Americans cried to the sergeant.

"Get his keyes," Karr ordered Espinosa, the soldier standing closest to the jailer. The soldier stepped alongside the policeman, keeping the M16 in his right hand directed at the man, its muzzle pressed hard into the policeman's ribs. With his free hand, the soldier removed the ring of keys from the jailer's leather belt.

Espinosa quickly unlocked the cells one by one. As the hostages collected in the tiny hallway, Karr called Warner with the radio built into his helmet; Karr reported that they'd reached the hostages. He completed his message and then spoke to those around him, "OK, folks—" Karr paused as the explosion of an LAW shook the outside of the building. "We're here to take you home."

A weak cheer went up from the hostages. All of them crowded toward the door leading out of the prison section.

"Follow this soldier here," Karr tapped Dexter on the shoulder. "Head for the roof. Our helicopter will pick you up. We'll take you to the beach on the northside of the island and, from there, to an American aircraft carrier. Now go."

As the people formed a line to climb the stairs

to the roof, Karr's helmet radio sounded in his ear, "Banshee Delta Three, this is Banshee Mother."

"This is Delta Three," Karr said.

"You've got three Hind-Ds headed your way. Keep the hostages inside."

"Will do," Karr said, shoving his way around the people closest to him. "Hold it, Dexter!" the sergeant hollered. "We've got trouble headed this way. We'll have to stay off the roof. You people," he told the hostages around him, "return to the prison area. It's safer there. There'll be a delay but we're going to get you out of here."

The sergeant faced his men. "You three guard the hostages. Keep them in there until I give the word to move them. Don't let anyone in or out. Amero?"

"Yes, Sarge."

"Come with me. Let's see how good a shot you are with that Dragon."

With the heavy antiarmor Dragon slung across his back on a shoulder strap, Amero followed the sergeant up the wooden stairs to the roof.

The Hind-Ds, their undersides lit by the city's streetlights, went streaking over as Karr peered out the door. He watched the heavy choppers launch their TOW missiles and hit one of the two MH-60Ks that circled the police station. The MH-60K was struck by a crippling explosion and went into a wide-curving flight path that ended as it crashed into the street below, its belly scraping nosily along the pavement and its blades whipping apart on the granite-faced hotel.

The rocket missed the second MH-60K. The

American helicopter went into a wide turn and gained altitude. After completing the maneuver, the pilot of the American chopper discharged a salvo of seven 2.75-inch rockets at the four Hind-Ds that continued to fly in close formation.

Most of the rockets missed, but two struck and severely damaged one of the Hind-Ds. It abruptly tumbled in its flight with three of its five main rotors coming apart and ripping into the cabin of the helicopter. The wreckage fell into the street beyond the police station.

The American helicopter launched another fusillade of rockets that struck the passenger compartment of one of the remaining Hind-Ds. With a muffled explosion, corpses and body parts spewed from the chopper's hold to rain over the buildings below. The damaged aircraft ascended over the police station, splattering Karr with hot engine oil as it passed. It continued its flight over the city and started a winding path to the airport for an emergency landing.

As Karr and Amero worked at preparing the Dragon rocket for firing, the two undamaged Hind-D helicopters managed to turn and fire at the MH-60K as its pilot struggled to gain altitude. A TOW missile from each of the Soviet-made helicopters jetted upward at the American aircraft. The MH-60K pilot went into a violent turn, narrowly missing the top floor of the hotel. He eluded the first missile that raced by him, which slammed into the hotel's flag pole with a terrific blast that sent the steel rod twirling into the air to plunge into the street.

The second missile hit the tail section of the helicopter as it cleared the edge of the hotel. The chopper whirled out of control as the explosion tore off its rear rotor. The pilot managed to cut his power so the aircraft slid along the flat roof of the hotel with a rending of metal and concrete. The chopper dropped onto its side and its rotor blades cut into the building's surface. The MH-60K finally came to rest with its nose hanging over the far edge of the hotel roof.

"Get that Hind-D," Karr ordered Amero, pointing to the nearest helicopter that was circling the police building, firing at the soldiers on the street below. The American soldiers on the avenue fired several LAW rockets but missed the chopper. The Hind-D's chin-mounted 12.7mm machine gun returned their fire, chewing the pavement and men below with heavy slugs.

Amero balanced the M47 Dragon rocket launcher on its bipod and sat on the hard surface of the roof. He uncovered the sight of the weapon and looked through it. "Clear!" he warned since the weapon's backblast was quite dangerous.

"All clear," Karr yelled over the racket of the firing from the street and the Hind-D.

Amero centered the Hind-D in the crosshairs of the tracker, held his breath, and fired the missile. There was a terrific backblast as the rocket vaulted from its launch tube. The soldier continued to keep his face plastered against the tracker, guiding the rocket toward its target with the electronic signals being conveyed over the hair-thin wire that was uncurling from the missile. The soldier guided it carefully.

An inferno lit the sky as the warhead struck the fuel compartment at the rear of the Hind-D. The Delta troops in the street ran for cover as the burning wreckage dropped to the ground.

There was a thundering in the air behind the police station and the blacktop roof seemed to disintegrate around Karr and Amero. The two men stared upward at the last Hind-D as it thundered toward them, its chin gun blazing.

Karr felt a 12.7mm projectile rip into his heart; he was dead almost before he sprawled to the roof. Amero jumped to his feet, tossing the empty launching tube aside. He was halfway to the stairs when he tumbled like a rag doll hit by a baseball bat.

35

Before the attack on the police station had started, Oz's helicopter and the AH-64 Apache had waited in the dark soccer field's parking lot for what seemed hours, even though a quick glance at his luminous watch told the pilot it had only been minutes.

"Banshee Three and Four are in place," Warner had told Oz over the AATF command net letting the pilot know that the assault on the police station was about to begin. That meant that Grant was ready to hit the island's radio station and the A-6F Intruders were on their way to initiate their bombing runs. "Banshee One and Two, start your final run," Warner continued. "Do not answer. Over and out."

Oz switched to his ABN UHF channel and spoke to the pilot in the helicopter in front of him. "Let's go."

The engines of the two helicopters came to life, their blades flopping in slow circles that quickly picked up speed. They lifted into the air with stomach-wrenching speed. "Banshee One to Banshee Two, let's proceed to our LZ."

"That's a Roger," the Apache pilot said as his chopper darted onto the flight path that would take them to the Presidential Palace.

High above the island, the Grumman EA-6B Prowler shut down all the radio channels except those reserved by the American AMC net; Grant's team destroyed the radio transmitter and telephone system. In the Hawkeye, Warner watched as the helicopters under his command got into position and the A-6F Intruders started their bombing runs.

"We're nearing the SP," Death Song announced.

Oz nodded and flipped on his radio, "Banshee Mother, this is Banshee One. We're nearing our SP."

The pilots dropped their choppers slightly to follow the nap of the earth flight route that had been created for them. Oz guided his MH-60K through a depression in the hillside, hurtling past a tall palm that rose out of the dark foliage beneath them.

Death Song checked his mission control computer on his CRT. "Here's the SP."

"Banshee One, this is Banshee Two," the pilot in the AH-64 Apache called. "We're taking some small-arms fire."

Oz glanced out his window and saw the small flashes to his left. "Continue on," he said over the radio. "We'll mop up on our way back."

"We're getting some hits, too," Death Song announced. A warning light on the console had started blinking indicating that bullets had struck several areas of the helicopter. Although these generally weren't of consequence, extensive hits might chance to strike critical areas of the helicopter or damage some of its redundant controls, thereby weakening it. Oz hoped they'd be out of range before such damage occurred.

The nighttime sky flashed as the bombs of the first A-6F Intruder hit the airport. A moment later, a second pair of flashes marked the bombing of the mansions.

Warner's voice crackled on the radio as the harmonics created by the Americans' jamming interfered with their own radios, "Banshee Mother to Banshees One, Two, Three, Four, and Five. You are cleared to fire. We took out the mansions. The strike on the airport didn't get all the Hind-Ds. A few are in the air, but they're not close to our forces. I'll keep you posted. Over and out."

As Oz watched the area ahead of him, there was a dip in the terrain, so he shoved down on the collective pitch lever. The craft dropped into the cover offered by the tree-canopied valley. As the valley ended, the pilot pulled the MH-60K SOA up.

"O.T. and Luger," Oz finally said. "Almost there."

"We're ready," O.T. announced.

The helicopter zipped down the hill and Oz spied their ACP landmark, an old British fort that was brightly lit for the tourists in the town below to see.

"There's the ACP," Oz said.

He followed the AH-64 Apache as it angled around the granite fortress and sped into the last leg of their route toward the Presidential Palace.

Death Song glanced at his CRT. "RP coming up."

"Lieutenant Ovelar," Oz contacted the Delta squad leader on the intercom, "we're going in."

"We're ready and waiting," Ovelar said. He checked the safety on his M16 and then twisted the knob on the Aimpoint scope mounted on his rifle, bringing the dot in the reticle to a point of red light.

"Banshee Two here," the pilot of the AH-64 Apache said. "I've got a Jeep at two o'clock."

"I see it," Oz said. "It's got a machine gun on it and it's headed toward our LZ. Take it out." The pilot slowed down so that the AH-64 Apache would have time to launch a guided missile.

There was a fiery blast from the pod of the AH-64 Apache ahead of them and a rocket hissed out through the darkness. The guided TOW rocket dipped and struck the Jeep.

Flames erupted in the trees ahead of them. The AH-64 Apache returned to its lead position and regained its speed as both American helicopters hurtled over the burning wreckage of the Jeep.

Oz pushed forward on the control column, increasing the four main blades' pitch for maximum speed. Simultaneously, the pilot used his left hand to push down on the collective pitch lever, dropping the helicopter down the hill, toward the Presidential Palace compound.

"I see a guy with a hand-held rocket!" O.T. warned. "He's tracking us. He's going to fire."

Oz jerked the MH-60K to the side in a violent turn. The rocket skidded past them, barely missing.

Close, Oz thought. Must be pretty green troops to launch rockets so near to the ground. It was probable that the rocket wouldn't have been armed in such a short distance. But it would have caused damage and might have had a delay device to cause it to go off after becoming lodged in the helicopter. He guided the chopper into a tight turn to come back behind the AH-64 Apache.

Ahead of the choppers at the Presidential Palace, Andrea pulled a T-shirt over her naked torso, jerked into an old pair of jeans, and struggled into her shoes as she staggered toward the hallway.

"Hurry!" Kellerman yelled at her as he pulled on his leather boots. "They're almost here. We won't stand a chance if we stay inside."

The two broke into a run down the winding stairs of the Presidential Palace in the cavernous grand hallway. Smiley was hollering something unintelligible from the balcony. A BRDM's engines were noisily firing up, and the American helicopters sounded as if they were almost on top of the palace.

Kellerman and Andrea trotted across the checkered tile floor and pushed through the heavy wooden front doors.

"Get into that hedge row," Andrea ordered three guards who stood in confusion on the porch of the building. "Give me that," she said, snatching an FN FAL from one of them.

She and Kellerman jumped off the porch.

The two American choppers wheeled along

the tree line, dark shapes against the nighttime sky. They swooped over the Presidential Palace and gunfire erupted on the ground as Andrea's men tried to hit the aircraft.

One of the BRDMs came chugging around the side of the palace firing with its 23mm cannon and machine gun at the MH-60K that trailed the attack helicopter.

"They'll never hit it while they're driving," Kellerman called, raising his voice and leaning toward Andrea as they continued to race toward the tree line.

Above the palace grounds, Luger yelled from his position at the right gunner's port, "BRDM next to the palace at one o'clock." Knowing it was too close to engage with rockets even if Oz had had the time to maneuver, he added, "I've got it."

The BRDM raced along the ground below him, its 23mm cannon continuing to fire wildly into the nighttime sky. Unlike the small-arms fire, the 23mm shells flashing by the helicopter were capable of bringing the aircraft down with just a few hits.

Luger jabbed the triggers of his spade-gripped Minigun as the MH-60K dropped into the clearing. The six barrels of the machine gun rotated in a blur as it fired strings of ten rounds each time Luger pulled the trigger. The hot casings and belt links spewed from the chute beneath the gun, dropping into the darkness below the chopper.

Luger's salvo chewed into the armored personnel carrier. The gunner fired until his armor-piercing rounds took effect and the vehicle suddenly swerved and stopped firing.

"We're taking more hits," Death Song cautioned as the warning lights on his display panel lit.

From the ground below the helicopter, Andrea watched the MH-60K circle the compound, coming in for a landing. A long blur of flame spit from the helicopter's Miniguns as it settled to the earth. The mercenaries in the brush ahead of Kellerman and Andrea screamed in pain as the fusillade chopped into them.

The American Delta troops jumped from the chopper and charged toward the Presidential Palace, firing their weapons as they ran.

"Our men have had it," Kellerman yelled as he and Andrea reached the brush. "Stay down, they have night-vision equipment. They'll be able to see us if we don't stay down."

Kellerman fumbled in the darkness. His fingers stabbed at the wet, sticky mess that had been a man's face before the helicopter's Minigun had raked the area with bullets. Kellerman continued to grope in the shadows until he located the dead man's rifle. He grasped the rifle and shouldered it to fire at an American soldier running across the grass. He was satisfied to see the man drop.

Andrea shouldered her rifle and tried to fire. She cursed, then cycled the bolt back. She raised the gun again and shot in unison with Kellerman. Two more American soldiers fell to the earth.

"Too bad no one else in our group can shoot," Kellerman remarked as he dropped down to avoid

the angry hail of bullets their shots had triggered
from the Delta troops.

The AH-64 Apache swooped in and fired four
2.75-inch rockets into the Presidential Palace.
There was an explosion that killed most of the mercenaries inside the front of the palace. Flames
licked to life inside the structure.

A string of Andrea's men rushed toward the
Delta troops leaving the grounded helicopter; both
groups of men fired their guns. The mercenaries
were cut to ribbons by the M16s. Two of the Americans stumbled and fell as they were hit by the
enemy's salvo.

Inside the helicopter, O.T. informed Oz over
the intercom, "Troops are all out."

"I'm taking her up," Oz said. The helicopter
shot skyward.

"Enemy troops downhill at seven o'clock,"
O.T. advised via the intercom. "Looks like there's
another BRDM with them."

"I've got them," Oz said, rotating the helicopter around to face the threat as they lifted from the
ground. The pilot fired the twin 7.62mm guns in
the weapons pod to his right. The bullets chattered
out and plumes of earth erupted around the foot
soldiers charging at them, cutting the men down
as they sprinted forward.

Watching the FLIR screen, Oz launched a
salvo of rockets toward the BRDM. The rockets
hissed forward and hit the vehicle; a microsecond
later hot metal erupted into the vehicle's interior,
killing the crew and setting off the fuel tank. The

secondary explosion lit up the night and debris tumbled through the air.

O.T.'s gun started firing, indicating that he had seen something threatening. Oz could hear bullets thumping against the side of the helicopter near him, stopped by the armor plating on the side of the aircraft.

"Banshee One, this is Banshee Mother. Pick up Delta One and move to reinforce Banshee Three and Four. They've hit some stiff resistance and need reinforcements. You've got to get the troops and scoot. Wait a second . . . You've got three, repeat three Hind-Ds approaching from the south. Better take them on before you pick up the dogs."

"Banshee One copies," Oz said.

Before Oz could radio the pilot of the AH-64 Apache, the man cut in, "Banshee Two copies. Want to help me on this, Banshee One?"

"Will do," Oz said, turning his helicopter to face the threat. "We'll ride shotgun on your left." Oz switched the radio to the frequency used by the ground troops. "Delta One, you'll have to wait a minute. We've got some Hind-Ds coming in."

"We'll wait. No problem."

The AH-64 Apache and MH-60K SOA rose into the darkness, gaining altitude to face the oncoming helicopters.

"I've located them," the pilot of the AH-64 Apache said. "At eleven o'clock."

"I see them, too," Oz said, eyeing the dark shapes in the distance. "Hang on a few moments before you launch. They're over a heavily popu-

lated area. Let's wait just a few more seconds . . .
We'll take the one on the left. OK, they're clear
now."

Below and behind the American helicopters,
Andrea yelled, "Smiley! Over here."

Smiley came running toward them in the darkness that was lit by the flickering flames coming
from the burning Presidential Palace. He carried
an RPG launcher with a rocket in it. Two more
rockets were under his arms.

"Let me have that," Andrea ordered, taking
the RPG-16 from Smiley.

"What the hell are they doing?" Kellerman
asked.

"Who?" Smiley asked.

"The American choppers," Kellerman said.
"They're getting ready to face our Hind-Ds!" Kellerman pointed. "Look. There on the horizon."

"I see them," Andrea said. "Three. They
ought to be able to take the Americans, shouldn't
they?"

"Maybe," Kellerman answered. He started to
fire another shot at the Delta troops, then thought
better of it. Obviously, the Americans were going
to gain control of the complex. Drawing fire would
accomplish nothing.

Kellerman turned back toward the approaching Hind-Ds.

In the American MH-60K, Death Song spoke
over the radio, "I'm going to aim for the one on
the left."

Oz held the MH-60K steady in the air. "That's
affirmative."

Death Song jerked the TOW controls and viewscreen toward himself. "Hold it steady," he told Oz.

Oz instantly froze the helicopter in the air.

Death Song launched the TOW. The rocket hissed forward in the darkness, leaving a fiery trail etched into the night-vision goggles. The navigator observed the high-resolution VID in front of him. Using the joysticks, he adjusted the flight of the missile through electronic signals conveyed in the fine wire that spooled out behind the rocket.

A TOW missile flew from each of the American helicopters. Each cut through the darkness, streaking on tails of fire, speeding toward the outermost Hind-Ds. The enemy helicopters wheeled out of their V formation, dropping to the right and left as they tried to avoid the missiles.

Death Song and the AH-64 Apache gunner expertly continued to guide their rockets to negate the maneuvers.

The missiles reached their targets. One of the Hind-Ds exploded, its wreckage scattering in the darkness as it fell into a park, making a patch of dispersed flames across the grass and bushes.

The second missile disabled its target, sending the enemy helicopter into a tight circle, rushing toward the earth as its pilot struggled unsuccessfully to keep the twelve-thousand-kilogram chopper aloft.

The damaged Hind-D slashed at the ground as troops jumped or were thrown from its open doors. The machine crumpled into the earth and burst into flames, throwing long shadows from the palm trees surrounding it.

The third Hind-D held its position and fired an AT-2C/6 TOW missile toward the AH-64 Apache.

Oz wheeled the nose of his MH-60K helicopter toward the Hind-D, discharging his machine guns and two 2.75-inch rockets in an effort to distract its gunner so he wouldn't hit his target.

The enemy helicopter held its ground for a moment, ignoring the rockets that hissed by it. Then its pilot panicked and pulled the helicopter to one side. The TOW missile suddenly veered off, missing the AH-64 Apache.

The American AH-64 Apache helicopter wheeled to follow the Hind-D.

Below the battling helicopters, Andrea yelled at her pilot, "Damned coward!" She brought up the RPG-16 as the AH-64 Apache turned in a wide path in an effort to come in behind the veering Hind-D. As the American chopper circled and dropped, Andrea rotated the safety over the trigger guard into its fire position. She gave the proper lead ahead of the chopper using the range stadia of the sight reticle. She squeezed the trigger. The rocket from the RPG-18 jumped from the launcher, dipped, then hurtled forward as its main rocket fired several yards ahead of her.

The rocket flashed forward, catching the AH-64 on its side. There was a detonation as the rocket struck the rotor drive shaft in the helicopter. The aircraft pinwheeled out of control to plummet across the dark sky south of the burning Presidential Palace.

"Let's get out of here," Kellerman said.

"There's a Jeep over there." Smiley pointed.

"Smiley, you stay here and help out," Andrea ordered as they neared the Jeep.

Smiley watched helplessly as Todd and Kellerman drove off.

The AH-64 Apache continued to lose altitude. "Mayday, mayday, Banshee Two is hit and going down," the pilot radioed matter-of-factly, his panic undetectable in his voice.

The AH-64 plummeted into the foliage.

As the AH-64 had gone down, Oz had hurled his helicopter toward the last Hind-D, approaching it in a curving path that brought them to its side. Now he launched three more 2.75-inch rockets. This time, one of the unguided missiles found its mark. The rocket exploded over the pilot's canopy, slashing the pilot and gunner with shards of plastic, glass, and metal, killing them instantly.

Oz jerked his helicopter aside as the out-of-control aircraft accelerated toward them. The Hind-D passed under the MH-60K, the mercenaries inside throwing its doors open and firing upward toward the Americans as they proceeded.

O.T. returned their fire, raking it with a salvo that caused the mercenaries to fall back into the belly of the pilotless chopper or tumble out its open door. The Soviet-made helicopter dropped toward the ground until it finally crashed beyond the Presidential Palace in a small conflagration.

"Banshee One," Warner called on his radio, "how soon can you lift out your ground forces?"

"The LZ is pretty hot," Oz answered.

"We've got four more Hind-Ds."

"Should we take them on?" Oz asked.

"Negative, Banshee One. They aren't headed for you. They're headed for Banshee Three and Four. They've already lost most of their ground forces. Can you get your dogs back on board and reinforce Three and Four?"

"We'll get to them ASAP."

"Roger that," Warner responded. "Over and out."

To the humming din of O.T.'s Minigun, Oz jerked the helicopter around, steered for the Presidential Palace, and switched to the frequency of Lieutenant Ovelar's helmet radio. "This is Banshee One to Banshee Delta One. How hot is it down there?"

"We've taken out the BRDMs and snipers," Ovelar reported. "But the PZ is still hot and several of them have rocket launchers, so be careful up there. We've taken some casualties."

"Cover us, we're coming down," Oz warned the lieutenant as the helicopter circled the compound. "We're needed to reinforce Banshee Three and Four."

Ovelar swore. "If you have to you have to, but it's really hot. We'll cover you the best we can."

Oz switched the radio, "Delta One, we're headed down."

C H A P T E R

36

Andrea floored the accelerator of the Jeep and sped down a narrow street, angrily honking the horn at a tourist who stood on the pavement with a small poodle on a leash. The wide-eyed tourist cried out as he jumped aside and the jeep bumped over the yelping dog.

"The airport's that way," Kellerman yelled as Andrea whipped around a corner, scraping against a delivery van in the process.

"They'll have the airport closed down by now," Andrea shouted, pushing a lock of long hair out of her eye. "Our only chance is to steal a boat."

Kellerman said nothing but nodded in agreement.

Andrea raced the car down the narrow route leading toward the harbor. Suddenly, she slowed the Jeep.

"What's wrong?" Kellerman asked, pulling out his Hi-Power and looking up and down the nearly empty street as they stopped.

"We need some insurance," Andrea said.

"Insurance?"

"There." Andrea pointed to a thin woman.

At the sight of Kellerman's pistol, the woman Andrea pointed to stepped back into the shadows of a closed souvenir shop. The woman squatted in the darkness, barely lit by the store's lights, tightly clasping her two small children to her as Kellerman's gaze fell upon them.

"Yeah." Kellerman laughed. "That might be just the ticket to get us through a roadblock and off this stinking island. Just a minute."

He leapt from the jeep and crossed to where the woman cowered in the shadows.

"Come on," he ordered her, motioning to the Jeep with his pistol.

She clutched her children more tightly and remained where she was.

Kellerman placed his pistol against her boy's temple. "Either come with us or . . ."

"Don't hurt us," she pleaded. "We'll go with you. Please don't do anything to hurt us."

"Just do what we say," Kellerman ordered. "Get into the Jeep and shut up."

He motioned the woman into the front seat beside Andrea, then picked up each of the children with his bony hands and roughly set them into the back of the automobile.

"Let's go," he said, climbing into the backseat and smiling at the sobbing girl and boy on either side of him.

37

Oz's helicopter had raced toward the police station, approaching behind a Hind-D. Oz pulled the helicopter into a hover in the darkness and helplessly watched as Sergeant Karr and Amero were cut to pieces.

"Ready with the TOW," Death Song said as the two Delta troops dropped lifelessly to the roof of the police station.

"Get those bastards," Oz told him.

"Just keep her steady." The last TOW rocket hissed out of its pod and streaked toward the rear of the Hind-D as it hovered over the surface of the police station roof. As the rocket neared the Hind-D, O.T.'s Minigun started firing from behind Death Song.

There was an explosion on the underside of the MH-60K. The controls shuddered in Oz's hands as the helicopter rocked to the side. The motion caused Death Song to accidentally flex the guidance controls for the TOW. The missile zigzagged to the side, missing the Hind-D in front of them.

O.T.'s gun fired a long burst, then he spoke over the intercom, "BRDM's 23mm cannon hit the passenger compartment. We've got four or five minor casualties. I knocked it out, but not soon enough."

Oz fought the controls that had become sluggish in his hands. Knowing he might be going down and probably wouldn't get another chance to fire at the Hind-D in front of him, he launched the remainder of his 2.75-inch rockets as he struggled to gain control of the wildly lurching aircraft.

The swarm of missiles flashed from their pod and sailed at the enemy helicopter. All but one missed. It crashed into the belly of the chopper as the aircraft started to rotate toward the MH-60K.

"We're losing it," Death Song warned. "The transmission fluid pressure is dropping and several backup systems are erratic."

Oz kicked a rudder pedal to keep the nose of the MH-60K pointed toward the Hind-D as they circled the smoking aircraft. The American pilot fired his machine gun at the enemy helicopter that lumbered about in an effort to get its heavy nose gun and missiles aligned for attack. The American pushed his helicopter upward and to the side to avoid the Hind-D's sights.

"I'm going to try to get us above the Hind-D," Oz told his crew. "We're out of rockets and ammunition up here, so hit it with all you've got as we cross by, Luger."

"I'm about out of ammunition, too," Luger warned.

"Use it all," Oz said. "We won't stay in the air much longer. Lieutenant Ovelar."

"Yes, sir."

"Have your troops fire their guns from the open side door. Maybe we'll get lucky."

As the MH-60K rose, the men on the right side of the craft discharged their guns at the Soviet-made helicopter. The bullets crashed into the Hind-D, but did only minor damage to the machine. It continued to turn, flames jetting from inside its passenger compartment. Oz watched as it slowly gained on the MH-60K.

He switched his radio to the AATF command net. "Banshee Mother, this is Banshee One."

"Roger, Banshee One."

"We've taken a 23mm hit and are barely in the air. There's one Hind-D after us."

"I'll scramble a Tomcat. Can you hang on?"

"Doubtful. But we'll try to take it as far away from the ground fighting as we can."

"Hang on," Warner said. "ETA for the Tomcat is . . . five minutes."

"We're hanging on. Over and out." He switched off the radio knowing they would be lucky to stay in the air, let alone out of the Hind-D's sights, for another five minutes.

"Captain," O.T. said over the intercom. "Can you take us directly over the Hind-D? I have an idea."

"I'm not sure," Oz said, "but I'll give it a try."

"Get my side right over it," O.T. said. "We'll try a little old-fashioned bombing back here with grenades and rifle fire."

A long shot, Oz realized, but they had nothing to lose. He glanced at the instrument panel that was full of blinking lights and gauges in red. He fought the chopper's sluggish controls, practically forcing it upward with brute strength.

The Hind-D fought to overtake the American helicopter that continued to rise above it. Finally, Oz managed to bring his aircraft forty meters above the larger chopper. As the MH-60K crossed over the enemy helicopter, the soldiers behind Oz dropped hand grenades out the open door.

The grenades exploded beside or below the enemy aircraft with little effect, the shrapnel bouncing harmlessly off its armored sides. Their grenades exhausted, the Delta soldiers leaned out of the helicopter, firing on the Hind-D, pocking its top and rotors and spalling the pilot's and gunner's windows.

Still the Hind-D followed the American chopper in its rising spiral.

"Son of a—" O.T. muttered over the intercom in a strained voice. The man lifted his now-empty Minigun from its pedestal, struggling with its weight as he heaved it across the edge of the gunner's port. He gritted his teeth as he watched out the port, the cool air causing tears to form in his eyes.

The city was far below them. Its lights were tiny gems in a sea of black. O.T. stood like a statue watching the dark shadow of the Hind-D as it circled below them. He waited until the enemy chopper crossed directly under him.

He released the Minigun.

The machine gun seemed to hang in the air, then plunged downward. It glanced into the swiftly rotating main blades of the Hind-D without apparent effect and then was flung into the darkness to vanish from sight.

O.T. studied the aircraft below them. It seemed undamaged. The warrant officer fell into his gunner's chair, exhausted and hopeless.

Then the American soldiers in the passenger compartment behind O.T. started to cheer. The gunner rose and leaned out the empty port beside him to stare downward.

The Hind-D below was wobbling like a child's top, its rotors shaking apart with the strain created by the blow from the falling Minigun. Two rotor blades broke loose, colliding with the tail of the helicopter as they flew outward, causing the tail rotor to quit functioning. As its tail blades lost speed, the whole body of the helicopter rotated in counter motion to the wobbling main rotor. The Hind-D coasted forward for a few seconds and then fell, whirling unchecked, the blaze in its hold becoming an inferno as it plummeted toward the bay far below.

"O.T. got it!" Luger shouted over the intercom. "O.T. bombed them to hell!"

"Pure luck," O.T. admitted in a tired but happy voice.

"If our luck holds," Oz announced, "I think we're going to make it to the ground in one piece. Luger, tend to the wounded and get everyone buckled in back there. O.T., better close the side doors. I suspect we're going to have a pretty rough landing."

38

"The airport's still hot. Can you get your chopper to the harbor?" Warner asked Oz over the ABN frequency after Oz had contacted the AATFC and explained the situation with the MH-60K.

"I think we can," Oz answered as he fought to keep his damaged chopper in the air.

"The SEALs have secured sector Zebra-Zero-One," Warner said, giving them the coordinates. "You took out the last Hind-D and all the BRDMs appear to have been destroyed, too. We have the SEALs' HH-60H helicopter ferrying a load of our Delta casualties back to the *America*. They'll be returning in about fifteen minutes for your wounded."

Oz glanced at his HSD on which Death Song had punched up the coordinates for the SEALs' position. "We'll head for Zebra-Zero-One, then."

"Good. Delta Four and what's left of Delta Three have commandeered several vans and are taking the hostages they freed to the airport. I'll have the SEALs release smoke to mark your LZ. They'll give you any security if you need it."

"We'll watch for the smoke," Oz said. "Over and out."

They passed above the now-quiet city of Coopersville. From the air, Oz observed the people milling about in the streets. The Americans had broadcast a recorded message from Noble to his people on the frequency of the island's radio station. The message that the Americans had come to free the island seemed to be having the desired effect: Many of them waved at the American helicopter as it passed over the streets.

Oz dropped his chopper lower as they neared the harbor. He sighted the smoke grenade that the SEALs set off. The smoke marked an intersection surrounded by low, single-story buildings bordering the harbor.

"We're going down," Oz warned his crew. He slowly brought the stiff control column to its center position so they hovered over the LZ. Then he slowly pressed on the collective pitch lever with his left hand. The helicopter responded by wobbly sinking to the pavement.

"Made it," Oz muttered to himself. Over the intercom: "Let's get everyone out back there, O.T. and Luger. Lieutenant Ovelar?"

"Yes."

"The HH-60H and several Seahawks will arrive at Palm Island to ferry your wounded to the *America* in about twenty minutes."

In the distance, Oz heard the low thumping of a .50-caliber machine gun. He hoped it didn't signal a serious problem. He started to shut down the helicopter when Warner's voice sounded in his headphones.

"Oz, you still on line?" Warner asked.

"Roger, Mother Banshee."

"We've got a problem. A couple—sounds like Kellerman and Todd—passed the Delta caravan and shot up one of the vans. They're headed toward the harbor in a Jeep. They're holding two children and a woman with them as hostages. The Delta troops couldn't stop them for fear of wounding the civilians."

"How well are they armed? We're totally out of ammunition and rockets here."

"According to Delta Four, they have several rifles and a .50-caliber machine gun that's mounted on the jeep. If we put some of the SEALs aboard your chopper, can you get into the air to block their escape?"

"We've got lots of red lights. The transmission's drained of fluid and will be burnt out in another few minutes. But the engine's still running. We might keep in the air for a short time. It's your call."

Warner was silent for a moment. Oz turned to Death Song. "Get that SEAL machine gunner aboard. I think we're going to need some armament."

"Cut them off, Banshee One," Warner ordered.

Because of the risk of crashing, Oz quickly ordered O.T. and Luger to stay on the ground. The only others with Oz in the MH-60K were Death

Song and a lanky SEAL who climbed aboard with an M60 machine gun.

Oz gently lifted on the collective pitch lever with his left hand. The helicopter shook, the engine whining in complaint, and then wobbled into the air. Oz booted his right pedal and swung the helicopter to face away from the harbor toward where Kellerman and Todd would be coming from. "Anyone see anything?" Oz asked over the intercom as he swung the chopper around in a half circle and then took them over the narrow street running parallel to the edge of the harbor.

"There, at twelve o'clock," Death Song said.

"I see them," Oz said. "They're not headed for the SEALs. Must be making for that private marina to the right. They've still got the hostages—"

"We're losing power," Death Song warned. The chopper's engine made an ominous noise and the aircraft dropped slightly.

39

"There's a damned chopper!" Kellerman yelled from the backseat of the Jeep as Andrea shoved the accelerator. The vehicle raced past a parked car and clipped a garbage can lying in the street, sending it clanking along the pavement. The woman and two children who were in the Jeep closed their eyes, too fearful to watch as they tore through the avenue forcing a heavy truck to stop for them.

Andrea glanced over her shoulder. "They're going to catch us there in the open."

"Just head for the wharf." Kellerman laughed as he held onto the machine gun mounted to the roll bar of the Jeep. "Keeping the wolves off the sled has always been simple." He leaned over to the front seat and grabbed the hair of the woman sitting next to Andrea.

The woman gasped in pain and fear.

"We toss these people out," Kellerman said to Andrea, "and that chopper will stop to try to help them." He took out his Hi-Power, placed it against the woman's shoulder. He waited a moment until they entered the large parking lot along the marina and then pulled the trigger.

The blast splattered blood onto the windshield of the Jeep. Kellerman pulled hard on the woman's hair and she fell out of the speeding Jeep, rolling limply on the pavement at the entrance of the parking lot.

Andrea slowed and shot down the main lane running through the parking lot leading to the marina.

"And now you." Kellerman turned to the crying boy beside him. The man grabbed the front of the six-year-old's shirt, lifting him in the air, and then hurled him at an approaching car. The driver of the car swerved, crashing into a parked pickup. The screaming child crashed into the pavement in a tangle of arms and legs.

The small child left in the backseat with Kellerman wailed as he tossed her out. She hit the hood of a parked truck with a sickening thump.

"It's working," Kellerman yelled as they neared the marina. "The chopper's slowing."

As they had been following Todd, Kellerman, and their three hostages, Oz had been feeding Warner a verbal description of what was happening.

"We'll stop and help the victims," Oz radioed his commander as Kellerman started throwing the helpless hostages from the speeding Jeep. The helicopter dropped as its engine lost more power trying to overcome the friction of the overheating transmission. Oz pulled the chopper to the left to miss a light pole.

"Negative," Warner told him. "Get Keller-

man and Todd. I'll get a couple of SEALs in.
They're capable of administering first aid."

"Will do," Oz replied. He switched to his intercom. "Are you ready back there?" he asked the SEAL in the passenger compartment.

"I'm more than ready to take that bastard," the SEAL said, fighting to control his voice. He had watched from the helicopter as the hostages were thrown from the Jeep. Now he was so angry his hands shook as he held his weapon.

"I'm going to pass over them and block their path to the marina," Oz told him. "I'll turn so you can fire out the left side door. You'll have to get them quickly. If he gets that machine gun trained on us, we've had it at that range."

"Get me a clear shot," the SEAL said. "I'll take care of the rest."

The MH-60K swooped above the Jeep. Oz brought back the control column, pushed downward on the collective pitch lever, and kicked the left rudder pedal. The chopper barely cleared the Jeep. The helicopter raced ahead and then dropped almost to the pavement forty yards ahead of the Jeep.

Andrea continued forward at full speed.

The helicopter hovered a few feet over the pavement; the SEAL fired a short burst that spalled the Jeep's windshield, but then his gun suddenly quit.

"It's jammed!" the SEAL yelled over the intercom and then swore a long stream of curses.

Oz fought the sluggish controls of the helicopter to lift it. But it refused to respond.

"She's going to ram us!" Death Song warned as he watched out his side door window.

Andrea pushed on the accelerator, the Jeep surged toward the side of the MH-60K. Kellerman stood and brought the .50-caliber BMG around. He pulled the weapon's trigger. The belted cartridges shuffled into the machine gun's side as the half-inch slugs burst from its muzzle in a stream of fire.

The heavy bullets cracked through the open passenger compartment, shredding the SEAL as he worked to clear the jam in his machine gun. As the gap between the vehicles narrowed, Kellerman trained his weapon on the cockpit of the MH-60K.

Oz tugged on the collective pitch lever and the helicopter shuddered and then finally lifted into the air. The .50-caliber slugs tore through the windscreen of the cabin as the chopper rose.

Most of the heavy bullets were diverted or stopped by the armor incorporated into the side of the cabin and the copilot's bucket seat. But two projectiles snapped through the Plexiglas of the door. One glanced off the edge of Death Song's helmet, jerking his head to the side and knocking him unconscious. The bullet continued on, knocking the night-vision goggles off Oz's helmet. The second slug tore into Oz's shoulder after bouncing off the armor in his chair.

At the same time the bullets entered the cockpit, Oz shoved on his right rudder pedal, turning the nose away from the approaching Jeep and its blazing gun.

Andrea pushed the Jeep forward, expecting to

go under the helicopter as it continued to rise. Instead, the nose of the chopper lifted and the tail dipped downward as Oz pulled back on the control column.

Andrea screamed as the tail of the helicopter swung toward her.

Andrea threw herself across the seat next to her and slammed on the brakes; the wheels locked and the jeep slid toward the whirring tail blades. Kellerman continued to fire the machine gun, a twisted smile frozen on his bony face.

The tail rotor turned so quickly it was invisible as it slashed over the Jeep. As if by magic, Kellerman's head, shoulders, and chest disappeared into a mist of blood and bone that was sprayed through the air by the churning tail rotor.

The .50-caliber machine gun was suddenly silent. Kellerman's decapitated body stood by itself for a moment as the Jeep rolled to a complete stop. What was left of the man plopped over and rolled out of the back of the Jeep, leaving its severed arms still hanging from the spade grips of the machine gun for a moment before they dropped into the backseat.

Oz forced the MH-60K into the air. It circled the parking lot like a crippled hawk as the pilot surveyed the damage he'd done. "Banshee One to Mother Banshee."

"What's going on, Banshee One?"

"Kellerman's dead. But he got us bad with his machine gun before I clipped him with the tail rotor. The SEAL with us is down—probably

dead—I can't see back there. Death Song is out;
I don't see any injury but—"

"The HH-60H is close to you. I'll divert it and
let the medics they're bringing in check your guys.
The HH-60H is almost there."

"Hang on, I've spied Todd," Oz said. "I'm
going to try to get her. Over and out."

Todd was making a dash for the marina, a rifle
in her hand. Oz struggled to bring the helicopter
around to cut off her escape. The engine made a
clanking noise and the power train failed. Oz carefully let the blades freewheel and set the helicopter
down quickly. Ignoring the pain in his shoulder,
he released his harness and turned to extract his
PK-15 from its rack behind his seat.

"Mother Banshee, this is Banshee One. My
chopper's conked out," the pilot said on the radio.
"Send the HH-60H to the marina at the southeast
end of Coopersville ASAP. Both men need medical
attention. I'm going after Todd on foot."

Before Warner could reply, Oz pulled off his
helmet, opened his door, and jumped out. He
jerked back on the charging handle of his PK-15
and twisted the power knob on its Aimpoint scope.

Todd was almost to the dock. Oz lifted his rifle
and centered the glowing aiming dot on her back.
He started to squeeze the trigger . . .

A van drove up. Its brakes squealed as it
stopped and blocked his sight picture.

"What's going on?" the driver asked. "You
need some help?"

"Get back!" Oz yelled as he tried to wave the
van out of the way.

"He's got a gun!" the passenger beside the driver hollered.

Oz quickly ran around the van, whose driver sat behind the wheel unsure what to do.

Oz got around the van, but Todd was nowhere to be seen. The pilot raced across the parking lot toward the marina.

Halfway to the marina, Oz heard the sound of a small boat's engines coughing to a start. The engines revved and a long cigarette boat sped away from the dock.

Oz came to the edge of the wharf as the boat thundered into the darkness. He could barely distinguish Andrea behind the wheel.

Oz dropped to one knee and aimed. The boat bounced over the choppy ocean, nearly swallowed in the shadows. The short rifle cycled fifteen 3-round bursts as Oz emptied its magazine at the speeding boat.

He didn't bother to reload the weapon. Although he could hear the small boat, it was lost in the darkness of the open sea.

40

Oz's arm ached unmercifully as he reached his helicopter. The HH-60H had arrived and a medic was checking Death Song.

"How is he?" Oz asked as he pulled an emergency field dressing from its pouch and opened its pack.

"Concussion," the medic said as he helped a Navy orderly lower the unconscious Death Song onto a stretcher on the pavement. Oz didn't ask about the SEAL in the passenger compartment. He was obviously dead.

"Let me look at that shoulder," the medic said, studying the bloody hole in Oz's uniform. "That's pretty serious."

"It can wait," Oz said as he pushed an emergency field dressing against it to stop the bleeding. Oz turned and climbed into the HH-60H.

"I need to speak to Mother Banshee," Oz told the startled warrant officer in the Navy chopper.

The warrant officer spoke to the pilot over the intercom as he handed another headset to Oz.

"We're patching you in to Mother Banshee," the pilot told Oz over the intercom.

Oz waited a moment and then spoke, "Mother Banshee, this is Oz."

"Did you get her?"

"Negative. She got away in a small boat. But I think we could catch her in Banshee Five. It's here in the parking lot. I could guide them to it."

"Banshee Five?"

"We heard," the pilot of the HH-60H answered.

"Go get her."

Minutes later, the HH-60H circled the warm Gulf waters. Oz guided the helicopter over the intercom. Oz stood behind the pilot and copilot, watching their FLIR screen over the pilot's shoulder.

"There she is," the pilot said. He brought the helicopter around and approached the boat.

"She's firing at us," the copilot said. "Some people don't know when to quit."

"Permission to attack," the pilot called to Warner. He had overheard Oz's account of how Todd and Kellerman had treated the woman and her two children as the HH-60H had been on its return flight to the island. Now the Navy pilot wanted revenge.

"Permission granted," Warner's voice came back.

The helicopter circled again, then turned to face the cigarette boat that continued to speed away.

"Arm the torpedo," the pilot ordered.

"Torpedo armed."

"Fire when ready."

The MK 46 torpedo dropped into the ocean below the helicopter and charged its target, leaving a white wake to mark its trail on the FLIR screen. Seconds later, a fiery explosion rocked the ocean.

The HH-60H circled the wreckage. A few dolphins appeared on the FLIR. But the men in the air saw no sign of Todd's body.

CHAPTER

41

The Rangers arrived on the C-5A Galaxy cargo planes several hours after Oz had returned to the island on the HH-60H. President Noble's broadcast had the desired effect: The islanders helped the Rangers round up the last of Todd's men who, thanks to a hasty agreement between Noble and the US Government, would be deported to the US to stand trial.

As the sun was rising on the island, more C-5A cargo planes transported a crew of US Army engineers and their Sikorsky S-64 "Skycranes" to the island. The S-64s buzzed about the island like giant bumblebees, ferrying wrecked BRDMs, Hind-Ds, and jeeps out over the ocean and dropping them into the sea. The island was quickly cleaned of shattered military vehicles; one BRDM that still ran was parked alongside the police station. US Rangers stored the ammunition and small arms in the station as they collected them from the last of Todd's men.

Oz wore a heavy bandage on his shoulder and carried his arm in a sling. The wound hurt, but the medic was positive there was no permanent damage. The pilot ignored the pain in his shoulder as he studied the island one last time before turning to board the C-5A. The cargo plane would take him and the rest of the Night Stalkers and the Delta teams quietly back to Fort Bragg before news reporters from around the world converged on the island.

Across the airfield, Oz could barely discern the throng of American hostages who he'd helped to rescue. The freed Americans crossed the field to board a TWA 747.

O.T. glanced across the field, then turned and flashed a crooked grin at Oz. "I'd say we done good."

Oz nodded but said nothing as he stepped up the cargo plane's ramp. O.T., Luger, and Death Song followed him into the belly of the C-5A.

Duncan Long is internationally recognized as a firearms expert, and has had over twenty books published on that subject, as well as numerous magazine articles. In addition to his nonfiction writing, Long has authored a science fiction novel, *Antigrav Unlimited.* He has an MA in music composition, and has worked as a rock musician; he has spent nine years teaching in public schools. Duncan Long lives in eastern Kansas with his wife and two children.